DEAD GORGEOUS

MALORIE BLACKMAN

Dead Gorgeous

DOUBLEDAY
London · New York · Toronto · Sydney · Auckland

DEAD GORGEOUS
A DOUBLEDAY BOOK 0385 600097

Published in Great Britain by Doubleday,
an imprint of Random House Children's Books

This edition published 2002

1 3 5 7 9 10 8 6 4 2

Set in 12/15 pt Bembo

RANDOM HOUSE CHILDREN'S BOOKS
61–63 Uxbridge Rd, London W5 5SA
A division of The Random House Group Ltd

RANDOM HOUSE AUSTRALIA (PTY) LTD
20 Alfred Street, Milsons Point, Sydney,
New South Wales 2061, Australia

RANDOM HOUSE NEW ZEALAND LTD
18 Poland Road, Glenfield, Auckland 10, New Zealand

RANDOM HOUSE (PTY) LTD
Endulini, 5A Jubilee Road, Parktown 2193, South Africa

THE RANDOM HOUSE GROUP Limited Reg. No. 954009

A CIP catalogue record for this book is available from the British Library.

Printed and bound in Great Britain
by Mackays of Chatham, Chatham, Kent

To Neil and Lizzy, with love

1. Liam

A storm was coming. I could smell it in the brackish air, hear it in the growl of the waves, see it in the darkening clouds. Josh picked up a stone and tried to skim it across the foaming water. It sank immediately. A wave raced up the beach towards us as if in protest.

Josh laughed and picked up another stone. 'Wow! Look at that!'

A salt tang caught at the back of my throat and I had to cough slightly to clear it before I could speak.

'Look! Look!' Josh pointed.

'At what?'

'The sea.'

'What about it?'

'It's like a huge pot of spaghetti, boiling and bubbling!'

I looked away and shook my head, biting back on the words that just itched to leave my mouth.

'Amazing! Check the sky!' Josh continued.

I automatically looked up at the strange yellowy-grey clouds. It was as if the tops of the clouds were solid and on fire and all the resultant soot and ash were falling to the bottom of them. It was quite common to see the clouds like that over the coast where we lived but I'd never seen them like that anywhere else, and certainly not inland. Not that I'd been to that many places. Not that I'd been anywhere really. The sky matched my mood. Unsettled. Restless.

'What about the sky?' I said, unable to keep the impatience out of my voice.

'Isn't it terrific? Like . . . like . . .'

'Oh, for heaven's sake, Josh. Not again,' I snapped like an old elastic band. 'Why're you always going on about the skylight and

the twilight and the moonlight? No wonder you're always getting picked on at school.'

Josh looked up at me like a wounded dog I'd kicked when he was down. 'I like . . . looking at things.'

'Fine. But that's no reason to drip on like a snotty tissue about them,' I said viciously.

Josh winced at my words and I wasn't sorry. I was glad. I liked to look at things too, but you didn't hear me going on like a girly about them. Josh had to toughen up — fast. I wouldn't always be there to watch his back at school, or anywhere else for that matter. Didn't he understand that?

'I'll shut up then,' Josh replied quietly.

'Thank you,' I said. 'I'd appreciate it.'

Josh's nose began to run. Another reason why my brother always gets picked on. Whenever he's upset, his nose dribbles. It drives me crazy.

'Wipe your nose,' I ordered.

Josh swiped the sleeve of his jumper across his face. He picked up another stone and skimmed it across the water. After a moment I picked up a stone, my hand clenching tightly around its icy smoothness. I knew I was just taking out my bad mood on my brother, but who else was there?

No one.

I shook my head.

My whole life was so pointless. It didn't matter. I didn't matter. I was like one of the small pebbles on the beach, battered smooth by day after month after year of wave upon wave. Except in my case, the wave was my dad. He picked on and criticized and disapproved and condemned every breath I took, until the effect was just the same. I was battered smooth, but that was only on the outside. Inside I was rough and jagged and all corners. And Josh was the only one I could hurt. So I often did. And as much as I hated myself afterwards, it never stopped me from doing it again. And again.

8

I clenched the stone in my hand even more tightly. Josh sniffed beside me. I wanted to turn to him and hug him and hold him and tell him that he was my brother and that meant something to me. But I didn't. We stood there, together but apart as it began to rain. No gradual build-up from a light spray, but great beads of icy water as big as my fingernails. We were soaked in seconds. The waves lashed up the beach, laughing at us. Or maybe they were angry with us. Or maybe they couldn't care less one way or the other. We picked up smooth stones and skimmed them across the rough water as the storm bashed at us.

It was better than going home.

Sooner or later, we'd have to turn round and head back. If we were lucky, Dad would be round the pub and we'd be able to change our clothes without ructions. If we were lucky. And once again, it'd be left to me to cook up some pasta or some bacon, beans and toast for dinner – which was OK as long as we could eat our dinner in peace before Dad got home. I turned to look at Josh, wondering what he was thinking. As if he sensed me watching him, he wiped his nose again with his sleeve. It was raining quite hard now. The yellow tinge to the clouds had disappeared. Now there was only dark charcoal-grey.

'Come on, Josh,' I shouted above the noise of the waves and the rain. 'Time to head back.'

'Liam, I don't want to go home,' he shouted back.

'Come on.' I started walking up the beach. I didn't need to turn round to know that my brother was standing there watching me. 'Come on, or I'll leave you to it,' I yelled.

Josh started to follow me. I slowed down so that he could catch up. When at last he did, I turned round to him and smiled. He smiled back. Without warning, I grabbed him and put him in a headlock.

'Get off!' he shouted.

After messing up his short locks good and proper, I let him go. Josh had to take a step forward, his hands stretched out before him to stop himself from falling. He sprang up and grinned at me. And just like that, some of the weight was lifted from my shoulders. But not much. And not for long.

'Time to go home,' I sighed.

Josh's smile vanished. And I'd done that. I was always the one to wipe the smile from his face. Sometimes, I really hated being the older brother. Sometimes, I wondered how it would feel to just be me. By myself. No one else to consider. No one else to worry about. Just the thought of it made me ache inside. To be on my own and left alone. Now that would be a real slice of heaven.

2. Nova and Her Dad

Nova had to read the wretched notice her dad had just put on the hotel notice board twice before the full horror of it sank in. What had she done to deserve such a father? Was she someone despicably mean in another life? Just who had she cheesed off? Obviously someone really high up in the pecking order of things, because she was sure paying for it now. It was like every night, Dad dreamed up unique, bizarre and very effective ways to embarrass the hell out of her. And the trouble was, he always succeeded. Nova sighed — one of the deep, long-suffering sighs that she was rightly proud of. She stretched out a hand to remove the notice.

'Nova, don't even think about it,' Dad called out, leaning over the reception desk.

'Dad, you can't leave that there.'

'Why not?'

'Anyone thinking of staying here will think this place is a nut-house, that's why.'

'Any new guests will be impressed by the hygiene standards at our hotel.'

'New guests? Dream on!' Nova muttered. She scowled at Dad's notice. It had to come down. Embarrassing didn't even come close to describing it.

POLITE NOTICE TO ALL GUESTS OF
PHOENIX MANOR

There are some devices which are being underused in this hotel due to an obvious lack of knowledge or technical awareness. I realize that these features come without a user guide, so I thought I might offer some advice.

★ The white or wooden handle on the rear wall of each toilet cubicle is not decorative, nor is it the handle of a fruit machine or a firing mechanism for an ejector seat. It has the express function of sending your sausage to the seaside. No matter how proud you may be of the fibre content of your diet, we at this hotel don't want to see the evidence. Flush the ruddy thing!

★ Loobrushaphobia continues to be a real problem for some of you. Hold the narrow white or wood-veneer end of the brush and use the bristly end to remove whatever excreta may have avoided 'the flush' (see above).

★ When you use the last piece of toilet paper in the dispenser, it would be a noble, charitable and friendly act to replace it from the large stock provided in each bathroom. Please do NOT phone me or any member of my family at Omigod o'clock in the early hours of the morning and ask where the spare toilet rolls are, as happened two nights ago. And if you do run out of toilet paper and find there is no more available in your current location, please do NOT shuffle down to the reception desk with your trousers around your ankles – yes, you, Mr Burntwood. (My wife is still having nightmares.)

★ The fact that fresh urine is almost sterile does not entirely mitigate the practice of spraying it around the toilet seat and/or floor like some randy tomcat. In other words, 'If you sprinkle when you tinkle, keep it neat and wipe the seat.'

If there are any technical issues for which you require further information, please call me on ext. 100 or try www.social.hygiene/how-to-use-the-ruddy-toilet.bum

Tyler Clibbens – Hotel Owner/Manager/General Dogsbody

Nova stretched out a hand towards it.

'Nova, I'm watching you,' Dad yelled, leaning even further over his desk.

'Dad, please.' Nova was desperate. 'Besides, you don't want Mum to see this, do you?'

'So what if she does?' Dad looked around furtively. He stood upright, shoulders squared, lips pursed and set. 'Besides, what I say goes.'

'Only when Mum isn't here,' replied Nova.

'Well, she's not here now so that notice stays. The job's a good 'un! Leave it alone.'

Nova recognized that belligerent tone of voice. She was familiar with the gritty, stern look. She had thought that throwing Mum into the conversation would make Dad back down – it usually did – but he was obviously having one of his 'I'm the man and not under my wife's thumb' moments! Nova couldn't help shaking her head at the notice one last time, before turning to make her way to the kitchen.

Mr Jackman bumped into her and carried on walking without saying a word.

'Excuse me all over the place,' Nova huffed at him.

Mr Jackman hadn't altered his pace one bit. Nova didn't even know if he'd heard her. What was that man's problem? He shuffled around the hotel as if he had the weight of the world on his shoulders. He wasn't even that old. Nova didn't think he'd reached his thirties yet. Early to middle twenties at the most. But he moved like a man at least three times his age. If he tried smiling occasionally he might actually be passable. Short, dark-brown hair, and once, when he'd actually looked at her rather than slinking past, head down, she'd noticed with a start that he had one brown eye and one dark blue. The start was because he'd been at the hotel for a few days by then and it was the first time Nova had caught a clear glimpse of his eyes. She had never seen a mixed race guy with different coloured eyes before. It made Mr Jackman seem even more mysterious.

Now he'd been in the hotel for over a week and when he did put in an appearance – which wasn't often – he always wore immaculate black jeans and a T-shirt, usually white, even in the unusually chilly autumn weather.

'Ah, Mr Jackman, will you be staying on with us for a while longer?' Dad called out, leaning over the reception desk and craning his neck.

Mr Jackman nodded and carried on towards the stairs.

'Can you give me some idea how long you'll be with us?' Dad leaned out even further, one hand waving to attract Mr Jackman's attention.

But the initial nod was all Dad was going to get. Mr Jackman walked up the stairs as if Dad hadn't spoken. As if Dad wasn't even there.

'Er . . . Mr Jackman . . . Mr — Arrggghhhh!' Dad tipped right over the reception desk to land in a heap on the other side.

'Hello, Nova.'

Nova jumped at the sound of the voice behind her. She whipped round, surprised then not surprised to see Miss Dawn standing behind her. Both Miss Dawn and her companion, Miss Eve, had the weirdest knack of appearing

14

behind you almost out of nowhere. Miss Dawn was an elderly black woman, her black hair streaked with honey-brown and burgundy highlights. She was about as tall as Nova's sister, Rainbow, though Miss Eve was taller.

'He's a strange man, isn't he?' said Miss Dawn.

'Are you talking about my dad or Mr Jackman?'

Miss Dawn smiled in Dad's direction, watching as he cursed up a blue streak while he struggled to his feet. She turned to watch Mr Jackman's back disappear round a bend in the stairs. 'Well, in this instance I was referring to Mr Jackman.'

'He's not very friendly, is he?' Nova said.

'Maybe he's got a lot on his mind,' Miss Dawn suggested.

'And all of it bad, from the look on his face.'

'What he needs is a good friend, my dear. Someone like you,' said Miss Dawn.

'I'm sure the very last thing he wants is to be bothered by me.'

'Don't you believe it. We all need someone to talk to, someone to share things with and sometimes . . .'

'Yeah?'

'Sometimes, no one sees things more clearly than a child.'

'Excuse me, I'm not a child. I'm nearly thirteen.' Nova bristled.

'Oh, of course, my dear. My mistake.' Miss Dawn's eyes twinkled. 'My point is just that sometimes younger ones like you see more clearly than us . . . wrinklies.'

'Tell that to my dad – ' Nova indicated with her head – 'then maybe he'll let me take down that notice.'

'Oh, no! You don't want to take that down. Your father's quite right, my dear.'

'But . . . but it's *embarrassing*!'

15

'What's embarrassing about using the toilet?' asked Miss Dawn with perfect seriousness. 'It's something to celebrate rather than be ashamed of. We all do it! And toilets are a fantastic invention. So useful. So *comfortable*!'

Nova's face grew hotter by the second. That was not the sort of thing old women should talk about. 'If you say so.' She took a discreet but wary step backwards.

'I do! I've spent many a happy hour sitting on the toilet, reading or sewing or just contemplating the infinite!'

'Er . . . I think I hear Mum calling me. Bye!' Nova turned and raced for the kitchen.

'Nova, don't run!' Dad yelled. 'Health and safety!'

'I wasn't about to give you a graphic demonstration, my dear,' Miss Dawn called out. 'I was just talking about them, that's all.'

Nova didn't stop running until she'd reached the kitchen. If it weren't for the weird guests at the hotel and the even more weird behaviour of her dad, the hotel might actually be a reasonable place to hang out!

3. Nova and Her Mum

'When I was at school, my cookery teacher told us the secret to rolling out good pastry was "Short, sharp strokes away from you! Short, sharp strokes away from you."' Mum matched the words to the actions, her hands on the rolling pin moving in brisk, precise strokes across the pastry on the kitchen table. 'And I find it actually works! I've never rolled out uneven pastry in my life!'

Nova entered the kitchen, only to stop short at the sound of her mum's voice. Mum was a cookery superstar again! Whenever she was alone in the kitchen, she always pretended to be some really famous cook whose every culinary move was watched by millions to copy, learn from and enjoy.

'And I find there's something very soothing about cooking foods high in carbohydrates. Beating cakes. Kneading dough. Rolling pastry. Very therapeutic. Very satisfying,' Mum continued, totally unaware that she was being watched. 'Take this pastry I'm rolling, for instance. Now, the guests brave enough – or broke enough – to eat dinner here may say that my puff pastry is as light as a brick, but they're missing the point. Making pastry stops me from throttling some of them. Beating cake mixture works out all the little stresses and strains of everyday life. And as for kneading bread dough – now that's a life saver. I even keep batches of bread dough in the fridge in case of emergencies. I have a little song I made up which goes to the heart of what I'm trying to say. It goes like this.' Turning her head away from the pastry before her, Mum coughed a couple of times to clear her throat before she began:

'When the kids start,
When the bills come,
When the guests complain.
I simply remember where I've put my dough,
And then I'm as right
As rain!

'Oh, yes, there's nothing like a big dollop of bread dough,' Mum concluded.

'Mum, that's about seventeen signs of madness all rolled into one, that is!'

Mum jumped so high, Nova thought she'd have to scrape her off the ceiling. 'It's not polite to listen to private conversations,' Mum ranted, when her feet touched the ground again.

'And it's not sane to pretend you're being filmed every time you break out a saucepan,' Nova pointed out.

'Was there something in particular you wanted or are you just here to make my life a misery?' Mum asked.

'What're you doing?' Nova came further into the room.

'Making pastry, dear. What does it look like?'

'Who cheesed you off then?'

'No one. Sometimes I make pastry because I'm cooking something that requires pastry.' Mum frowned. 'Besides, you're the one who's got a funny look on your face.'

'No I haven't.'

'Yes you have. Your eyebrows are knotted together so tightly, it'd take Alexander the Great to sort them out.'

'Who's he then? A footballer?' grinned Nova.

Mum shook her head. 'What do they teach you at school these days?'

'Things that are far more useful than the dreary stuff you learned,' Nova replied. 'And I know who Alexander the Great was. He was the son of Alexander the Average.'

'You were telling me why you've got a face on?' Mum said patiently.

'I had to get away from Miss Dawn.'

'Why?'

'She was going on and on about toilets and how lucky we are that they're so comfortable!'

Mum burst out laughing.

'I like her but she is really strange.' Nova shook her head.

'She's in the perfect place then. Strange is what we do best at this hotel,' said Mum.

'Yeah, but there's something very odd about her. And that other woman, Miss Eve. Why do they travel around together? They're always sniping at each other,' Nova wondered out loud.

'At least they don't stab each other in the back,' Mum pointed out. 'They're nasty to each other's faces.'

'But why go around together then?'

'Why not? And at that age, maybe it's better than being alone.'

'Is it?' said Nova.

Mum shrugged. 'Some people will do some really foolish things or put up with a great deal rather than be lonely.'

'Would you?' Nova asked.

Mum considered. 'No, I don't think so.'

'I don't think I would either.'

Mother and daughter exchanged a smile of perfect understanding.

'D'you want a snack?' asked Mum. 'I've bought some

rock buns or there're some doughnuts next to the bread bin.'

'No thanks.'

'Not hungry?'

'Not especially,' Nova replied.

'You never are,' said Mum. 'You only ever eat at meal times – that I've seen, anyway.'

'That's good, isn't it?'

'Yeah, but it's not normal. Not for a twelve-year-old at any rate!'

'I'm the most normal one in this hotel,' Nova said indignantly.

'Which isn't saying much!'

'True,' Nova agreed with a grin.

Mum's smile faded. 'So why d'you never eat snacks?'

Nova sighed with impatience. 'I do eat snacks. I stuff myself with snacks.'

At Mum's raised eyebrows, Nova insisted, 'It's true.'

'You don't seem to have much of a sweet tooth either. It's not natural,' said Mum, more to herself than otherwise.

'Oh, for heaven's sake!' Nova marched over to the bread bin and helped herself to a jam doughnut from the paper bag next to it. She took a huge bite out of it, chewing rapidly as she said, 'See!'

'Yes, dear.' Mum smiled and returned to her pastry. Nova finished her doughnut in four bites before licking her sugary fingers clean like a cat licking its paws.

'Want another one?' asked Mum.

'Maybe later.' Nova drifted around the kitchen, looking for something to do that would require little effort and less thought. 'Dad's put up one of his notices again.'

Mum sighed. 'Oh dear! What's this one about?'

'Using the toilets properly.'

'First Miss Dawn, then your father. Why is everyone fixated on their nether regions today?' Mum frowned.

'Don't ask me. D'you want some help?'

'No, I've got it all under control,' Mum said hastily. 'No offence, love, but you helping out in the kitchen is like a bull helping out in a crystal glass shop!'

'Well, thank you very much. And when I don't offer —' Nova got no further.

Jude and Jake raced into the kitchen, crashing into her. 'Ow! Can't you two watch where you're going?' she stormed at them.

Only seconds behind them sprinted Rainbow, Nova's older sister. 'Mum, tell those little nappy squirts to stay out of my room or I'll . . . I'll torture them,' she raged, snatching at her brothers.

Jake and Jude ducked under and around the table, trying to keep out of reach of both Rainbow and Nova. The twins hid behind Mum as Rainbow did her best to grab first one, then the other, without much success.

'Raye, calm down. Nova, they bashed into you by accident so back off. OK, you two, what've you been up to?' Mum had to sidestep, then front-step to keep between Rainbow and the twins. It looked as if she were line-dancing.

'They've been in my room, searching through my things – that's what they've been doing,' Rainbow fumed. 'Mum, I want a lock on my door and if you don't get someone to do it, I'll do it myself.'

'Jude, is that true? Were you two searching through Raye's bedroom?'

'Only a little bit, Mum,' Jude admitted.

'In a pig's eye!' Raye exploded. 'They've been through all my stuff and my room's a mess.'

'How can you tell?' Mum wasn't trying to be sarcastic.

At least, Nova didn't think she was. From the instantly apologetic look on Mum's face, it'd obviously just slipped out. But it'd slipped out far enough for Rainbow to hear. Rainbow glared at Mum before she turned and marched out of the kitchen.

Mum turned to the twins. 'Could you two please, *please* stay out of Rainbow's room for the sake of my blood pressure? Not to mention my sanity!'

The twins grinned at her. 'At least we give Rainbow something else to worry about apart from boys!' said Jude.

'So what did you get this time?' Nova said eagerly. 'Anything interesting?'

'Raye's writing poems,' Jake informed her solemnly.

'No! Did you manage to get one?'

Jake lifted up his jumper and a piece of paper immediately fluttered out and onto the floor.

'Let's see.' Nova bent to snatch at it but Jake got there first.

'We'll read it,' he told her.

'I wouldn't do that if I were you,' Mum warned. 'It doesn't belong to you and if Raye finds out you've got it, you're on your own!'

'She won't find out, Mum. Don't worry. Ready, Jake?' said Jude.

'Ready, Jude,' Jake replied.

'I really, *really* don't recommend this,' Mum began.

'Never mind her. Read it,' Nova ordered, her eyes ablaze with possibilities.

'I want nothing to do with this.' Mum went back to rolling out her pastry.

'You start, Jake,' said Jude. 'We'll take half each.'

Jake grinned at Nova, then he began, 'Raye's poem:

'I'm a lanky, tall girl
With a cellulite body.
I've got a bulging stomach,
And my bum's big like a lorry.

I've got biceps like a boxer
I've canoes instead of feet,
And when I fart — look out!
'Cos my bottom isn't sweet!'

'Well, that bit is certainly true.' Jude nodded vigorously as he handed over the sheet of paper to his twin.

'My parents are as mad as loons,
My sister's a real pain.
My brothers are the worst of all
They're driving me insane.

What gives me inspiration as
My life heads down the tubes?
The two things that I wouldn't change,
My colour and my —'

'Give me that.' Mum snatched the poem from Jude before he could protest. She glanced down at the writing on the page. 'Oh, dear! Is that really how Raye sees herself?'

'What's she talking about — her bum's big like a lorry!?' Nova scoffed. 'She's thin as a pin. Any skinnier and I'd be able to pick my teeth with her.'

'Why on earth would she think her dad and I are mad? I'm the sanest person I know!' said Mum.

'Mum, you talk to your pastry and Dad is always hanging up peculiar notices for the guests. If that's not barmy, then what is?' said Nova.

'You're a pain! You're a pain!' said Jake to Nova glee-fully.

'And we're driving her insane,' said Jude with equal delight. 'Yes!'

Jude and Jake gave each other a high five as a salute to a job well done.

'Look, you two,' said Mum urgently, 'I don't want Raye finding out that you snaffled one of her poems, d'you hear? She's going through enough as it is.'

'What's she going through then?' Nova asked.

'She's a teenager,' Mum replied. As far as she was concerned that explained everything.

'I can't wait to be a teenager if it means I'll get away with all the stuff Raye does,' said Nova.

'You've always been stroppy, Nova, so your dad and I have had a lot of practice in dealing with you. Your sister, however, is different.'

'Thanks a lot!' Nova stormed.

'I didn't mean it like that!' Mum amended quickly. 'I just —'

'What does stroppy mean?' asked Jude.

'Awkward, stubborn, difficult — basically a pain in the neck,' Nova supplied.

'I just meant —' said Mum desperately.

'Save it, Mum!' Nova flounced over to the fridge.

Mum raised her eyes heavenwards.

'Are we going to be like that when we become teenagers?' Jake asked hopefully.

'Yeah, are we?' added Jude, with equal alacrity.

'Over my dead body,' Mum told them at once.

'How come the girls get to do it and we don't?' Jake pouted.

'Yeah, how come?' Jude added.

Mum said in a long-suffering voice, 'Why do I have the

sudden urge to bake enough bread to feed every mouth in the country?' She turned back to Rainbow's poem, the crease between her eyebrows deepening.

Jude and Jake grinned at each other. Mum was now softened up nicely!

'Mum, can we go and play in the attic?' Jake asked casually.

'Not in my bedroom,' Nova said quickly. Half the attic space had been converted into her bedroom and she guarded her space ferociously. The other half was used for storage and contained old-fashioned trunks and dusty boxes and piles of papers that only Jude and Jake enjoyed going through.

'Yeah, can we?' asked Jude.

'Can you what?' asked Mum, preoccupied.

'Play in the attic.'

'OK,' said Mum.

Stunned, Nova stared at her. Mum's brain obviously wasn't switched on. As the twins turned to run out of the room, Mum suddenly realized what she'd been asked. She moved at greased lightning speed to grab both of them by the arm.

'Just a minute, you two. No dropping water bombs on the heads of the guests, no dust sheets over your heads and pretending to be ghosts, no strange noises, no banana skins, no itching powder, no fake dog poo, no real cock-roaches, no stink bombs, no worms in any of the beds, no fart alarms, no frogs in any of the baths. NO NONSENSE. Is that understood?'

'Ma'am, yes, ma'am!' Jude and Jake saluted in unison.

'I mean it. If I hear from any of the guests that you two have been up to your usual antics, you're both in BIG trouble.'

'We heard,' Jake sniffed.

'No need to go on and on,' Jude added, dusting the flour off his arm.

They both ran off with Mum eyeing them suspiciously. She directed a worried look at Nova.

'Don't worry, Mum,' Nova said. 'Between me, Raye, Dad and the other guests, they probably won't get away with too much. Probably.'

'That makes me feel a whole heap better,' Mum replied dryly.

Nova grinned at her.

Dad burst through the door. 'Karmah, has Mr Jackman deigned to tell you how long he's staying with us?' he asked.

'No, he hasn't. And as long as we have his credit card details, he can dither as long as he likes,' Mum replied.

Nova wondered if she had time to slide out, tear down Dad's latest notice and duck out of sight for an hour or so until he calmed down. It was worth a try. Edging behind him, she started to sidestep silently towards the door.

'I'm not happy with guests not letting me know how long they plan to stay. How am I meant to schedule in future bookings if I don't know when the guests are going to leave?' Dad complained, adding without turning round, 'Nova, for the last time, leave my notice alone. D'you hear?'

'What future bookings?' Nova piped up from behind him, peeved.

Mum glared at Nova, her expression piercing. Nova knew exactly what that look meant. They'd been at the hotel for almost two years now and Dad had tried just about everything to make Phoenix Manor more popular, but nothing really took off. The hotel was set high up on the gently sloping St Bart's Head, overlooking St Bart's Bay. To the front of the hotel there were stunning views across the bay to the sea beyond. The formal gardens behind the hotel merged into Siren's Copse. Underground tunnels criss-crossed the land for miles around — tunnels where, centuries before, smugglers were rumoured to have brought silks and brandy ashore from continental Europe, using the secret underground passages to hide from the authorities. There was meant to be a tunnel entrance hidden in the bay somewhere and another one in Siren's Copse, but no one had ever found them. In a setting steeped in local history, the hotel should've been a dead certainty for success — but it wasn't. Business was slow, not to mention a constant worry. And as Mum pointed out, Dad didn't need his family constantly moaning on and making him feel like a failure.

'We do all right, Nova,' Mum said, an edge to her voice.

'Yeah, right.' Nova headed for the fridge. 'I'm thirsty. Any juice or something fizzy in there?'

'Nova Alexandra Clibbens, don't even think about it!' said Mum as Nova raised the orange juice carton to her lips. 'Use a glass.'

'What's that?' Dad pointed to the piece of paper, now covered in flour, beside Mum's pastry.

Mum picked it up. 'Oh, that's —'

Raye marched into the room. 'Mum, I want you to — Is that one of my poems?'

Nova wasn't surprised that Raye had spotted it. Her sister always did have eyes like a hawk.

'Yes, but I . . .' Mum spluttered.

'Mum, how could you? My poems are private and personal.' Raye snatched it out of her mother's hand, directing a look at her that would've had a weaker person gasping for breath. 'You're worse than the twins.'

'So what's so good about your boobs that you wouldn't change them?' Nova couldn't resist asking.

'Mum, I can't believe you! You let Nova read it?' Raye asked, scandalized.

'Why d'you want to change your boobs, Rainbow?' asked Dad, getting hold of entirely the wrong end of the stick. 'I hope you're not thinking of plastic surgery or some other such nonsense at your age.'

'Leave my boobs out of this,' Raye said furiously, her beige cheeks now fiery red.

'Raye wants to have her boobs done,' Nova sang.

'I do not!'

'Raye wants to have her boobs done!'

Raye used sign language to tell Nova exactly where to go and what to do when she got there.

'Rainbow, that's quite enough of that,' Dad admonished.

After glaring at Dad and scowling at Nova, Rainbow turned her attention to Mum. 'I'm not going to forget this in a hurry,' she snapped. 'Thanks a lot for showing me up in front of everyone.'

'Now wait just a minute . . .' Mum said, once she'd scraped her jaw off the floor.

But she was talking to the closing kitchen door. Rainbow was long gone! The kitchen was stony silent as Mum turned to see Dad and Nova watching her. Nova drank her orange juice, looking away so she wouldn't be blamed for what had just happened. Dad moved in to stand behind Mum.

'What you need is a stress-relieving massage,' he said, his fingers already digging into Mum's shoulders.

Mum winced and tried to pull away, but nothing doing. Nova felt sorry for her. She had already experienced Dad's massages at a time when she used to suffer from leg cramps. The cramps were less painful! Mum tried again to shrug out of his grasp, but Dad just held on tighter.

'Ah!' There was no mistaking the satisfaction in Dad's voice. 'Isn't that much better? Let's just work out those kinks.'

'The kinks are all gone,' Mum said hastily, trying to pull herself away. 'Let go, dear. I'm getting pins and needles up and down my arms.'

'Nonsense. Five minutes of one of my massages and you'll be smiling for the rest of the week.'

By which time, Mum had had enough. She raised her hands to prise Dad's fingers off her protesting muscles, starting with his little fingers first. 'Tyler, back off! I'm not being funny but your massages are hellish!'

Dad's hands dropped to his sides. 'Pardon?'

'Every time you give me a massage, it feels like a golden eagle has landed on me and is trying to tear off bits of my body.' Mum rubbed at each of her sore shoulders in turn.

'I see,' Dad said with icy politeness.

Nova raised her eyebrows. Today obviously wasn't Mum's day for tact, but Nova could see she was still trying to work through the pain in her shoulders as she spoke!

'If that's how you feel, I'll take my eagle's talons some-where else.' Dad stormed out of the kitchen without another word.

Nova fought down a grin. 'Shall I break out the bread dough, Mum?' she asked.

Rubbing her throbbing temples, Mum replied, 'Please!'

4. Liam

I marched down the hallway, grabbing my jacket off the banister on my way to the front door.

'Liam, get back here.'

I kept striding, pulling open the front door. Dad rushed up behind me and pushed it shut, painfully jerking my fingers in the process.

'Liam, you'll do as I say. This is still my house.'

'Your house?' I scoffed. 'Mum left it to me. Or are you too drunk to remember that?'

Dad's face went seven shades of red. He looked like one of those DIY paint charts. 'Don't talk to me like that, boy. I'm still your father.' Spittle flew out of his mouth to land on my cheek.

'I wish to God I could forget.' I took a great deal of pleasure in scrubbing at my face with the back of my hand. I let my eyes blaze, making no attempt to hide what I was feeling. 'Look at you. You'd be a joke if you weren't so pathetic!'

I glared down at Dad, silently daring him to try something. At sixteen, I was several centimetres taller than him and I was glad for every single one of them. Burning spots of pink appeared on Dad's cheeks as his glance slid away. He obviously couldn't take the way I was looking at him. Good!

'I do my best for you, Liam,' he sighed. 'I know you don't believe that, but I do.'

'You save your best for the local pub. You've no interest in anything or anyone except yourself.'

'That's not fair —'

'Fair!' I exploded. I pointed to my brother, who couldn't stop sniffing as he sat on the top stair, taking it all in. 'Every stitch of clothing on Josh's back was bought by me. If it wasn't for my Saturday job, we'd be walking around in rags.'

'I do my best,' Dad repeated.

'Oh, do me a favour.' I shook my head. 'You have no idea what I want, what I'm doing, nothing. I passed all my mock exams but you weren't even interested enough to ask me how I did.'

'I . . . well done . . .'

'Don't strain yourself, Dad.' My contempt sliced into him with every word. 'The first chance I get, I'm outta here. I'm going to pass my exams and go on to college and, I swear, you will never see me again.'

'Liam, take me with you.' Josh's voice rang out from above us.

'No way. It's time I looked out for myself instead of putting you first all the time. If it wasn't for you, Josh, I'd've left this dump long ago . . .' Josh flinched at my words. I regretted them the moment I said them. Josh's face crumpled. Tears rolled down his face. His nose started to drip again.

'You don't have to worry about your brother. Josh is my responsibility. I'll take care of him,' Dad insisted.

I stared at him. Did he really believe what he was saying? Couldn't he hear himself? My head was full of bitter words which tripped and tumbled over each other in their haste to leave my mouth. There were too many of them, darting back and forth much too fast. They hurt so much they made my eyes sting. I clamped my lips together. Silent moments passed.

'Dad, get out of my way,' I said, when I could trust myself to speak without making a fool of myself.

On the stairs Josh's sniffing was getting louder and more fre-quent. I glanced up at him, watching with quiet desperation as the tears trickled faster down his cheeks.

'I've got to get out of here.' I could hear the despair in my voice and despised myself for it. Wrenching open the door, I ran from the house, leaving the door open behind me.

31

'Liam, take me with you,' Josh called out from behind me. 'Please, take me with you.'

I ran faster. Ran and ran until my heart roared like a wounded lion. But even the roar couldn't drown out Josh's words.

'Liam, take me with you . . .'

I covered my ears with my hands as I ran.

'Liam, take me with you . . .'

I can't, Josh.

I can't.

5. Rainbow

Rainbow was still steaming. Why couldn't she live with a normal family in a normal house in a normal neighbourhood? Preferably somewhere in a big city where there were actual things to see and do. Instead she was stuck out in the middle of nowhere-by-the-sea with the brothers from hell. After nearly two years Rainbow still missed her old school and her old friends. She was beginning to wonder if she'd ever get used to life in Phoenix Manor. She always felt like she was fifteen minutes ahead of everyone else at the hotel. She just didn't fit, no matter how hard she tried. And the twins weren't helping.

'If I catch those two in my room just once more . . . I swear! And no jury of girls my age would convict,' Rainbow ranted in an undertone. 'I am so fed up with . . . with — Omigod! He's gorgeous!'

Rainbow came to an abrupt, complete halt and stared. The boy standing at the reception desk had her full attention. Those lips! Oh, those kissable lips! And that nose. Strong and masculine. And those eyes! Omigod, those beautiful brown eyes. Like mysterious pools of . . .

'Er, excuse me, love, but d'you know where the staff are? We want to book in,' said a man's voice from far away.

'Sorry?' Rainbow had to drag her gaze away from the angel in front of her. A short, reasonable-looking man and a slightly taller, sour-faced blonde woman stood behind the Boy Wonder. The man had brown hair flecked with abundant silver strands and wore a genuinely amused smile on his face. The woman next to him didn't though. She was not so much frowning as scowling at Rainbow.

'D'you know where the staff are?' the man repeated.

'I'll book you in. That's no trouble.' Rainbow immediately moved behind the reception desk. No way was she letting Mr Snog-Me-Until-I'm-Breathless out of her sight until she had his name, age, mobile phone number and star sign.

'D'you work here then?' the man asked dubiously.

'My family runs this hotel,' Rainbow informed him, with false modesty. This was one of those rare occasions when she actually volunteered the information.

'And those are your room rates?' He pointed to the sign behind her.

Rainbow nodded. What did he expect to find under a huge sign with the heading ROOM RATES? Second-hand car prices?

'We're Mr and Mrs Stanley and this is our son, Andrew. We booked a room a fortnight ago. Does the family room come with a double and a single bed or three singles?'

Rainbow stopped listening after she'd heard the hunk's name. 'Hi, Andrew.' She turned on what she hoped was a casual yet friendly smile. Not too forward, but not too reluctant. Not too eager, yet not too formal. A genuine smile from the eyes. With just a hint of mystery and a dash of promise.

'Hi. Good to meet you. What's your name?' Andrew asked. And his voice was deep and flowed like honey. Wow! Gorgeous all over.

And then Rainbow realized what he'd asked her. Her heart sank. 'My name? My name is . . . er . . . Raye . . . All my friends call me Raye. You can call me Raye too if you like.'

'Excuse me, but d'you think we could book in some time before the end of the century?' his mum cut in.

Rainbow glared at her. How rude! 'Could you fill in

this registration form, please?' She handed Mrs Stanley the form with a painted-on smile, then turned back to Mr Tall, Dark and Drool-Slobber Handsome. 'Will you be here for long?'

Please! Please!

'Two days. We leave on Sunday,' Andrew replied.

Yes!

'Well, I hope you have a pleasant stay. If there's anything you need, anything at all . . .'

'Thanks, Rainbow. I'll take over now.' Dad practically pushed her to one side as he smiled at the new guests.

'Rainbow?' Andrew raised his eyebrows.

Rainbow's face immediately began to radiate heat. She could've died. 'My dad's idea,' she informed him quickly. 'I hate it.'

'I don't,' said Andrew. 'It's original. Unusual. It suits you.'

'D'you think so?'

Andrew nodded. And for the first time since Rainbow was about seven, she didn't mind her name.

'We'd like a family room,' said Mr Stanley. 'I was asking your daughter if your family rooms come with a double and a single bed or three singles?'

'A double bed and one single,' Dad replied. 'But as we're not too busy at the moment, I can let you have a double room with an adjoining single for the same price, if you'd like?'

'My own room. Great! Perfect,' Andrew enthused.

'I'm not sure about that . . .' Mrs Stanley began.

'Mum, I'm perfectly old enough to stay in a room of my own. I'll behave,' Andrew said silkily. 'I promise.'

A strange feeling came over Rainbow as she watched Andrew and his parents regard each other. There was something going on, some strange undercurrent that Andrew's words had provoked.

'That's OK then. I'm very keen on guests who behave themselves!' Dad laughed.

And just like that, the tension in the air vanished. Rainbow wondered if maybe she'd imagined it. She wasn't sure. But she didn't think so.

'Rainbow, could you . . .? Rainbow?' Dad prodded his daughter's arm to get her attention.

'What?'

'If you can stop fluttering your eyelashes for five seconds, could you get me the keys to the Dickens and the Austen rooms please?'

Rainbow's cheeks began to burn – badly. Honestly! She could've kicked Dad in the shins. 'I am not fluttering my eyelashes,' she hissed, before turning to get the keys.

'Dickens room?' Mr Stanley asked.

'All our rooms are named after famous writers. Dead ones. I don't want to be sued. It was my idea actually. It came to me about a week after we took over this place and the minute I thought of it, I said to myself, "Tyler, the job's a good 'un!" And fortunately my wife agreed. You'll meet her later. Her name is Karmah. She's in the kitchen at the moment — Ow! Rainbow!'

'Here are your keys.' Rainbow thrust them into Mr Stanley's hand. She'd had to step on Dad's foot in the process to get him to shut up. He was burbling on like talking had just come into fashion.

'Will you be dining here tonight? My wife is a great cook,' Dad smiled.

Rainbow stared at him. How could he just open his mouth and lie like that?

'Er, I don't —' began Mrs Stanley.

'Go on, Mum,' Andrew interrupted. 'I'm a bit tired. I'd like to stay in this evening.'

'Tired? Are you sure you're OK?' His mum was all flustered concern. 'Is there anything I can do?'

'No, Mum. Stop flapping.' Andrew smiled to take the sting out of his words.

Rainbow was not impressed with Mrs Stanley.

'OK.' Mrs Stanley turned back to Dad. 'Can we book a table for eight o'clock, please?'

'Certainly. I'll make a note of that. The dining room is just through those double doors,' said Dad, pointing past reception to his right.

'And we'll need a table for three for eight tomorrow,' Mrs Stanley added.

'Pardon?'

'For three people, for eight o'clock tomorrow night,' Mrs Stanley explained impatiently.

She was getting right up Rainbow's nose and no mistake.

'It's Andrew's birthday tomorrow,' said Mr Stanley, smiling apologetically at Rainbow and her dad.

'How old will you be?' Rainbow asked Andrew directly.

'Sixteen,' he replied with a smile.

'Just a year older than me.'

'You look older.'

'Thanks.' Rainbow couldn't believe how he always knew exactly the right things to say. It was uncanny.

'Maybe it would be better if we went elsewhere,' said Mrs Stanley, glancing frostily at Rainbow before turning back to Rainbow's dad. 'Can you recommend a good restaurant?'

Before Dad could say a word, Andrew got in first. 'No, Mum. I want my birthday dinner here. This is just fine.'

'You're sure?' Mrs Stanley asked doubtfully.

'Positive. And it is *my* birthday.'

'If you insist.' Mrs Stanley shrugged.

Andrew winked at Rainbow, who smiled back. His mum was a gorgon but he more than made up for her.

'D'you need help with your bags?' Dad asked hopefully.

They might have thought he was going out of his way to help them, but Rainbow knew the hope in his voice was because he was praying not to have to carry their luggage. Dad had a bad back and lifting heavy suitcases was not what the doctor ordered.

'No thanks. We can manage.' Andrew spoke before his parents could. 'Raye, will you be eating at eight too?'

I am now. 'I might be,' Rainbow smiled. After all, it didn't pay to seem too, *too* eager.

'Hope to see you later then,' said Andrew. He and his parents headed up the stairs.

Count on it, Rainbow thought. Even if she had to drag him to the dining room by his hair roots, they'd meet up again later.

'Ah! Young love!' Dad sighed.

The sigh quickly changed into a cough when Rainbow turned the full force of her outraged glare at him.

'Something wrong, darling?' Dad asked, his face all innocence.

Rainbow marched off without deigning to answer.

'Something I said, Raye?' Dad laughed after her.

Rainbow kept on walking. And not once, not once did she realize she was being watched.

6. Nova and Miss Eve

Nova sighed, the way she always did when she thought about her sister. Less than a couple of years ago they'd been so close. What'd happened since then? It would've been so fantastic to go to the beach or go shopping or just hang out together in the hotel. But nothing doing. Over the past year or so Raye had backed right away from doing anything with Nova. She didn't even want to be seen with her. Not in the hotel. Not at school. Nowhere. No way!

'Nova, stop swinging on the banister!' Dad called out from the reception desk.

Nova carried on rocking to and fro, her hands wrapped around the bottom banister post. Nova the pain. That was her new name. So now Raye was too old to hang out with and the twins were too young. The half-term break was dragging more than usual this time round. Nova usually longed for school holidays and they ended much too soon – but this time not much had been going on at the hotel. Friday morning and nothing dawning.

'Nova, am I talking Martian? Get off the banister,' said Dad.

Nova sighed again, but did as she was told this time. She thought for a moment. The gardens. She'd go for a long walk across the gardens and after that maybe down to the beach. She headed across the hall towards the front door.

Miss Eve emerged from the hotel lounge. 'Ah, Nova, my poppet. How are you today?'

Nova bristled with indignation. How many times did

she have to repeat herself before Miss Eve got it? 'Poppet' was out, OUT, OUT!

'Fine,' Nova muttered in a voice that suggested she was anything but.

'I wonder if I might have a word?' Miss Eve continued.

'Any word in particular?'

'Pardon?'

'Nothing,' Nova replied hastily. She didn't want to spend the next ten minutes explaining. She looked at Miss Eve but her glance quickly slid away again. There was something about the elderly woman that set the hairs at the back of Nova's neck bristling. Miss Eve had off-white, blue-rinsed hair which matched her pale blue eyes. Ice-cold eyes, Nova always thought. She was tall and straight and laughed a lot, but very rarely smiled. Miss Dawn was the opposite: she smiled a lot but very rarely laughed. Miss Dawn seemed the sadder of the two.

'Where're you off to?' asked Miss Eve.

'I was going to take a walk in the garden. A long walk.' Nova hoped that would put the old dear off. 'A long, long walk.'

'Excellent! I was just thinking of doing the same thing myself. Let's walk together, poppet,' suggested Miss Eve.

Nova's heart and hopes sank. She had wanted to spend some time by herself, not spend the next half hour listening to Miss Eve rabbit on about her various aches and pains and varicose veins. 'Are you sure you're up to it, Miss Eve?' Nova couldn't give up without a fight. 'I'll be walking quite quickly.'

'My dear poppet, I have more stamina than you might think.' Miss Eve's eyes twinkled wickedly. 'Why, if I were to tell you some of the things I've got up to in my time—'

'Please don't,' Nova interrupted. 'I mean, please don't

bother yourself. You should save your energy. For the walk.'

'Of course. Shall we go then?'

'Maybe you should go and get a cardie? It looks a bit nippy out there.' Brilliant! Nova congratulated herself on her ploy. While Miss Eve was off getting herself a cardigan, Nova would be out of there faster than a rat up a drainpipe. Perfect!

'No thanks. I'm just fine,' replied Miss Eve. She linked arms with Nova and set a brisk pace for the door. 'Don't dawdle, poppet. As you quite rightly said, it's not a proper walk if it's not bracing.'

Nova turned her head, searching for something, someone, *anyone* to rescue her. But there was only Dad at the reception desk. Nova threw him her best beseeching look, mouthing, 'Help!' in the process.

'Enjoy!' Dad called out, grinning maliciously as he waved goodbye.

Nova was sink, sank, sunk – without a trace. She glared at Dad as Miss Eve continued to drag her out the front door.

Miss Eve stood on the top step looking around at the autumn countryside. Nova looked around as well. She never got tired of this view. The front of the hotel stood tall and still like a faithful sentinel. It was set back about two hundred metres from the cliff edge but was impressive enough to be seen from boats heading in and out of St Bart's Bay. In past times fishermen in their vessels had been the ones to admire or envy the Manor House, as it had been called. Now leisure boats and small yachts sailed out, not even giving Phoenix Manor a backwards glance. At the back of the hotel were the hotel grounds, over an acre of formally landscaped gardens. But the best thing of all was that from the front step, no matter what the weather, you could see or hear or taste the sea. Nova loved the way the sea shone like a shattered mirror when it was calm or rose up in a fury in stormy weather. Sometimes she went down to the cliff edge and leaned against the wall overlooking the bay and just watched the sea for hours on end. And sometimes she almost believed that the sea lay there watching her as well.

Nova remembered how she'd complained incessantly about moving away from her school and her friends. She'd been worse than Rainbow and that was saying something – until she'd stood on this top step and savoured the view. And with the view, all thoughts of her previous life had faded to a place where they didn't hurt any more.

Nova inhaled deeply, her eyes closed as she drank in the salty tang in the air. Next to her Miss Eve did the same, only to start coughing almost immediately.

'Ah, smell that fresh sea air. Doesn't it make you feel sick?' asked Miss Eve. 'Doesn't it make you long for car fumes mixed with the gentle waft of stale burgers and backed-up, overflowing sewers?'

'Did you originally live in a city then?' Nova asked to be polite.

'Oh, I've lived everywhere, poppet. Miss Dawn and me, we like to travel.' Miss Eve laughed like a woman possessed, though for the life of her, Nova couldn't see what was so funny.

'Private joke, poppet. Private joke,' Miss Eve supplied when she saw the way Nova was looking at her.

She tugged Nova down the stairs. They turned left to walk round the side of the hotel to the gardens at the back. Miss Eve was striding along as if she were on a route march. Nova had to trot beside her to keep up.

'You said you wanted to talk to me?' Nova gasped.

'Oh, yes. Nothing terribly important. I just wondered

whether Miss Dawn had spoken to you recently?' Miss Eve asked lightly.

'Yeah. Earlier today.' Where had those tiny beads of sweat prickling her forehead come from? Was it just the fast walk or something else? What was it about this woman . . .?

'What did she say?' asked Miss Eve.

'Good morning.'

'Good morning to you too, my poppet. But what did Miss Dawn say to you?'

'She said, "Good morning",' Nova explained patiently.

'Anything else?'

'Like what?' Nova asked, curious now in spite of herself. The beads of sweat still kept coming, even though it wasn't that warm and Nova wasn't trotting that quickly any more. It was as if every cell in her body was on alert.

'Did she mention any of the other guests at all?' asked Miss Eve.

Nova stopped trotting altogether and pulled away. Miss Eve turned with a ready smile on her lips. 'I just wondered, that's all.'

'I can't remember.' Nova frowned. 'I think she said something about Dad falling over the reception desk but not much more than that. Why?'

'As I said, I'm just curious.'

'Why would she mention any of the guests to me?' asked Nova.

'No reason.' Miss Eve started walking again.

Nova's suspicions were well and truly aroused. What was this all about? What was Miss Eve after? Why all the questions and the interest in what Miss Dawn might have said about any of the guests? Miss Eve turned as if she felt Nova studying her. Nova forced herself to smile and walked to catch up.

'When you get to my age, my poppet, poking your nose into other people's business is one of the few pleasures left in life!' said Miss Eve.

Nova nodded, then shrugged.

Miss Eve glanced down at her watch. 'Oh, silly me!' she continued. 'I've got some letters which I need to finish off if they're going to catch the next post. D'you mind if I cut short our walk, poppet?'

'No! I mean, that's fine,' Nova said in all seriousness.

'We'll have a nice long walk and talk some time soon,' Miss Eve smiled. 'OK?'

'OK,' agreed Nova, thinking, Like when my toes learn to chew gum!

She watched as Miss Eve walked back towards the front of the house. Talk about a lucky escape! There was definitely something about Miss Eve ... Something that made Nova careful of every word she said, and every move she made. Once Miss Eve had rounded the corner of the hotel and was out of sight, Nova turned away, breathing a huge sigh of relief – only to walk straight into someone's chest.

'Ow!' Nova stepped back but it didn't stop her from falling backwards to land on the gravelly path with a thump.

The teenage boy she'd just bumped into stared at her in stunned amazement. His mid-brown eyes were wide with shock. He had short, dark hair and the creases around his mouth indicated either a ready smile or a ready frown – Nova wasn't quite sure which.

'Why don't you look where you're going?' she demanded furiously.

'Why don't you?' the boy replied.

'Because this is my hotel,' Nova said stiffly.

'That shouldn't stop you from looking where you're

going,' said the boy. 'And anyway, I live here too.'

'No. You might be staying here, but this is my home.' Nova tried to scramble to her feet.

The boy put out a hand to help her up. Nova reached out to take it but before she could grab hold, he withdrew it sharply. Nova's bum bounced off the stony ground again.

'Sorry,' said the boy, his hands behind his back.

Nova scowled at him, her eyes ablaze.

'Jeez! If looks could kill . . .' And the boy started laughing.

'You moron!' Nova jumped up. 'I bet your shoe size is bigger than your IQ.'

'It's not, actually. My IQ puts me in the genius category. I've been tested.'

'If you're a genius, I'm the Queen of Sheba,' Nova scoffed.

'Your majesty!' said the boy, bowing slightly.

'When you've quite finished.' This boy was getting more and more irritating. The longer Nova was around him, the more she longed to be somewhere else. She didn't care if she never saw this idiot again. 'Excuse me.' She tried to go round the boy, but he stepped in front of her, blocking her path. To her surprise, he waved his hand in front of her face.

'What's your problem?' Nova asked, eyeing him suspiciously.

'What do I look like?'

Nova stared. 'Pardon?'

'What colour's my hair?'

Nova began to feel just a little bit anxious. This boy definitely had more than one screw loose. Best to humour him. 'Black.' Nova looked closer. 'No. Dark brown.'

The boy took a step forward. Nova took a step back.

'What colour are my eyes?'

'I dunno.' Nova leaned forward for a better look, only to pull back immediately. 'Brown.'

'How tall am I?' The question was fired at Nova.

'What is this? Don't you know what you look like?'

'Just checking.' The boy suddenly grinned from ear to ear.

A couple of eggs short of the full hotel breakfast and no mistake, Nova amended silently. 'Excuse me, I have things to do.' She turned and walked quickly back the way she had come, towards the front of the hotel.

'Wait. I want to talk to you.'

Nova kept walking. She most certainly didn't want to talk to that weirdo. What was it about her that had all the nutters for miles around flocking to her? Maybe she should try a different soap! What was he doing? Watching her leave? Nova turned round. The boy had vanished. Startled, she looked around. He couldn't have reached the other side of the hotel already, not without running – and if he'd run then Nova would've heard his footsteps crunching on the gravel path. And he hadn't cut across the gardens, otherwise he'd still be in sight. Not even an Olympic gold medallist could sprint out of sight that fast.

Nova took another look around. Nothing. Seriously spooked, she quickened her pace as she headed back to the front entrance. Only when she was back inside the hotel did she dare to breathe a sigh of relief. Who was that creep? With a little luck she'd never have to see him again. There was something about him that put her on edge. Mind you, he wasn't bad looking. But that was the only thing he had going for him.

'Dad, who's the boy with — ?' Nova was heading for the reception desk, but then she stopped abruptly.

Weirdo was back and standing right next to Dad behind the reception desk. He was peering over Dad's shoulder, but at the sound of Nova's voice he looked up and waved.

'What're you doing behind there? Come out!' Nova demanded furiously.

'Huh? I work here.' Dad frowned.

'Not you, Dad. How did you get back in here before me?' Nova asked the boy.

'I never left,' Dad replied, bewildered.

'Not you, Dad. *Him*.'

Dad looked round. 'Nova, who're you talking to?'

'I thought guests weren't allowed behind the reception desk?'

'They're not.' Dad's frown deepened.

'Then tell him to move.'

'Tell who?'

'Him,' Nova said impatiently, pointing at the boy, who now had a beaming smirk on his face.

Dad turned in the direction of Nova's pointing finger. 'Nova, there's no one here except you and me.'

'Dad, this isn't the time for a wind-up.'

'My feelings exactly. Go and wind up your mother instead,' Dad huffed.

'Why did you let him behind the desk?' Nova asked, exasperated.

'Who?'

Nova was just about to explode when Weirdo put his finger up to his lips. The gesture momentarily took the wind out of Nova's sails – but only momentarily.

'Dad —' She got no further.

Weirdo walked right *through* Dad and the reception desk to stand in front of Nova. 'I wouldn't bother if I were you,' he said. 'It seems that you're the only one in this dump who can see me. Hi, I'm Liam.' And he held out his hand.

Two seconds maximum of stunned silence, then Nova opened her mouth – and screamed blue murder!

Liam grimaced and stuck his fingers in his ears. Nova screamed until her throat felt like it was on fire, but even then she didn't stop.

Dad ran out from behind the reception desk. 'Nova? Nova, stop it. What's the matter? Nova, talk to me.'

Mum ran in from the kitchen. 'What's happened? What on earth is going on?'

'I thought you of all people would take it better than that!' Liam shouted above the din, fading out to disappear altogether.

Nova's head was spinning and she felt sick. Was she going to faint? Was this what it was like to be on the verge of fainting? Her heart was trembling and her blood was racing and everything around her was moving in and out of her vision like a telly moving back and forth on roller skates. Nova took a deep breath, then another, still staring into the space where Liam had just been.

'Nova, what's wrong?' Dad repeated frantically.

Hotel guests appeared on the stairs and from the hotel lounge.

'Nova?'

Her heartbeat began to slow down from frenzied to merely frantic. Her mum and dad stood in front of her, anxiety and concern written all over their faces.

'Nova, darling, what is it?' Mum said urgently.

'Nova, talk to us. What's wrong?' Dad pleaded.

'He's . . . he's a ghost!' said Nova at last. 'Dad, there was a ghost standing behind you and he walked right through you!'

48

Dad straightened up, his expression incredulous. 'You saw a what?' he repeated. 'A ghost?'

The other guests looked at each other, startled. Mrs Stanley drew her cardigan closer to her, looking around anxiously.

'You saw no such thing,' Mum warned Nova sternly.

'But, Mum, I —'

'Nova, your joke has gone far enough. You're frightening the guests – OK?'

Nova looked round. The guests were all peering at her. A couple of them looked amused; Mrs Stanley and most of the others didn't.

'I'm sorry, Mum. It wasn't really a ghost. It . . . it was a spider – above Dad's head.'

The guests melted away with disapproving shakes of their heads or sympathetic smiles. Mum's look of incredulity melted into something else. Nova knew she was in trouble.

'It was an enormous spider. It was the spider from hell!' Nova tried to defend herself.

'Go to your room,' Mum said furiously. '*Now!*'

Nova set off up the stairs, muttering to herself. Well, what was she supposed to say?

'That is your daughter!' Mum and Dad spoke in unison, pointing at each other in a very accusatory manner.

'If you must know,' Nova called out from the top of the stairs. 'I didn't see a spider. I really did see a ghost!'

'Enough nonsense,' Mum snapped. 'Go to your room.'

'Nova, do as you're told,' Dad ordered. 'You're in enough trouble already, without adding to it.'

Nova's attic bedroom was up another flight of stairs but she ran all the way. She paused outside her bedroom door, puffing and desperately trying to gulp down air to catch her breath. The boy she'd seen – the *ghost* she'd seen – was he real or was she still asleep and dreaming the whole thing or was she imagining things? Nova dismissed the last two options. She never imagined things, well, hardly ever. And she'd seen the boy – what did he say his name was? Liam? Well, she'd seen him as large as life. *Hadn't she?* With a sigh, Nova opened her bedroom door – and gasped. There, sitting on her bed, was Liam.

7. Liam

I walked and walked. Down by the sea front. Along the pier. Back past the railway station. Through Jubilee Park. Just walking, trying to outdistance my thoughts. I kept hearing Josh say 'Take me with you.' I couldn't get his words out of my head. They played like an undying echo.

'Take me with you . . .'

Why, Josh? So you can end up a loser like me? And the worst thing of all was, I knew I was throwing my life away. I was angry all the time, resentful all the time. All I wanted to do was hit out, hit back, at school, at home – it didn't really matter where. That's why I had to get away – before I choked on all the feelings inside me. Josh would be OK. He'd survive. Besides, Josh is the brains of the family. The obvious brains! Good school reports. Good test results.

'Josh is very intelligent . . .'

'Josh is a pleasure to teach . . .'

'Josh has a keen interest in the subject . . .'

He'd never had a bad report in his life. And it didn't take a genius to figure out what all those school reports were really saying.

'Josh isn't like his older brother . . .'

No, he isn't. He hasn't a clue how to look after himself. I've always done it for him. I've done nothing else but look after Josh since Mum died. Just call me Polyfilla – filling all the gaps in Josh's life so he wouldn't miss Mum as much as I did.

Do.

My brother is the artistic one, the sensitive one, the articulate one. Me? I'm Conan the Barbarian compared to him. I know that's how I'm considered. And you know what, I don't care. I can look after myself. No one ever asked me to be artistic or poetic. A couple of silly pranks at school and that was it — my card was marked. They were never going to give me a chance after that. Never in a million years. I was even sent for a test — what they called a psychological evaluation. Dad hit the roof, of course. Until it became clear that I wasn't a moron, or even average. The tests showed I had a well-above-average IQ. That shocked everyone. Even me, to be honest. I'd spent so long listening to everyone tell me how useless I was that even I'd started to believe it. My IQ rating is the only reason they didn't kick me out of school, I reckon. But after the test, I really let rip. I was untouchable. I was invincible. And some of the things I got up to . . . Silly, hurtful things. Not that I'm making excuses. But taking the test and everyone's reaction to it did something to me. I realized that before the results, nothing was expected from me. No talent, no hard work, no commitment, no brains, no sense, no ambitions — nothing. So I decided that if everyone expected nothing, that was precisely what they were going to get.

I don't walk all over people. But I don't let them walk all over me either.

Poor Josh! Being lumbered with a brother like me. I tease him and wind him up something chronic, and he still adores me. Silly beggar! My friends call him the lapdog — even to his face 'cos of the way he follows me around. I can't change direction without tripping over him first. Josh, the anchor. Josh, the chain. Josh, the lapdog. Josh, the pain. Josh, my brother. Josh, the one thing in this world I really care about.

Sometimes . . . sometimes I feel like I want to just demolish things because there's so much inside me that I want to say and do but I can't get it out. I want to make things, build things. I want to climb. I want to fly. But my brother keeps me tethered to the ground. So I smash things instead.

'Take me with you.'

How can I, when because of you, I never leave? Take you

where? Take you to nowhere. Take you to nothing. You don't need me, Josh. Sooner or later, you'll fly on your own. And I'll be stuck here, down on the ground, watching you fly. And hating you. I don't want to hate you. You're my brother. I care about you.

But I'm afraid. You scare me, Josh.

Where am I?

Jeez! Manor Hotel. Have I really walked that far? Manor Hotel used to be the Manor House, owned a couple of centuries before by Count whoever or Lord someone-or-other. It was converted into a hotel about thirty years ago, though, passing from one person to another, none of whom seemed to want it. The last owner (a woman, I think) closed it down over nine years ago and it has stood empty ever since.

But I love this place. It's derelict and practically falling down, but it's such an excellent place to hang out. Me and my friends used to run riot around here. Breaking windows. Spray painting the walls. Making our mark. It was our hide-out. A home away from home. I haven't been over this way in months though. Who put all this wire-mesh fencing up? It's too high to get over. I'll go round. Hopefully the original wire fence at the back is still there and they haven't replaced it. That was always our way in – the gap in the wire security fence over by the gardens. Gardens! The polite way to put it! They looked more like an overgrown wasteland than anything else. But there's something about this place, set on the sloping cliff top, with the sea before it and the so-called gardens behind. What I didn't tell my mates was that sometimes, when things got really bad at home, I'd come up here by myself and just wander around and explore. It was somewhere to be away from things. To escape. Manor Hotel. I haven't been up here for months. I can't believe I haven't been up here for months. Maybe that's why I feel so stressed.

Oh please! Look at that! What a useless sign! Is that really meant to put anyone off?

```
WARNING!
THIS SITE IS DANGEROUS. NO
TRESPASSING.

SECURITY GUARDS AND PATROL DOGS
ARE EMPLOYED ON THIS SITE.

TRESPASSERS WILL BE
PROSECUTED.
```

Yeah right! That sign has been there for the last five years and in all that time, I've never seen a single security guard or dog. Who're they trying to kid? Not that it'd put me off even if there were guards. I really don't want to go home tonight.

How about if I stay here? Just for one night. It'll do Dad good to think I really have gone. And as for Josh . . . he'll survive without me for one night. Just one night. Manor Hotel is a bit of a wreck but I'll find somewhere warm and dry. I know this place like the back of my hand. Don't worry, Josh, I'll see you tomorrow. I just can't face going back home tonight, that's all. One night won't hurt. One night won't hurt anyone.

I'll see you tomorrow, Josh.

8. Rainbow

This sucks!

It's not fair!

What am I going to wear? I need some new clothes. This top is so five minutes ago! I hate my life. Look at the state of my hair. Look at the state of me. I need something to wear for tonight. Something to knock Andrew's eyes out. Something to convince him that I'm the girl of his daydreams. A fantasy girl! Yeah, I like the sound of that. So what should I wear? This may be the back of beyond but that's no reason to go around looking like something the dog dug up – or threw up.

I wonder if I can get Mum or Dad to cough up for a new outfit. Not that I'd get much round here. I'd need to go to the city to get some really decent gear. And that's not going to happen in the next couple of hours, is it? Maybe with some carefully applied make-up I can take the focus off my outfit. I wouldn't have to do any of this if we lived somewhere with a couple of decent clothes shops.

It's not fair.

This sucks!

9. Nova and Liam

'If you're going to scream again, could you warn me first? My ears are still ringing,' said Liam.

A long, long pause.

'Well, aren't you coming in?'

Nova stood right where she was.

'You're not afraid, are you?' Liam asked, amused.

Nova visibly bristled at that. She took a deep breath and walked into the room.

'Are you going to scream again?' asked Liam.

Nova slowly shook her head.

Silence. More silence!

'Are you just going to stare at me all year or will you be speaking some time soon?'

Nova shook her head, then blinked hard. She still couldn't believe it. Here she was, standing in the middle of her bedroom – and there was an actual ghost sitting on her bed. Nova moved forward and waved her left hand in front of Liam's face. She leaned forward and waved her hand right through his head. Jumping back like a scalded cat, she continued to stare at him. Taking another step forward, she waved her hand through Liam's head again. It didn't feel any different to normal air. Slightly cooler perhaps, or maybe that was just her imagination. Nova drank in the sight of Liam. He was really there, wasn't he? She wasn't cracking up, was she? If she was, she'd conjured up a dead good-looking guy. He had the warmest, clearest brown eyes she'd ever seen. He was almost as tall as her dad and that was saying something. Nova waved her hand through his head once more.

'You really *are* a ghost, aren't you?' she whispered. 'A real, live ghost!'

'The pleasure is all yours,' Liam said.

'A real, live ghost in my room,' said Nova. 'What tricks can you do, apart from fading and walking through people, that is? Can you make yourself invisible and move things? Can you change into different animals? Can you shoot fire out of your eyes and fly around the hotel?'

'I'm a ghost, not a mutant X-man.' Liam frowned.

Nova sat down next to him. 'So, is that it then? Can you only fade out and walk through people and objects? Big deal!'

'You were very impressed less than ten minutes ago!' Liam pointed out.

'That was then, and this is now. Well? Can't you do anything else?'

'How about I tell you what you can do instead?'

'All right! All right! Only asking,' said Nova.

But her mind was fired up with possibilities. Liam might just be the answer to a prayer. A hotel with a real, live ghost. Guests would definitely flock to see that – and they'd pay through the nose and ears for it too. OK, so five minutes ago the guests in reception hadn't seemed too keen on the idea of a ghost in the hotel. But Nova hadn't handled that right. If Liam could appear on cue – and disappear, of course – then the guests would know what to expect and wouldn't be afraid. They'd just be . . . thrilled! She'd have to get Liam to appear to her mum and dad. Wait till she told them her plans! Things were definitely looking brighter.

'Hang on! If you're a ghost, how come I bumped into you in the garden?'

Liam turned his head and looked almost embarrassed.

Nova waved her hand through his body again. 'Can you make yourself real any time you like then?'

'I'm already real.' Liam frowned. 'I'm just a ghost, that's all.'

'Why can't I touch you now then?'

'Because, if you must know, Miss Eve stresses me out,' Liam admitted. 'And when I get in a stress, or I get angry or upset I seem to become "real" again – to use your word.'

'Real?'

'Solid. I can touch things and pick up things and others can see me and touch me. But it only lasts for a few minutes at most. And afterwards, I'm totally wiped out.'

'Can Miss Eve see you too?'

'No. At least, I don't think so,' said Liam.

'Why does she stress you out?'

Liam shook his head. 'There's something about her . . .'

'What?'

'I can't explain it. She makes the hairs on the back of my neck stand on end.'

How strange! That was exactly how Nova felt about Miss Eve as well.

'What about Miss Dawn?'

'There's something about her too, but she doesn't freak me out,' Liam admitted. 'At least, not in the same way as Miss Eve.'

'How come Mum and Dad have never seen you?'

'I told you. I can only materialize if I get upset or something.'

'You mean – emotional!' amended Nova.

'I mean upset or something,' Liam corrected briskly. 'And I like to keep myself to myself. Anyway, I don't want your family and the others in this place gawping at me. I'm not some kind of freaky sideshow.'

'No, of course not,' Nova said, hoping he hadn't guessed the plans she'd been busy making in her head. She'd have to pick the right moment to try and persuade him to give her plan a try.

She reached out a tentative finger to prod Liam. Her finger passed straight through him, like moving into the cool space in an empty fridge. 'A real, live ghost!' She drew back her hand, before jabbing it forward once more to prod him. She didn't know what she was expecting. Was she hoping to catch him off guard and find he was solid after all? Nova tried poking him once more.

'Could you stop doing that?'

'Why? You can't feel it.'

'It's still irritating!'

'Are you still feeling stressed then? How come I can still see you?'

'Actually, I was wondering that myself. I'm back to normal now. At least, I feel the way I always feel, so you shouldn't be able to see me,' said Liam, scrutinizing Nova. 'Have you ever seen a ghost before?'

'Not as far as I know,' said Nova.

'You must be more sensitive than most to ghosts. And now you've seen me, it's like you can't stop seeing me – if you see what I mean!'

Nova nodded, adding, 'You could've warned me that you were a ghost. Dad thinks I've lost my marbles.'

'I didn't know you'd freak like that.'

'How did you expect me to react? You walked straight through my dad!'

'It didn't hurt him, did it? So what's the problem?'

'You scared me,' Nova admitted.

'But you're not scared any more, are you?' asked Liam.

Nova considered, then shook her head. Liam looked harmless enough. A bit smarmy and full of himself, but then he was a boy, and a teenage boy at that – so what else was new! But he was strange looking though – mainly because he wasn't strange looking! He didn't float centimetres above the ground or carry his head under his arm. He wasn't dressed in a dazzling white suit, nor was there a glow or an aura around him. In fact, for a ghost he was a bit of a disappointment. He was wearing faded blue jeans and a matching blue-buttoned shirt. His trainers were grubby in places and of an old double-striped design. But even so . . .

'Can I ask you a question?' said Nova.

'Was that it?'

'No.'

'Go on then!'

'I've always wondered something about you ghosts,' Nova said, her brows creased. 'How come you can walk though walls and pass through objects and yet you can still walk on a floor without passing straight through it?'

Liam stared at her in disbelief. 'Because I just can.'

'That's not an answer.'

'It's the only one I can give you,' said Liam. 'It's like asking a bird how come it can fly or a fish how come it can swim. 'Cos it just can – and it's the same with me.'

'Well, that doesn't really explain much,' Nova said, disappointed.

'I can't help that,' Liam said dryly. He sat in silence as Nova regarded him for a long while. 'You'll know me the next time you see me, won't you!' he said at last, clearly irritated.

'How long have you been . . . here?' Nova was going to ask how long he'd been a ghost but somehow it didn't seem quite right. At least, not yet.

'No idea. I think it's been quite a while but it could be a month, could be a year. I don't know.'

'Why not?'

'Time doesn't pass the same way for me as it does for you,' said Liam. 'It goes a lot more slowly.'

'Oh, I see,' said Nova. She didn't really but she let it pass. She sat watching him for a while longer. 'How did you . . . er, come to be here?'

'I had a quarrel with my dad,' said Liam bitterly.

'Pardon?'

'I had a big fight with my dad.'

'And what? You had a heart attack or something?' asked Nova.

'No. Look, I don't want to talk about it.'

'Was it your dad's fault then?'

Liam turned away without answering.

'Sorry. I didn't mean to pry,' said Nova.

'I'll live!' said Liam.

Nova burst out laughing. Liam stared at her. Then he realized what he'd said and smiled. Nova still couldn't believe it. Here she was, chatting to a ghost in her room. She was doing something no one else in her family had ever done. She was the first. A first in itself. 'A real, live ghost . . .' she breathed.

'Yeah, you keep saying that.' Liam frowned. 'I still can't believe you can see me. I've been trolling around this dump *for ever* and no one's ever seen me before.'

'Lucky me!' Nova sniffed. 'And this place is not a dump, thank you very much.'

'I've heard you call it worse.'

'I can 'cos this is my home.'

'It's my home too,' Liam pointed out.

'It's still not a dump,' Nova bristled.

Liam smiled unexpectedly. 'No, it's not. You're right. It used to be, but your family have done a good job.'

'Hmm!' Nova murmured, only slightly placated.

'Sorry. OK?'

'OK,' said Nova reluctantly. 'So why're you here?'

'What d'you mean?' asked Liam.

'Why aren't you in Heaven or Hell or some place where teenage ghosts go? Why're you still here?'

'I don't know.' Liam stood up and walked over to the window. 'You get a good view of the sea from up here.'

Puzzled, Nova was determined not to let the subject drop. 'Do you like it here so much that you don't want to move on?'

'Are you kidding?' Liam rounded on her at once. 'I hate it here.'

'Why don't you leave then?'

'How?'

'I don't know. Just go. Fade out. Disappear. Walk away – or whatever it is that ghosts do.'

Liam turned back to the window. 'I've tried all of those. They don't work.'

Nova considered for a moment. 'You were outside. Why don't you just head off in one direction and keep going?'

At first she thought Liam wasn't going to answer. 'Because the further I go, the darker everything gets. And then I pass out and when I wake up, I'm right back here. And I have no idea how I got back, or who brought me back or how much time has even passed. D'you have any idea what that's like?'

Nova couldn't even begin to imagine what it must be like. She shook her head, but Liam seemed to have forgotten that she was even there. He carried on talking, more to himself than anyone else.

'It's like walking up a long flight of stairs and never, ever getting to the top. Or starting a race and running as hard and as fast as you can and never even getting past the starting line.' Liam's voice was getting softer and softer. 'It's like dying – over and over again, without ever being born.'

And now there was nothing left of him but his voice fading away into nothing. Melting into nowhere.

Nova looked around. 'Liam? Come back. Liam . . .?'

But she was alone.

10. Liam

*The sun was low down in the sky now. Another few minutes and
it'd set. But there was still enough light to see the Manor Hotel.
It was just as I remembered it. Standing in front of it made me
feel strange — almost homesick. And heartsick — though I'd never
be dibby enough to let anyone know that. How could anyone let
the place get into this state? With a bit of TLC it could be
halfway decent. The wire-mesh fence might have been reinforced
but it still couldn't hide the fact that there was mud and debris
and neglect and decay everywhere.*

My place.

*I mean, where else was I meant to go? I wasn't going home,
that's for sure.*

The tunnels.

*None of my friends knew about the tunnels. Only me. In the
cellar of the hotel there were a number of empty, rotting, wooden,
floor-to-ceiling wine racks, but behind one of them was a door. I'd
only found it by accident when I leaned against one of the stone
slabs on an adjacent wall. The door behind one of the wine racks
sprang open. It scared the hell out of me at the time and then
some. But of course, once I'd got over the shock, I just had to go
exploring. I mean, what kind of person would pass up a chance
like that? I swung back the wine rack, most of it crumbling to so
much dust as soon as I touched it. It was pitch black in there so
I only took a few steps inside before I bottled . . . I mean, before
I decided to be prudent. After all, I didn't want to break a leg or
something.*

*The next day I came back with a torch, spare batteries and
some string so I could do a Theseus and the Minotaur. I spent
not just hours, but days exploring those tunnels. Every spare*

64

chance I got. They ran back and forth under the hotel and grounds, into the copse on one side and down to a cave set in the cliff by the sea front on the other. Apart from the hidden exit by the sea front, I've only ever found two other exits — but I knew enough to realize that was just the tip of the iceberg. Who knew how many more exits and how many more tunnels ran underground for kilometres around?

I never used the copse tunnel. Too many animals had made it their home over the years and it stank to high heaven, plus I didn't think it'd be too safe with animals burrowing back and forth through it. They didn't seem to venture much beyond the copse though.

The exit I used was in the hotel gardens beneath a hollowed-out slab where some old, weather-worn benches had been dumped. I spent ages clearing them away but it was worth it. Now I could come and go without even entering the hotel building. It was like another world down there. Dry and warm, with a mouldy-earthy smell it didn't take me long to get used to. The tunnels were my favourite part of the Manor Hotel, because I instinctively knew that no one knew about them but me. They were all mine to discover and explore and make my own. You wouldn't believe how good that made me feel.

I walked to the end of the fencing and carried on along the road. If I cut round by the copse, skirting the edge of it, I should be able to double back and make it round to the back of the hotel where the grounds were. Me and my mates had fixed the short wire fencing round the back so that we could get in and out without anyone realizing. All we had to do was push the wire mesh back into place when we'd finished.

Once my mate Dave was stupid enough to try and get through without pushing the mesh all the way up and the wire sliced through his leg like a sharp knife through a squishy tomato. You should've seen the blood pour. I tied my belt around his leg to try and stem the bleeding and then we had to practically carry him *all the way back to the main road. Stopping at the first house we came to, we finally managed to call for an ambulance. They rushed him to hospital but fast. He needed twelve stitches and a blood transfusion. My mates weren't too keen on the place after that. But something kept drawing me back. It was a great place that deserved a good owner. Someone who would take care of it as it should be taken care of.*

But the tunnels were mine.

At least for a little while.

At least for tonight.

11. Andrew

'Yeah, that's right! The wrinklies are next door. Hang on a sec!' Andrew flopped down on the bed, swinging his legs around so that he lay prone. He moved his mobile phone to his other ear, away from the wall, announcing, 'In this dive, the walls are probably as thin as tissue paper.'

'Your mum still flapping over you?' asked Kieran at the other end of the phone.

'What d'you think? Still, at least I've got my own room – not that it's up to much.'

'What's the hotel like?' asked Kieran.

'Have a guess! If we weren't leaving on Sunday, I'd be tearing my hair out. Goodness knows why Mum thought it would be such a great birthday treat for me. But guess what? There's a girl here—'

'That didn't take you long!' Kieran laughed.

'You know me! Anyway, her name is Rainbow but she calls herself Raye.'

'Rainbow? Love and peace, man!' laughed Kieran. 'So what's she like?'

'She's OK, actually.'

'Ooh!'

'I mean, she's a bit of a whippet but in a land of dogs, she's the least canine . . .' Andrew amended hastily.

'A whippet?'

'Yeah, you know – skinny. You could probably use her ribs as a toast rack. But she'll do.'

'High praise indeed!'

'I'm not joking. From what I've seen so far, the girls

67

down here should walk around with paper bags on their heads and do us all a favour . . .'

Kieran's burst of laughter over the mobile phone could be heard from across the room. 'So, are you going to make a move on her?'

'Of course. I've got nothing else to do.'

'I bet her parents watch her like a hawk.'

'So? She fancies me something rotten so that's half my work done for me already!'

'I bet you don't even get the chance to pucker up!' Kieran scoffed.

'Wanna bet?'

'You're on! I bet you don't get to snog her before you leave on Sunday.'

'Oh, please! Don't insult me. Can't you come up with something a bit more challenging than that?' Andrew said disdainfully.

'Talk is cheap.'

'What kind of cheap are we talking about?' Andrew challenged.

'What did you have in mind?' Kieran asked.

Andrew laughed before mentioning a sum of money.

'The last of the big spenders!' Kieran was not impressed.

'That's all any of the girls down here are worth,' said Andrew.

'Right then. You're on! But you've got to provide proof that she kissed you.'

'How do I do that?'

'That's your problem,' said Kieran.

'OK,' Andrew replied. 'I almost feel guilty about taking your money off you. Almost . . . but not quite! The girl's practically eating out of my hand already. You should've seen the way she looked at me. She obviously has first-class taste and knows a good thing when she sees it!'

'You don't think much of yourself, do you?' said Kieran.

'If I don't love myself, who else will!'

'Hmm! So how d'you plan to do this?'

'I'm going to find Rainbow and chat to her. Let her see my sensitive side.' Andrew grinned.

'Good luck, but don't forget, it doesn't count unless you can prove it.'

'Don't worry. I and my proof will be with you on Monday!'

Andrew hung up, throwing his phone down on the bed. Placing his hands behind his head, he smirked up at the ceiling. And in the corner of the room, unseen by Andrew, stood Liam, listening to every word.

12. Acquaintances

'Miss Dawn, will you be leaving any time soon?'

'Miss Eve, I might ask you the same question.'

The two elderly women sat regarding each other, smiles serene, eyes like diamonds, minds like steel traps. They were closer than sisters, but they weren't friends. They called themselves 'acquaintances'. To everyone else they were travelling companions and rarely apart. The two women were currently sharing adjacent rooms at the Phoenix Manor Hotel.

'So who have you got your eye on now?' asked Miss Eve.

Miss Dawn scrutinized Miss Eve before answering, 'Mr Jackman – as if you didn't know. I saw you talking to Nova earlier. What were you doing? Asking about me – or Mr Jackman?'

'What makes you think you have anything to do with it?' Miss Eve huffed. 'The world doesn't revolve around you, you know.'

Miss Dawn smiled serenely. Miss Eve glowered at her.

'So you're after Mr Jackman, eh?' asked Miss Eve, trying to show that she wasn't rankled. 'Now, he's definitely edible!'

'Put him down! Besides, he's mine!'

'I do like to see a woman of your advanced years still living in hope,' taunted Miss Eve.

'Hope is my middle name,' Miss Dawn said silkily. 'You should know that by now.'

Miss Eve considered her companion. 'So you reckon you'll get him?'

'I know I will.' Miss Dawn's smile had returned.

'That's what you said about the last three, and it didn't happen, did it? I got them.'

'It'll be different this time. I can feel it in my vitals.'

'That's what you said the last three times.'

'I have faith,' said Miss Dawn.

'Faith?' scoffed Miss Eve.

'Yes, faith.'

'An extinct commodity.'

'Dormant perhaps, not extinct.'

'On the way out,' argued Miss Eve.

'Or on the way in. It all depends on your point of view.'

Miss Eve tried and failed to keep the irritation out of her voice. 'Why d'you always have to argue?'

'Why do you?'

'You really are the most aggravating creature.'

'I know!' Miss Dawn's serene smile broadened.

'I could always move on, you know.'

'Not without me you couldn't,' said Miss Dawn. 'Where one of us goes, the other follows – remember?'

Miss Eve glared at her companion, then suddenly smiled. 'I don't know why I'm worried. Mr Jackman *is* going to disappoint you.'

'Why?'

'Why what?'

'Why're you so sure he will?'

'You expect too much. You always do.'

'He'll do the right thing,' said Miss Dawn. But was that the faintest trace of doubt in her voice?

'Ah, but his idea of the "right thing" might not be the same as yours,' Miss Eve said with glee.

'We'll see,' said Miss Dawn. 'We'll see.'

13. Liam and Rainbow

'Hello, Rainbow.'

Raye whirled round, ready to do battle with whoever it was using her full name. Only her words of rebuke withered and died on her lips. Omigod! Another gorgeous guy, with short black hair and the most beautiful brown eyes she'd ever seen. Attractive guys to the left. Handsome guys to the right. This was much more like it!

'It's Raye. I prefer Raye.'

'Of course. I prefer Raye too. Rainbow is a bit "hippy chick", isn't it!'

'Excuse me?'

'Not that I don't like Rainbow too. I do,' the boy amended hastily. 'It's just . . . it's just time for me to shut up now!'

'Can I help you with something?' Raye asked, her tone decidedly cool now.

'You can help me take my foot out of my mouth!'

Raye smiled reluctantly. 'So you're a guest here? Did you arrive this morning?'

'No. I've been here a while. I live . . . round here.'

'Really? I haven't seen you before,' said Rainbow.

'Nova has. I like to walk around the grounds. I love it up here. I hope that's OK?'

Raye shrugged. 'It's fine with me. So how come you know my name?'

'I made it my business to find out. I'm Liam.'

Raye held out her hand. 'Hi, Liam.'

Liam put his hands behind his back. Raye's hand dropped to her side. What was this guy's problem?

'I'm sorry. My hands are dirty,' said Liam quickly, his hands now lightly clenched at his sides.

Raye glanced down. Hmm! His hands didn't look particularly dirty to her. 'Why did you make it your business to find out my name?' she asked.

'I just did. Look, there was something else I wanted to talk to you about.'

'I'm list —' Raye's head snapped back with sudden shock. For the briefest of moments she could've sworn she could actually see *through* Liam. She shook her head and blinked heavily. The light in the reception hall was playing funny tricks with her eyes.

'I don't have much time,' Liam said in an enigmatic rush. 'Just watch out for Andrew, OK? He's a liar.'

'I beg your pardon?'

'He wants to use you to win a stupid bet.'

'How d'you know that?'

'I just know, that's all.'

Raye regarded Liam. 'You're just trying to stir things, aren't you? What's your game?'

'I'm not the one playing games, Andrew is. Look, I have to go now,' Liam said apologetically. 'But I'm not lying.'

'And I'm not listening. The nerve of some people!' Raye turned and stormed off towards the dining room.

She turned to laser Liam with one last glare, but he'd vanished. Raye looked around, annoyed. He must've gone down the same rat hole he came out of. How come he knew Andrew? And why was he trying to make trouble between them? And if he lived round there, how come she'd never seen him before? Raye thought she'd thoroughly scouted out all the local talent – not that there was that much! So she would've definitely noticed someone like Liam.

Next time she saw him, he wouldn't get off so lightly. She'd have a few choice words of her own to say and Liam wasn't going anywhere until he'd heard every single one.

14. Nova

Nova sat on her favourite bench beneath a pergola at the far end of the hotel grounds. The pergola separated the bench from the direct gaze of the hotel and all around were the scents and sights of autumn – damask roses and late honeysuckle. Not that Nova was there to admire the flowers. Her head turned first one way, then the other, the expression on her face alert and watchful.

'Liam? Are you here?' Nova whispered. 'I'm sorry – OK?'

Nothing. Nova had been right through the hotel, calling out to Liam and looking for him. She'd even tried the guest rooms – at least, the ones that weren't locked or occupied. For all she knew, Liam could've been sitting right next to her at that moment. Nova reached out a tentative hand, only to drop it back down by her side. No, he wasn't there. Even as he had faded out in her room, she could still sense him. She'd known the moment he was no longer present and that had been several seconds after his voice had faded. He wasn't here. As far as Nova could tell, he wasn't anywhere. Nova heard footsteps turning the corner, crunching on the gravel path. She sprang to her feet.

Liam . . .?

'Oh, sorry. I didn't know anyone was here.' Mr Jackman was already turning round.

'It's OK,' Nova said quickly. 'I was just leaving.'

'You don't have to leave on my account.'

'I'm not. I really was going. I just like to sit here sometimes. It's peaceful.'

'I like it here too.' Mr Jackman nodded, looking around. 'And you can smell the sea, even if you can't see it from this spot!'

Nova was surprised at the sudden volunteering of information. She knew she should probably leave him to it, but for some reason her feet didn't seem to want to move.

'Don't you think the sea smells like a promise?' Mr Jackman mused. 'A promise of all the things it knows and all the things it might reveal.'

Nova frowned at him. What on earth was he going on about? Did he get all poetic with everyone who stayed around long enough? Maybe that was why most of the guests gave him a wide berth. Except Miss Dawn, who had taken him under her wing.

In a flash it came back to her. Nova now remembered the rest of what Miss Dawn had said to her that morning. It had been about Mr Jackman. And was that what Miss Eve had been trying to get out of her when they went for their walk which was mercifully cut short? Nova wondered at the elderly women's interest in Mr Jackman.

'I love this place,' said Mr Jackman on a sigh. 'Always have.'

'You've been here before?' said Nova.

A trace of a smile flitted over Mr Jackman's face. 'A while ago.'

'I can't remember seeing you before.' Not that Nova remembered every hotel guest who'd ever stayed at the hotel, but somehow she knew she would've remembered Mr Jackman.

'It was some time ago . . . Are your family happy here? Your sister?'

'Why d'you ask?'

'Just something I heard her say a couple of days ago,' said Mr Jackman. 'It sounded as if she wasn't too keen on the place.'

'Don't listen to Raye. She's never happy unless she's whingeing about something.'

'Your mum and dad are OK here though, aren't they?'

'They are now. They weren't at first – well, Mum wasn't,' Nova amended.

'Why did your mum and dad move down here then?' asked Mr Jackman.

'The hotel was left to my mum by a great-aunt,' Nova explained. 'It was called the Manor Hotel then. Mum and Dad decided to put all their savings into doing it up and opening it as a hotel again.'

'Yes, I remember the Manor Hotel,' said Mr Jackman thoughtfully.

'Is that when you stayed here last?'

'No. I used to live round here,' said Mr Jackman. 'I much prefer its new name – Phoenix Manor Hotel.'

'Mum and Dad decided to call it that.'

'It suits the place. Your name is Nova, isn't it?'

Nova nodded, surprised.

'And your mum's name is Karmah?'

'That's right. Dad wanted me and Raye to have names like Mum.'

'And what did your mum think of that?'

Nova laughed. 'Apparently they agreed that Mum should name any boys they had and Dad would name the girls. And a deal's a deal.'

'I see!' Mr Jackman smiled.

Nova smiled back. 'So where d'you live now?'

Mr Jackman turned to look at her. Really look at her.

'That was nosy,' Nova said quickly.

77

'No, you're all right . . . I have a flat in Manchester. I wouldn't say I live there, though. I travel around too much.'

'With your job?'

'Something like that,' said Mr Jackman. 'I like to keep moving – even when I don't have to.'

'Why?'

'I'm searching.'

'For what?'

'Someone.'

'Who?'

Mr Jackman looked at Nova and grinned.

Nova's face started to burn. 'Sorry! That was nosy too.'

'Yes, it was. But good for you!'

Nova studied Mr Jackman, not making any attempt to disguise what she was doing. Strange, but when he grinned, someone else's face had flashed through her mind quicker than summer lightning. Nova tried to remember just who it was Mr Jackman reminded her of, but it was gone.

'So who are you looking for?' she repeated.

She waited for him to answer her last question – but he didn't. As Nova watched his smile fade, she realized it was the first time she'd seen him smile since he'd arrived at the hotel. He didn't look like a man who smiled easily.

'I like your name,' Mr Jackman said at last. 'It suits you. Super Nova!'

Nova smiled wanly. If he was aiming for a subtle change of subject, he'd failed miserably.

'Sorry! I bet that's not the first time you've had someone say that to you,' said Mr Jackman.

'No.'

It was only about the fifty millionth time she'd heard

the same joke! They stood in silence for a few strangely unawkward moments. Nova continued to scrutinize Mr Jackman. She usually knew what to make of the guests within five minutes of spotting them. The arrogant, the shy, the considerate, those with something to hide, the pompous – it didn't take her long to suss them out. But Mr Jackman was different. Strange that he should now decide to talk to her – especially after Nova's earlier conversation with Miss Dawn. This was the most he'd said to anyone in the hotel since he'd arrived, as far as she knew.

'Are you here for a holiday or are you still searching?' she asked.

'Still searching,' replied Mr Jackman. 'I never stop. I never will.'

Nova waited and wondered if Mr Jackman was going to continue. It wasn't like having a conversation with anyone else she had ever met. Usually you could tell by what was said, and how it was said and the way the person looked, just where the conversation was going and whether or not it had finished. But not with Mr Jackman. With him it was all guesswork.

'I'd better be getting back,' she sighed.

Mr Jackman nodded, moving past her to sit on the bench she had just vacated. Nova glanced back at him. What was it Miss Dawn had said? 'We all need friends'? She wondered why Mr Jackman had suddenly decided to speak to her. Maybe Miss Dawn was right. But it wouldn't have surprised or upset her to learn that Mr Jackman had forgotten about her already. He had himself and his quest and he didn't seem to need anything else.

Nova headed back to the hotel. Why worry about Mr Jackman? He was old enough to take care of himself. He certainly didn't need her help for anything. But as Nova took one last look at him, it occurred to her that she'd never seen anyone look so lonely. Or quite so alone.

15. Mr Jackman

'I need your help . . .' Mr Jackman stared straight ahead but his thoughts were light years away in long ago. 'D'you hear me? I need your help. It's in your hands now. I've been everywhere. This is the only place left. And I'm not leaving. Not until I find you. You shouldn't have gone. It wasn't your fault, I know that. It was my fault. I drove you out. That's why I'm not leaving. But you have to help me.

'You have to.

'You just have to . . .'

16. Nova and Rainbow

'Rainbow, stop picking at your food and eat it properly.'

'My name is Raye,' Rainbow amended tersely. 'And I *am* eating.'

Mum frowned down at Rainbow's dinner plate. 'Eating what exactly? Air?'

'Food!' said Rainbow. 'And I'm fifteen, Mum, not five. I don't need you to tell me to eat my food. You'll be picking up the fork and feeding me next.'

'Raye, ten minutes ago you had a dollop of mashed potato on your plate, along with two sausages and baked beans – and none of them have moved,' said Mum.

'I've eaten some beans,' argued Raye.

'No, you haven't.'

Raye glared at Mum. Her voice dropped an octave as she mockingly said, '"I put it to you, Rainbow Clibbens, that you had one hundred and fifty beans on your plate at the start of the meal and there are still one hundred and fifty left." What did you do, Mum? Count them onto my plate so you could count them all off again?'

Nova slowly chewed on her sausage as she listened to her mum and sister argue. It was the same almost every meal time.

'Raye, I didn't stand in this hot kitchen all afternoon making you dinner for the fun of it.'

'Here we go.' Raye tutted and raised her eyes heavenwards. '"I spend all day in this kitchen, and do you appreciate it? Hell, no!"'

'Don't be so cheeky.'

'Stop bossing me about then.'

'I'll stop when you start eating. Or should I get your dad to have a word with you?'

Raye savagely pronged a sausage before stuffing the whole thing into her mouth in one go. 'Satisfied?' she mumbled, her cheeks bulging.

Nova and the twins exchanged a long-suffering look. Nova shook her head as she took another bite of her sausage.

'Can't you two stop arguing for two seconds?' Jake asked.

'Yeah! You're giving us a bellyache,' Jude added.

'And you're both giving me a headache,' Nova put in her twopence worth, glaring at her mum, then at Raye in turn.

'Fine! Right!' Raye piled creamy-white mashed potato onto her fork so that the fork was no longer visible beneath the huge mound. Then she pushed the whole lot into her mouth.

'Good idea, Raye,' Mum said sarcastically. 'Choking on your food will really show me!'

Raye sat in stony silence and continued chewing her food. Her eyes shot daggers at anyone who dared to look in her direction. Nova cut carefully into her second sausage, dissecting it into four equal pieces, before pushing one of the quarters into her mouth. She had a set routine. Peas, beans or tomatoes first, then the meat – whatever it might be, then the energy food (as Mum called it), or stodge (as Raye called it). Stodge like chips or rice or mashed potatoes or pasta. Nova never argued about eating her food. And she always finished what she was given. She looked down at her plate. Nearly there. She popped another quarter of sausage into her mouth.

'Mum, can I have some more milk?' asked Jake.

'Me too!' added Jude.

Mum turned round to get the milk out of the fridge. Nova spread some mashed potato over her last two pieces of sausage. She popped one into her mouth before pushing the remaining mashed potato into a miniature volcano-shaped heap in the middle of the plate.

'Mum, while you're in the fridge, can I have something fizzy to drink?' asked Nova.

'Like what?'

'Got any ginger beer?'

'There's one left,' Mum replied.

'I'll have that then. Thanks.' Nova put the last lot of mashed potato and sausage into her mouth before putting her knife and fork together in the middle of her plate.

'I see you've finished all your food – again. Creep!' Raye hissed.

'What's your problem?' asked Nova. 'Not enough fibre in your diet?'

'Crawly creeper!' Raye mustered as much venom as she could to inject into her words.

'I think you mean creepy crawler! You're such a pleasure to be around – really,' said Nova. 'I'm so proud you're my sister.'

'Bog off!'

'You first,' said Nova.

'That's quite enough of that,' Mum snapped.

Nova and Raye glared at each other. Jude and Jake shared a grin. Meal times were such fun, with everyone arguing and saying rude things.

'I'll help you to serve the dinner later, Mum,' said Raye, reluctant to tear the full force of her filthy look away from her sister.

'Catch me, someone,' said Mum, swooning. 'I'm fainting!'

'You're always going on about me helping around the

hotel more and when I do volunteer, you just mock me,' Raye fumed.

'You need a sense of humour transplant,' Nova muttered so she could be heard.

'And who was talking to you?' said Raye.

'Sorry, Raye.' Mum straightened up. 'You're quite right. I shouldn't have made fun of you. Thanks for volunteering.'

'She just wants to be with whatshisface – Andrew,' said Jake.

'Are you going to snog him?' asked Jude in all seriousness.

After one last razor-sharp look which scythed around the table, Raye flounced out of the room. Mum shook her head and handed a can of ginger beer over to Nova.

'I can't wait to be a teenager.' Jude grinned at his brother.

'Me too!' agreed Jake.

'Just drink your milk, you two!' said Mum, placing a full glass before each of the twins.

Nova drank as much of her ginger beer in one go as she could, until her stomach was full to the point of being bloated. She sat back and stared at her empty plate. Totally empty. Only a little tomato sauce from the beans showed there'd been anything on it. Nova rubbed her stomach. The gas from the ginger beer was making her feel really uncomfortable. It couldn't be a good idea to gulp it down so fast. The effect was always the same. Nova sighed and stood up. Standing across the table from her was Liam.

She jumped. 'How long have you been standing there?' she asked.

'We're not standing. We're still sitting,' Jude frowned.

'She's not talking to us,' Jake whispered in Jude's ear.

'I was talking to . . . Never mind.' No way was Nova

going to try and explain herself again. She turned back to Liam. 'How long have you been here?'

'Long enough,' Liam replied. 'I need your help.'

'To do what?'

'You've got to help me get my — get Mr Jackman out of here.'

'Out of the hotel?' asked Nova.

'Yes.'

'Why? What's he done?'

'Nova, who're you talking to?' Mum asked.

'No one. Myself.' Nova headed for the kitchen door. She'd have to watch it. If she started talking to Liam when her family were around, they'd all think she was barking mad. Well . . . even more barking mad than usual.

'Er, oh no you don't,' Mum called Nova back. 'It's your turn to help me load up the dishwasher.'

'But, Mum, I've got other things to do.'

'Tough!' said Mum, without a single shred of sympathy. 'It's your turn. Get on with it.'

'But, Mum . . .'

'Nova . . .'

Nova turned back to Liam with a regretful shrug, but he was gone.

17. Liam and Mr Jackman

'When're you going to leave?'

Mr Jackman sat at the small wooden table, its surface scratched and scarred, and continued to write. He didn't even raise his head.

'I want you to leave . . .'

Mr Jackman raised his head, a frown creeping across his face, but all too soon he carried on with his writing.

'D'you hear me? You're not wanted here. Why don't you go?' Liam shouted from the middle of the room. 'You made my life a misery when I was alive and now I'm dead, you're still doing it!'

Liam glared at the man before him in total frustration. He tried to force himself to focus so that he could materialize, but all the old feelings kept bubbling up inside him. It was so hard, deliberately appearing in front of people. It always seemed to happen by accident, when he lost his temper or experienced some other emotion equally potent. Except with Nova. Why did she see him so easily when no one else could? And now, unless he faded out and thought himself somewhere else entirely, Nova could see him whether he wanted her to or not. Liam sighed. What was the reason? There had to be a reason. Maybe she was more sensitive to his presence? Or maybe she just wanted to see him more than anyone else in the hotel. *Needed* to see him. Needed his help – just as he needed her help at this moment. Tentatively, he moved closer. What was this man doing? What was it that had him so engrossed?

Liam walked over to stand to one side of the man and

began to read over his shoulder. Horrified, he shook his head, unable to believe what he was reading – but it was there in black and white. He looked at the man beside him, hoping against hope that he'd misread the letter. Maybe he'd misunderstood what was written? But the sombre expression on the man's face told Liam that he'd done no such thing.

'Oh God!' Liam exclaimed.

He needed to find help – fast. And there wasn't much time.

18. Liam

I moved swiftly through the hotel grounds, looking around all the time to make sure there was no one else there. Luckily the slab that marked out the entrance to the tunnel didn't have too much debris over it. Just an old, discarded wheelbarrow, recently dumped. Shifting it to one side, I moved the slab covering the entrance. I sat down at the edge of the now uncovered hole, then twisted my body round to grab hold of the rope ladder which led down to the tunnels below. Moving down a couple of rungs, I leaned against the ladder and the dirt wall beyond that, until I was steady enough to pull the slab back into place. Even partially hollowed out, it was heavy, but nothing I couldn't handle.

I was careful to make sure the slab was back in place before I headed down the ladder. I didn't want anyone to find the entrance. I was the one who'd gone to the trouble of replacing the rotten, knotted rope which used to hang at the entrance. I'd made the ladder I was now standing on, buying several metres of rope and twisting and plaiting them into shape in my every spare moment until it was ready. So why should I give up this place?

The tunnels were warm and dry, just as I remembered them. But I'd barely taken three steps before my thoughts returned once again to Josh. I'd told him all about the tunnels, but until now I'd refused to show them to him. But why not? If I was going to show them to anyone in the world it would be him. After all, he is my brother and I care about him. Who am I trying to kid? I love him. There! I admit it! And strangely enough, I don't feel silly or soppy or even embarrassed. In fact, for some strange reason, it makes me feel . . . OK! Not just OK about my brother, but in a strange way, OK about myself as well.

So what was Josh doing now? Wondering where I was? What

was I worried about? The fact that Josh might be anxious about me, or the fact that he might not be? I smiled wryly as I thought about my younger brother. He had a lot to answer for! I shone my torch around. The dim, yellow torchlight was soon swallowed whole by the darkness. Ahead, behind, it made no difference. I could see no further than a metre in any direction. The torch was a whip, cracking silently to keep the gloom and shadows at bay. But I'd only been walking for about ten or fifteen minutes when it began to flicker. I turned the torch upwards to stare into its fading light. How could the batteries be dying? I'd changed them less than a fortnight ago. I shone it on the ground, looking for a patch of ground that was even. About a metre ahead of me was the perfect bed – ground that was even and solid. I lay down, taking off my jacket so I could use it as a pillow. Switching off the torch to save the batteries, I made myself comfortable and within moments I surprised myself by falling fast asleep.

I woke with a start and with that groggy feeling you get from too much sleep rather than not enough. I could hear a faint rumbling sound but I couldn't tell which direction it was coming from. It must've been the noise that woke me up, faint as it was. Usually the tunnels were eerily silent. I stood up, wiping the sleep out of my eyes. The tunnels were still pitch black but I instinctively knew it was now morning. I glanced down at my watch, forgetting I couldn't see a thing. I felt around for my torch, then shone the light down on it. Ten-thirty. I'd been asleep for ages. I must've been more tired than I thought. That probably explained why I'd been so ratty to my brother. Never mind. I'd make it up to him. I always did.

And maybe it was time to make up with Dad too?

To be honest, I was tired of fighting with him. Time to call a truce – if Dad would meet me halfway. He had to be just as sick of our quarrels as I was. When I was a lot younger, we'd go to the beach or the local museum, or play football, or just sit huddled up on the sofa watching the telly. Yes, he was my dad, but it was more than that. We were good mates. Until Mum died. He fell to pieces and our family fell apart. And stupidly I'd thought I could put everyone and everything back together. Sitting there in the torch-lit gloom, I saw more clearly than I ever had before. When Mum died, and Dad fell apart, I'd tried to take over his role. But I couldn't. I shouldn't have even tried. I needed help – Dad's help. I took a deep breath and let it out slowly, one fight, one quarrel, one bad thought, one frustration at a time. Time to let go. Time to go home. Time to start again.

I gathered up my jacket, switched on my torch and turned, heading back for the tunnel entrance. The torchlight was dim, but it'd last until I was out of the tunnels. After a couple of minutes I stopped abruptly. What was that noise? I stopped breathing, moving my head forward to listen into the silence. A faint crack-ing sound . . . What was it? And a rumble, like some kind of machinery, or thunder. What was going on?

Get a grip, I told myself. My imagination was starting to play tricks on me. Funny that! Mr Sugarman, my English teacher, was always whining at me for not having enough imagination.

'Liam, switch on your imagination when you write!'

'Liam, this poem lacks imagination. Don't you daydream? Can't you think above and beyond and outside your little box?'

Outside my little box! Patronizing twit! What did that mean, for heaven's sake? I had enough problems coping with my dad and Josh and everyday stuff without drifting along with my head in the clouds.

Without warning the torch went out and I was plunged into darkness. I shook the torch vigorously. Nothing. It was so dark, I couldn't even see the torch in my hand, let alone anything else. I looked around, careful not to move my feet, only my head. The darkness was an impenetrable, overpowering force, swallowing me up, eyes first. A darkness rich and thick enough to drink. I took a cautious step forward. I'd be OK as long as I didn't panic. I'd been in these tunnels a dozen times or more – so what was there to panic about? *One foot in front of the other. Face forward. Keep going. No problem.* I took another step — and another. See! This was easy. No string, no twine, no thread, no nothing. I didn't need it. Usually I only used twine if I was exploring a new part of the tunnels, but when I stormed out of the house, I didn't even know where I was going until I found myself at the hotel. I'd been in the tunnels before and I could find my way through the familiar bits with my eyes shut.

So as long as I didn't get lost . . . but I wouldn't. And if I did, I'd just call out until someone heard me, so I wasn't in danger. OK, I shouldn't have been in the tunnels in the first place but I could argue about that afterwards. The quarrel I'd had with Dad last night had been a scorcher — by both our standards. But if I could want to go home and face Dad, then I could face anything.

I started walking again, my hands out in front of me. I had to be only seconds away from the exit. I'd feel the rope ladder and be out before I could string five thoughts together. No problem. I shook my torch and tried switching it on and off again. Nothing. Then I dropped it.

'Hell!' The word exploded into the darkness around me.

I squatted down to fumble around in the dirt for my torch. I swept my hand across the dirt in ever-increasing arcs. My hand swept over something small and furry — and moving. Instantly, I drew back my hand, wiping it on my jeans. I couldn't help the shudder that ricocheted through me. I didn't even want to know what that was. My feet swivelled on the dry earth as I felt around again. Stupid Josh must've been playing with my torch and drained the batteries. My lips thinned into a angry frown. 'Just wait till I get hold of you, Josh,' I muttered.

At last I found the torch. I had to really stretch out to get it. It must've rolled away from me. But as I straightened up, I realized instinctively that I wasn't facing in exactly the same direction. My feet had moved slightly to the right. So all I had to do was move them a quarter turn to the left. Too much or too little? I couldn't be that off track. Just keep going. Whatever happens, just keep going.

I wanted to go home. I wasn't afraid, but these tunnels were like a maze, with tunnels off more tunnels, and I didn't want to get lost in the darkness. I carried on walking. I was OK. Just walk in a straight line back to the tunnel entrance. See! Easy!

Crack!

I stopped in my tracks and looked straight up. What was that?

Cra-a-ck! What felt like dry rain fell over my face. I leapt back and wiped the dirt and dust from out of my eyes. There was that sound again. And then panic grabbed me. And all I wanted to do was run. Move. Get out of there — as fast as I could. I started running. But before I could take more than three strides, the cracking sound turned into a deafening roar and the rain of dust and dirt was just the start of something far worse. I hit the ground, trying to protect my head with my arms as the world fell on top of me and all I knew was darkness and the sound of thunder. And then the world changed from pitch black to a cold, ice white which blinded me and froze every part of my body until I shattered into a million pieces.

19. Liam

Liam stood outside the toilet cubicle listening to the sounds of someone inside being violently sick. He shook his head, his frown cutting into his cheeks as he listened. It was like clockwork. Within half an hour of every meal time, she'd be in here, making herself vomit. He could set his watch by her – if it'd been working instead of permanently stuck at 10.37.

What was the matter with her family? Couldn't her mum and dad see what was going on? Didn't they notice the pattern to her eating? Insisting on certain foods with every meal and always eating them first. Always guzzling orange juice or fizzy drinks after eating. Disappearing after every meal and then reappearing a little while later to look listless and sombre. Being tired all the time. The signs were all there. And then there was the bingeing on snack foods. She'd sneak up to her room with two or three packets of crisps or a packet of custard creams or fruit shortcake biscuits, followed half an hour later by the famous disappearing act into her favourite toilet cubicle. Liam was sure that if he were her dad or one of her brothers, he'd have been very suspicious about her behaviour. OK, so her mum and dad were busy running the hotel, but that was a reason, not an excuse.

Liam shook his head again. The toilet was flushed and the sound was followed by a racking cough. Then came the sound of more retching. Liam turned away in disgust. He couldn't stay there all day listening to her cough her guts out – he had things to do. There had to be some way to solve his problem without involving her. But how? Liam faded out slowly, shaking his head.

Time was running out.

20. Dinner

'Can I get you anything else, Andrew?' asked Raye.

'No thanks,' Andrew smiled. 'And please say thanks to your mum and dad for such a delicious meal.'

'Yes, it was,' Mr Stanley chorused.

'It was lovely,' Mrs Stanley agreed after a pointed look from her husband.

'I'll tell Mum. It'll make a change, someone actually enjoying her cooking!' said Raye.

Andrew's smile was warm as Raye gathered up his plate. She stood beside him, returning his smile with interest as they regarded each other.

'Raye, I think we've finished as well,' said Mr Stanley gently.

Raye forced her eyes away. 'Yes, of course.' Reluctantly she moved away from Andrew and continued round the table.

'Any chance of us getting our dessert before I'm too old to have the teeth left to chew it?' Miss Eve called from an adjacent table.

'There's no hurry.' Miss Dawn smiled sympathetically at Raye.

'I'll be right there,' Raye promised. Very professionally, she gathered up the rest of the plates on Andrew's table and turned to head for the door.

'Remind me to come back as a boy next time,' Miss Eve grumbled. 'Then I might actually get some pudding from that girl this side of Christmas.'

Raye turned to glare at her, before she carried on out of the dining room. Andrew leapt up and ran across to her.

'Let me get that door for you,' he said.

'Thanks.' Raye's smile was dazzling.

Andrew held open the dining-room door, despite the fact that it swung open with the lightest push.

'Thanks again,' said Raye, wishing she could think of something more scintillating to say.

'Would you like to go for a walk with me some time tomorrow?' asked Andrew.

'Where?'

'Maybe down to the beach?'

'That'd be lovely,' Raye enthused. Her face fell. 'But I've got to help around the hotel in the afternoon and then I've got to finish my homework so I can probably only get away straight after breakfast.'

'That's fine with me,' Andrew nodded. 'I'll meet you just outside the hotel?'

'It's a date.' Raye's smile shone out.

'It's a date,' Andrew agreed and headed back to his mum and dad's table.

Raye did her best not to grin from ear to ear. If Mum saw she'd instantly start asking questions. Raye bustled into the kitchen, her tray stacked with dirty dinner plates, most of which were surprisingly empty. Nova was at the table, preparing more desserts while Mum refilled the coffee machine with fresh coffee grounds.

'Your pie is going down well,' Raye told Mum.

'It is, isn't it?' Mum looked dubiously at the two slices of pie she had left in the baking tray. More often than not, she made two trays-worth of food and at least one tray was still left over at the end of the evening. She'd have to try that tinned lamb as a pie filling again.

'Miss Eve wants her dessert,' said Raye.

'Over there on the counter.' Mum pointed.

Raye picked up a clean tray and placed two bowls of

97

peach and raspberry strudel on it – one with custard from a tin, one with soft scoop vanilla ice cream.

'Nova, can you manage that coffee for Mr Jackman?' asked Raye.

'No problem.'

'He's in the alcove,' Raye told her.

'Why d'you put him in there?' Mum turned to Raye.

'I didn't seat him. Nova did,' Raye defended herself.

'Before you have a go at me, he asked for it specifically,' said Nova. 'Said he wanted some privacy.'

'There's a surprise,' Raye muttered.

Nova shook her head. 'I wonder what's wrong with the poor man. I feel sorry for him.'

'Why?' Raye was scornful. 'It's his choice not to make friends with anyone.'

'Maybe it's not that simple —' Nova began.

'Oh, Nova, don't start!' Raye begged. 'You're always trying to create mysteries around people. He's just an anti-social loner, so let's leave him alone.'

'I was only saying,' Nova huffed. 'No need to jump down my throat.'

Raising her eyebrows in exasperation, Raye gathered up a number of dessert menus and headed out of the kitchen, followed by her sister. They both entered the dining room and split like a fork in the road to hand out their various items. Nova concentrated on the coffee on her small tray, determined not to spill a drop. A quick glance up to make sure she wasn't about to trip over anyone's leg or bag, and she made her way to Mr Jackman's table. The dining room was L-shaped, with a secluded booth at the end of the alcove that formed the shorter section of the room. Mum liked everyone to mix and mingle and never seated anyone in the alcove unless nothing else was available. But Mr Jackman always asked for the alcove table when he ate in the dining room with the other guests, which wasn't often. Nova kept her head down, her eyes still focused on her coffee. She turned the corner and made her way down to the last table. It was only when she'd dodged past the only other unoccupied table in the alcove that she glanced up again – and stopped dead in her tracks.

Liam was sitting opposite Mr Jackman at his table.

'Liam, what . . .?' Nova's lips snapped together. She had to remember not to talk to him in front of other people.

Mr Jackman stared at her. 'What did you say?'

'Nothing.'

Mr Jackman sprang to his feet. 'What did you say?' he urged.

Nova stared at him. She glanced at Liam, who vigorously shook his head. 'I just said . . . erm . . . what . . . what did you order to drink? I just wanted to check I've brought this coffee to the right table.'

Mr Jackman slowly sat down again. 'Oh, I see.'

Nova was glad he did, because she didn't. 'Is something wrong, Mr Jackman?'

'I thought you said . . . something else.'

'What?'

Mr Jackman shook his head. 'It doesn't matter. The coffee is mine.'

'There you are.' Nova put the cup and saucer down on the table, adding a small jug of milk and a tiny bowl of brown and white sugar cubes. It was so hard to carry on as if there was nothing unusual happening with Liam sitting there watching her every move.

'Nova, I need your help. You can't let him leave the hotel tonight. You must find a way to stop him,' Liam urged.

'What?' Nova wasn't sure if she'd heard correctly.

'I didn't say anything,' said Mr Jackman.

'D'you understand me, Nova? He plans to leave the hotel as soon as he's finished his coffee. You mustn't let him,' Liam pleaded.

'How am I meant to do that?'

'Who're you talking to?' Mr Jackman turned his head to where Nova was looking. 'Who's there?'

'I—'

Mr Jackman grabbed Nova's arm. 'It's him, isn't it? I know it's him. I can *feel* him.'

'You're hurting me.' Nova tried to pull away.

'Tell me who you're talking to!' Mr Jackman demanded.

'Let her go!' Liam sprang up, furious.

'Liam . . .' Mr Jackman immediately let go of Nova's arm. He stared directly at Liam, his eyes huge, his mouth open and slack with stunned surprise. 'Liam . . .'

Without warning Liam swept the coffee across the table into Mr Jackman's lap.

'Ahh!' Mr Jackman yelled and sprang up like a scalded cat, pulling his hot, soaking trousers away from his skin and hopping from foot to foot.

'What on earth . . .?' Raye appeared round the corner and took in the situation at one glance. 'Nova, what on earth d'you think you're doing?' she asked furiously, rushing over. 'I'm so sorry, Mr Jackman. Nova, how could you be so clumsy?'

'I didn't do it,' Nova said indignantly.

'I suppose Mr Jackman did it to himself,' Raye fumed.

'Don't worry about it,' Mr Jackman said through gritted teeth, pulling the fabric of his trousers away from his thighs.

'We'll pay to have your trousers cleaned,' Raye said quickly.

'I didn't do it,' Nova repeated, glaring at Liam.

Liam wasn't looking at her though, or at Mr Jackman. His eyes were on Raye, with the strangest look on his face that Nova had ever seen. Liam waved a tentative hand in front of Raye's face. Raye didn't bat an eyelid. She obviously couldn't see him. His expression changed, swinging between acceptance and disappointment like a pendulum. Mr Jackman looked around, looking straight through Liam, looking past him, looking without any real focus. And Nova realized that Mr Jackman could no longer see him.

'Is he still here?' Mr Jackman asked.

Nova regarded him. How should she answer? She didn't want to answer. Mr Jackman had called Liam by his first name. How did this man know him? Who was he? And why was Liam so frightened of him? Or was it frightened for him? It was hard to tell.

'Is he here?' Mr Jackman insisted.

'Is who here?' asked Raye.

Nova looked across to where Liam was standing. Liam shook his head frantically at her.

'*Is he?*' Mr Jackman asked Nova again, ignoring her sister.

Nova nodded. 'Yes.'

'Where?'

Nova pointed.

'Prove it.'

'How?'

'Ask him who owned our house,' Mr Jackman suggested intently.

'Nova, what's he talking about?' frowned Raye.

Nova turned to Liam, but he had eyes for no one but Mr Jackman. Raye looked from Nova to Mr Jackman in turn, completely baffled. 'Would someone please tell me what's going on?' she asked.

'It was my house,' Liam said at last. 'Mum left it to me.'

'Liam says it was his. His mum left it to him,' answered Nova.

The silence that followed was only broken by the merest of sighs from Mr Jackman.

'Who's Liam?' asked Raye, irritated. 'The boy I met earlier?'

'You've met him?' Nova asked, astounded. 'So you *saw* him?'

'Of course I saw him, but he's gone now.'

'I've wanted so much to find him. I've waited so long. But I never gave up hope. I always knew I'd find him — one day.' Mr Jackman didn't look happy at the prospect though. Far from it.

'My turn now,' said Liam suddenly. 'Nova, tell him I saw the letter he was writing this afternoon. Tell him he won't succeed and all he'll do is put himself in danger if he goes through with it.'

'Through with what?' Nova asked.

'Just tell him!' Liam roared.

'Excuse me all over the place!' Nova glared, before turning back to Mr Jackman. 'Liam says he saw what you were writing earlier. He says that you won't succeed and all you'll do is put yourself in danger — so don't do it!'

Mr Jackman turned in what he thought was Liam's general direction. 'It's the only way I'll be able to find you,' he said.

Nova could tell that Mr Jackman couldn't see Liam and was just guessing at his location, but his expression was indescribable. Such hope and misery and joy and despair warring with each other for dominance on his face.

'Liam, I have to find you. I can't think of anything else.'

'Nova, tell him to go home. Tell him I don't want him here,' said Liam, adding to, and for, himself, 'He can't do anything for me. No one can.'

'Look, what am I? An answering machine?'

'Please, just tell him,' said Liam, suddenly looking dog-tired.

'Mr Jackman, he wants you to go home. He thinks you should leave here now,' Nova said, unable to keep a trace of resentment from creeping into her voice.

'Have you all gone loopy or what?' said Raye belligerently. 'Nova, if you've got together with Mr Jackman or that stupid Liam to wind me up for a joke, then I can tell you now, I'm not laughing.'

'Raye, I never—'

'Save it!' Raye turned and strode off without another word.

'I'm not leaving, Liam. Not without you,' said Mr Jackman, looking in Liam's approximate direction.

'And that, Nova, is why I didn't want him to know I was here in the first place,' Liam told her bitterly.

'Don't blame me.' Nova tried to defend herself.

'Whose fault is it then? If you weren't such a Mouth Almighty, he might've given up and gone home.'

'You're the one who just poured coffee in his lap.' Nova couldn't believe her ears.

'Liam, what happened? I need to know,' urged Mr Jackman.

Casting a look at Nova that could kill, Liam faded from view. Nova sighed. So much for trying to help.

'He's . . . he's gone, hasn't he?' Mr Jackman said slowly.

'Yes,' Nova replied.

'I mean it,' Mr Jackman told her fiercely. 'I'm not

leaving this hotel without him. If he wants to get rid of me, he'll have to tell me what I want to know. Next time you see him, you tell him that.'

And with that, Mr Jackman marched past Nova and out of the dining room.

21. Liam

I got up slowly. For a terrifying moment, I had no idea where I was. No idea what the darkness around me could be. Where was I? I did have my eyes open, didn't I? I blinked a couple of times to make sure. And then I remembered.

The cave-in.

I looked around again. I still couldn't see anything. It was much too dark. But then an odd thing happened. The tunnels got strangely lighter. But not with daylight or even moonlight. This was like something I'd never seen before. It was like lying in my bed at home when it was dead dark and dead quiet, and slowly but surely being able to make out the outlines and the familiar silhouettes of the things around me. Only here, in this tunnel, I could see more clearly and more in focus than I ever could before – and it was all in the dark.

It took me a few moments to realize that.

It was as if a blue light shone out from my eyes onto all the things around me and then bounced right back at me. To be honest, it freaked me out a bit. Why could I suddenly see so clearly? There had to be blue light entering the tunnels from some place I hadn't yet been, somewhere I hadn't yet discovered. Or maybe there was some kind of luminous metallic ore in the rocks around me. Deep down, I knew I was clutching at straws but there had to be a logical explanation. I just needed to find it. Either way, I had to get out of here. Now. At once. I started walking, then running towards what I thought was the nearest exit. But I couldn't feel anything. It took a few seconds to realize that although my feet were making contact with the ground, I couldn't feel the ground against my feet, pushing back. I stopped abruptly and stared down at my feet in the cold blue semi-light.

I jumped tentatively. My feet left the ground, then seconds later they landed. I stopped. But I hadn't felt the ground that time either. The rock fall must've damaged some nerves in my legs or back. That's why I couldn't feel anything. But then, how come I could still walk and run? I didn't understand it. Terrified, I started sprinting again – in case I was running on adrenaline or luck only and one or both of them were about to run out. I should've been getting closer to the entrance by now.

But instead of getting lighter, it got darker and darker until I was racing as fast as I could, until my heart was burning and I had one hell of a stitch and still I kept running, until I was swallowed up by the dark, with nowhere left to run but onwards to nowhere.

22. Liam

Nova slammed her bedroom door shut. 'Liam, are you here?'

Liam slowly faded into view before her. 'What d'you want?'

'I want to know what all that was about?'

'All what?'

Nova's severe scowl was truly impressive. It was enough to sour milk and then some. 'Don't play games, Liam. How come Mr Jackman knows who you are?'

'That's my business,' said Liam, turning away slightly.

Nova strode towards him, aiming to grab his arm and turn him round to face her. But her hand went straight through his body. She inhaled sharply with surprise, then looked annoyed. 'I wish you wouldn't do that,' she grumbled.

'Can't help it!' Liam said with a trace of a smile.

'I mean it, Liam. What's going on between you and Mr Jackman?'

Liam's smile vanished. That was one question he wasn't going to answer. 'That's between me and him.'

'Not if you want my help, it's not.'

So that's how it was, eh? Liam scrutinized Nova carefully. 'We all have our little secrets, Nova. Even you.'

Nova suddenly grew still. 'What does that mean?'

'Never mind.'

'No, if you've got something to say, let's hear it,' Nova insisted. 'Go on.'

All right then. She'd asked for it. 'What d'you like to do in your spare time, Nova? Watch telly? Go for a walk?'

asked Liam after a pause. 'Or maybe you like to do something a little more radical? More gross but more radical?'

Nova clasped her trembling hands together in an effort to stop them from shaking.

'Shall I tell you one of my hobbies?' Liam continued. 'I love to go to the toilets on the second floor. You know, the ones at the back of the hotel? Listening to you make yourself vomit after every meal is better than watching a horror film on the telly.'

Nova's mouth fell open. 'You know?'

'Of course I know. You're in there three times a day at least, so it's either chronic long-term diarrhoea or vomiting.'

'How dare you? You have no right to spy on me!' Nova exclaimed, horrified.

'Spy on you? Do me a favour! D'you think I've got nothing better to do?'

'Obviously not!' Nova was furious. She looked like a cornered rat, looking for a fast escape route.

'Why d'you do it?' frowned Liam.

'None of your business.'

'You can dish it out but you sure can't take it, can you?' said Liam. 'How come you can ask me personal stuff, but not the other way round?'

'Because you're a ghost and ghosts don't have personal stuff,' Nova raged at him.

'Which ghost manual did you read that in?' asked Liam.

Nova clenched and unclenched her fists, desperately trying to find something to say.

'Why d'you keep making yourself sick? Is your mum's cooking really that bad?'

'It has nothing to do with Mum's cooking.'

'So what is it about then?'

'You wouldn't understand.'

'Try me.'

'It's nothing.'

'You make yourself puke morning, noon and night after every meal – but it's nothing. I believe that all right!'

'Liam, keep your nose out of my business.'

'No can do. Sorry.'

'Get out of my room.'

'No.'

'Get out of my room. Now!' Nova was fifty shades of furious.

'No!' Liam folded his arms across his chest.

'I'm not surprised you're dead!' Nova screamed at him. 'It wouldn't surprise me if someone had murdered you!'

A deathly chill flooded through Liam at Nova's words. She started to stride past him but, incensed, he grabbed her arm and yanked her back. 'Don't you ever, ever, as long as you live, say that to me again. D'you hear?' he hissed, fire dancing in his brown eyes.

Nova glared at him, but he scowled right back. She was the first to drop her gaze. 'I'm sorry. That was out of order.'

Liam's scowl didn't disappear by any means. If anything, it got worse.

'Jeez! If looks could kill . . .' Nova shot out, only to bite her lip. 'Sorry! I didn't mean that the way it came out.'

'You don't mean a lot of things, but it doesn't stop you from saying them.'

'Sorry. OK? I'm sorry. Sometimes my mouth kicks in before my brain switches on,' said Nova.

Moments ticked by as Liam struggled to control his feelings. He closed his eyes and took a concentrated deep breath. Only when he was sure he wouldn't bite her head off did he speak. 'Look, Nova, I want you to promise you'll stop all this vomiting rubbish. Apart from making your teeth rot and trashing your insides, you're too smart for all that.'

Nova pulled away from his grasp. 'What d'you know about it?'

'I know—' But Liam got no further.

'You don't know anything. People like you and my sister make me sick,' Nova interrupted harshly. 'You're all drop-dead gorgeous and you've never had to worry about more than the odd pimple. You don't know what it's like to hate every tiny bit of yourself.'

'What're you talking about?' Liam shook his head, bewildered. 'There's nothing wrong with you.'

'Yeah, right,' Nova scoffed. 'That's why when my aunts and uncles and grandparents come round, they all rave on about how beautiful Rainbow is and how sweet and cute the twins are and no one says a word about me – except maybe about how much I've shot up. "Nova, haven't you grown!", "We should call you bamboo, Nova!", "Nova, you'll soon be taller than me!"'

'What's wrong with that?'

'I hate it – OK? I hate it!' Nova shouted at him.

She ran for the door. Liam tried to grab her arm again but his hand passed right through her. He ran to get to the door first, standing in front of it to block her way. Not being able to control when he became solid was more than frustrating. Now that his initial burst of anger was over, he was back to being intangible, truly ghost-like. 'Look, I know what it's like to be compared all the time to someone else in your family,' he told her. 'I was always being compared to my younger brother, Josh. Everyone thought the sun shone from his one eye and the rest of the stars sparkled out the other.'

'And how did that make you feel?'

Liam didn't answer.

'Exactly!'

'I still . . . I still cared about him,' Liam defended himself.

'I care about Raye. 'Course I do. But sometimes, I can't stop myself from hating her too,' Nova admitted.

'And vomiting up every meal is going to sort all that out, is it?' asked Liam.

'I want to look like Rainbow.'

'What's wrong with looking like yourself?' asked Liam.

Quickly, Nova wiped her eyes. She stepped back and scrutinized him. 'Tell me something. What d'you think of my sister?'

Liam dropped his gaze, then turned his head. His beige-coloured cheeks had a reddish glow to them and the tips of his ears were a discernable fiery red. He instinctively knew he'd done the wrong thing. He should've looked Nova in the eyes when he answered her. 'I don't really know her,' he mumbled inanely.

Nova studied him before asking, 'D'you think she's pretty?'

'She's OK.'

'Liar!'

'All right then, she is pretty. In fact, she's way past stunning. Is that what you want to hear?' asked Liam.

'So why shouldn't I try and be like her?' asked Nova.

'Fine. Then be like her. She doesn't make herself sick after every meal.'

'She doesn't have to. She's so skinny, she probably has to jump about in the shower to get wet!' Nova replied. 'And I'm going to look like Rainbow if it kills me.'

'You stupid twit,' Liam hissed. 'That's exactly what it will do if you don't stop.'

'I don't care!' Nova shouted again.

'Oh, you fancy being like me, do you?' said Liam. 'You

fancy trolling around this hotel for the rest of eternity where no one can see or hear you? This isn't just about being dead, Nova. This place isn't just my coffin. This place is Hell. So go ahead, starve yourself, or give yourself a heart attack from all that vomiting. See if I care.'

Nova stared at him. With a sob, she ran straight through him, wrenching open the door to run away from his words as fast as she could. Liam stared after her, mentally kicking himself.

'Well done, Liam!' he muttered. 'Brilliantly handled. Well done!'

23. Nova

He knew. Liam knew. Someone knew. What was she going
to do? Nova ran and ran, down the stairs and out of the
house, and she didn't stop until she'd reached her favourite
bench in the garden. She flopped down, gasping to catch
her breath from all that running, and stared out towards
the copse, watching but not seeing the last rays of the sun
light up the leaves with a burnished gold. Funny, but she
never used to get so out of breath, running from the hotel
to her favourite bench. Everything exhausted her these
days. The reason was obvious. But now someone else
knew the reason.

What was she going to do?

But hang on . . . Maybe she was panicking about nothing. Liam was a ghost. Who was he going to tell? No one
else but her could see him. But he'd got so angry with her,
he'd actually been able to grab her arm. And when he got
upset with Mr Jackman he'd suddenly become visible,
right in front of him. What if he got angry again? Angry
enough to materialize and tell her mum or dad what she
was doing? Nova looked around nervously. Was Liam
there, watching her right now but not making himself
visible? And how long had he been watching her
make herself sick? A month? A year? How many times
had he watched her vomit? Nova shuddered with
shame at the thought. It was OK when she thought no
one knew, like a noble secret that was hers and hers
alone. But now that someone else knew it didn't seem
fine and noble any more. It was just shabby and horrible.
Had he watched all her little tricks? Like insisting on

113

peas or tomatoes or baked beans with every meal and always eating them first before anything else on her plate, so that when she was sick, she'd know when her stomach was truly empty? First in, last out. Did he know that she never ate chocolate? Not because she didn't like the taste like she'd told everyone, but because it smelt so awful when it came up again. Did he know about her having a fizzy drink with every meal, or oranges, or sherbet sweets – anything to fill her stomach with more acid or gas to make bringing up her food that much easier. All the little tricks and slips she'd learned over the last year, until vomiting had become more than a now-and-then pastime. Vomiting had become a way of life. A form of control. In fact it was more than a way of life. It *was* her life.

If things were going wrong it was because she hadn't got all the food out of her stomach. If she didn't do well in class, making herself sick was a way to make things better. And Nova knew it was doing bad things to her body. Her tongue was getting furry. Her breath now smelt so bad she was constantly chewing gum. She was tired all the time and any kind of exercise left her breathless and giddy. Look at the way she'd been left gasping for air, just from running up one flight of stairs at full pelt that morning. But Nova couldn't stop herself vomiting. She'd tried. But every time she tried to eat and keep it down, the food sat in her stomach like a boulder until she couldn't bear it any longer and out it came.

Liam didn't understand. How could he? Nova herself didn't understand. But Liam *knew*.

'Can I sit down?'

Nova didn't bother to turn her head at the sound of Liam's voice. Out of the corner of her eye, she saw him sit down beside her.

'I'm not judging you,' he said after a long pause.

'Aren't you?' asked Nova bitterly.

'I'm sorry,' Liam said. 'What I mean is, I didn't mean to judge you. I'm just trying to understand why, that's all.'

'It doesn't matter.'

'Of course it matters.'

They sat in silence as the sun sank lower in the sky.

'What's *your* secret?' Nova asked at last.

'Secret?'

Nova turned to Liam. 'You said we both have our little secrets. You know mine. What's yours?'

'It can wait.'

'No, it can't,' said Nova. 'Is it about Mr Jackman?'

Liam nodded.

'Is he . . .?'

But Liam began to fade out, becoming more and more transparent as Nova glared at him.

'Good way to avoid answering questions you don't like!' she bristled.

'Isn't it just!' Liam's grinning face was all that was visible before it too began to fade away.

'How nice to disappear whenever the going gets tough. Were you always this much of a coward?' asked Nova.

Liam's grin vanished. The rest of him didn't, though. His sudden snap back to opaqueness made Nova jump.

'How dare you? I'm not a coward,' he said heatedly.

'No? It's not the first time you've pulled your disappearing act at the first sign of something unpleasant,' Nova pointed out.

Liam glowered at her with a look on his face Nova had never seen before – and never wanted to see again.

'So are you going to answer my question now?'

'What question?' asked Liam belligerently.

'Why didn't you want Mr Jackman to leave the hotel?'

'He was planning to do something . . . stupid. Dangerously stupid,' Liam replied. 'He was going to explore the underwater caves in the bay to try and find me. And everyone round here knows that those caves are lethal. No one is stupid enough to go in them – especially at night – but m— Mr Jackman was going to try. I saw him writing an "if anything should happen to me . . ." letter.'

'You're joking . . .' Nova stared at him.

'I wish I was. He was convinced I was here even before he saw me.' Liam shrugged. 'But I think catching sight of me has changed his night-swimming plans. Although you confirming I was there didn't help get rid of him, which is what I wanted.'

'He'd already seen you and it was obvious he knew you.'

'But if you'd kept quiet, he might've thought he'd imagined seeing me.'

'Not very likely,' said Nova.

'But still possible.'

'Why're you so set against him knowing about you?'

'I want him to get on with his life,' Liam said quietly. 'I don't want him tying his life down and around me.'

'Why would he do that?' Nova thought of something. But it couldn't be that – could it? 'Liam, what's your surname?'

Silence.

'Liam . . .?'

'I should've guessed you'd figure it out sooner or later,' Liam sighed.

'So what is it?'

'Jackman.' The whispered word was all that was left of Liam as once more he vanished from sight.

24. Dad

Dad sighed, then quickly glanced up to make sure that his wife was nowhere around. He was in luck. There was only Mr Jackman hovering at the foot of the stairs. Dad glanced down at the computer on the reception desk again. He'd called up the month's receipts on his spreadsheet and it did not make heart-warming viewing. The hotel wasn't in trouble, but it wasn't far from it either. They just weren't getting the bookings they needed to keep afloat. Dad sighed again as he scrolled down the expenditure column. They were still spending too much and making too little. Cheap holiday packages abroad and the mystery that was English summer weather were combining to choke the life out of him. He had to come up with some way, some sure-fire way, for the hotel to make money. But what? Dad glanced up again. Mr Jackman was heading straight for him. That had to be a mirage for a start. Money worries were obviously affecting his brain.

'Hello, Mr Clibbens.'

Dad stared, totally astounded. Mr Jackman was actually talking to him! Flying pigs and blue snow would occur within the hour. 'Hello, Mr Jackman. Off for a walk, are you?'

'No. Not this evening. I thought . . . I'd stay in for a change. It really is a beautiful hotel.'

'Thank you. Yes, it is,' Dad agreed. What was this man up to? This was the most he'd said to him since his arrival.

'You must've spent a fortune on it,' said Mr Jackman.

'Every penny we had.' Dad hoped the truth sounded

more nonchalant than desperate. He allowed himself a faint satisfied smile. 'But it was worth it.'

'Did you have the place completely rebuilt?'

'No, the structure was still sound. But we had it gutted and completely refurbished. We moved rooms around, split some rooms in two, knocked some together, that sort of thing.'

'Any hidden staircases or secret passages?' Mr Jackman joked.

'Not a one,' Dad laughed.

'Shame!' said Mr Jackman, his smile fading. 'Secret passages conjure up so many images, don't they? Like memory mazes. Turn the next corner and catch the long forgotten scent of a dark-time dream or a daytime nightmare.'

'If you say so,' Dad said doubtfully. 'Are you into that sort of thing then?'

Mr Jackman shrugged. 'So how long did it take to renovate this place?'

'Over a year.'

'It used to be called Manor Hotel, didn't it?'

'That's right. We changed the name to Phoenix Manor – kind of like a new hotel rising out of the ashes of the old one. My wife thought of the name actually. But when she suggested it, I said, "Karmah, the name's a good 'un." And I was right. The name suits the place.'

'Yes,' Mr Jackman said, looking around slowly. 'Yes, it does. Well, I'd best be getting on.' Mr Jackman turned and headed for the stairs.

Dad studied him, unsure what to make of what had just happened. Maybe the man was finally mellowing out. And not before time either. 'Oh, just a minute,' he called after Mr Jackman. 'Talking of secret passages, there was one – well, sort of one – that was found soon after building work had begun.'

'Oh yes?' Mr Jackman was back at the reception desk in a flash. 'Where was that?'

'Down in the cellar, but it wasn't much of a passage. It stopped dead after about fifty or so metres and there was solid rock and earth after that.'

'Did you try to dig through it?'

Dad raised his eyebrows. 'Now why on earth would we do that? I wanted to rebuild the hotel, not tunnel under it like a mole.'

'Where's the entrance to this passage?' asked Mr Jackman. 'Is it still in the cellar? Can I see it?'

'I'm afraid not. It's kept permanently locked. We have a state-of-the-art wine cellar and storage facility down there, with some excellent vintages . . .'

But Dad was talking to Mr Jackman's back. Mr Jackman ran up the stairs, taking them two and three at a time. Well, so much for thinking the man was getting better. He was just as rude as ever. Dad turned back to his computer screen, then sighed deeply as he remembered what he'd been doing.

Money! How could the hotel make more money?

25. Nova

Nova just couldn't get comfortable. She tried her back, her front, then both sides – but nothing doing. She switched on her bedside light and tilted her alarm clock. It was past two in the morning. So much for sleep then. Maybe a glass of milk would help? Yeah, a glass of warm milk instead of something acidic or fizzy. And milk tasted absolutely foul when it came up again, so she'd be more likely to try and keep it down. And then Liam couldn't accuse her of not even trying to get better. So milk it was.

Wondering why she cared so much about Liam's opinion, Nova swung out of bed, pushing her feet into her fluffy purple slippers. She grabbed her matching dressing gown from the bottom of the bed before heading out of her room. The hotel would certainly be locked up for the night and the last thing she wanted to do was wake anyone up. The low-level lighting on the stairs and landing was more than enough to see by, but it was still strange walking through the hotel when it was this tranquil. During the day Nova sometimes had to fight to hear herself think but this was so different, it was unnerving. Pulling her dressing gown tighter around her against the cool night air, she carried on down the stairs.

She was on the top step just past the first-floor landing when she heard strange sounds coming from below. Peering over the banister, she strained to see who – or what – was making the noise. Then she tiptoed down the stairs, feeling strangely nervous, and leaned over the banister. The thuds were coming from the direction of the kitchen. It was probably just Mum or Dad or the twins up to one of their silly tricks – or Liam. It certainly wouldn't be anything for her to be afraid of. Liam was a ghost, for heaven's sake! And if *he* didn't freak her out, then nothing could.

Nova crept towards the slightly ajar kitchen door. A strange yellow light bounced on and off around the door. First it was there, then it wasn't – like a torch being shone around, or swung around. And then the light was gone. She waited for a few moments but the light didn't come on again. She pushed open the door. 'Dad, is that you?' she whispered.

Nothing.

No way was she going to go stumbling around in the dark. She switched on the light. The door leading down to the cellar was open and Mum always made sure she locked it at night before she went to bed. Nova walked across to the door and hesitated at the top of the stairs. The bad thing about the cellar was you had to go down the stairs to switch on the light. It was one of those things Dad was going to fix if he ever got round to it.

'Mum? Dad? Are you down there?'

Silence. But someone was definitely down there. The hairs standing up on the back of her neck told her that much.

'Liam . . .' Nova whispered.

But it couldn't be Liam. He didn't need to open doors to get through them.

'If you don't come out now, I'm going to get my mum and dad,' Nova challenged with far more courage than she was feeling.

A torch flicked on immediately. With all the light from it spilling forward, it was hard to tell who was holding it.

'The light switch is on the wall at the foot of the stairs,' Nova called out.

Still shrouded in shadow, the person moved towards the switch and moments later the cellar was flooded with light.

'Mr Jackman!' Nova frowned.

Nova and Mr Jackman regarded each other, neither of them moving, neither of them even blinking.

'What're you doing down there?' asked Nova, noting the torch in his hand.

'I was looking for something.'

'What?'

Mr Jackman didn't answer.

'Did you find it?' asked Nova.

'Not yet.'

'Maybe I can help you look for it?' Nova and Mr Jackman still didn't take their eyes off each other. It was as if they were saying one thing and talking about something entirely different – and they both knew it.

'I think you've found it . . . or should I say him, already.'

'You were looking for Liam in the cellar?' Nova wasn't quite sure she understood.

'Sort of,' said Mr Jackman.

'I'm not with you.'

Mr Jackman scrutinized Nova before speaking. 'I'm looking for an entrance to the tunnels your dad was telling me about earlier.'

'The tunnels? Dad had the entrance padlocked ages ago,' said Nova. 'And there was just one tunnel, not tunnels plural.'

'I was talking to Miss Eve earlier and she said there's supposed to be a whole network of tunnels running under this hotel and the grounds,' said Mr Jackman. 'If your dad and the builders only found one, then I think there must've been some kind of collapse or cave-in which blocked off access to the rest. And I need to find them.'

'Did you find the entrance in the cellar then?'

'Not yet. It's a big cellar and I'd only just started looking when you arrived.'

'But why? What's so special about the tunnels?'

'It's the only place Liam can be,' Mr Jackman said after a long pause.

'What're you talking about? Liam's all over the place. Believe me, I know. Nothing happens in this hotel without him knowing about it.'

'I'm talking about his . . . body.'

An ice-cold shiver shot up through Nova's body. Horrified, she stared at Mr Jackman. She'd never once thought about that. She'd never even considered the possibility that Liam's body was still somewhere in or around the hotel.

'I think that's why he's still at this hotel, why he can't leave,' said Mr Jackman.

'Who told you he couldn't leave?' asked Nova.

'Oh, come on. It's obvious. Why would he hang around this hotel otherwise?'

'Thank you,' Nova bristled.

'I'm not insulting your hotel. But if you had the choice, would you spend eternity in this place?' asked Mr Jackman.

Nova didn't answer. It was only now that the full impact of what was going on between Mr Jackman and Liam hit Nova. Mr Jackman was obviously Liam's dad. It explained so much. But wait a second . . . he couldn't be Liam's dad, could he? Liam was at least fifteen or sixteen and Mr Jackman didn't look like he was even thirty yet – not that Nova was any good at guessing adults' ages. Maybe Mr Jackman was really old but looked very good for his age?

'How did you know he'd be here in the first place?' asked Nova.

'I didn't. But this used to be one of his favourite places before your family took it over. I knew he wouldn't just disappear for all these years without ever trying to get in touch with me. So that meant only one thing.'

'That he'd died?' Nova whispered.

Mr Jackman nodded, his expression grim. 'That he'd died. So I've spent the last few years trying to find out what happened to him. If I could just find him and make sure he has a decent burial, then he might be able to rest in peace.'

'Dad's not going to let you go digging up his cellar and his gardens,' said Nova.

'Then you'll have to get Liam to tell me exactly where his body is,' argued Mr Jackman.

'I'll ask him. That doesn't mean he'll tell me,' Nova pointed out. 'I know . . . I know you're his dad but Liam really wants you to leave.'

Mr Jackman's mouth fell open. 'I'm not Liam's dad.'

'His uncle then.'

'I'm not his uncle either,' said Mr Jackman. 'My name is Joshua Jackman.' At Nova's blank look, he added quietly, 'Liam's not my son or my nephew. He's my brother.'

26. Nova

'Your brother . . .? But he can't be.' Nova couldn't take it in. 'Liam said he had a younger brother called Josh.'

'I'm his younger brother.'

'But he's sixteen at most.' Nova shook her head. 'You're way up there!'

Mr Jackman smiled dryly. 'I'm twenty-four in a couple of months.'

'Like I said!' Nova said, her point proven.

'Liam died over ten years ago,' said Mr Jackman. 'When he appeared to me he looked exactly the same as the last time I saw him . . . alive. Ghosts obviously don't grow older. But I do.'

'But . . . but . . .' Nova blinked like a dazzled owl as she struggled to grasp what Mr Jackman was saying. 'That's . . . that's . . . horrible. Poor Liam!'

Nova could hardly imagine what it must be like for Liam. How must he feel, seeing Mr Jackman and knowing who he was. Mr Jackman was Liam's younger brother, but now older and alive, while Liam was stuck. Stuck in the hotel. Stuck in time. Stuck like a fly in a spider's web. No wonder Mr Jackman was so desperate to free Liam – one way or another. Nova had assumed Liam had only been at the hotel for a few months, a year or two at most. And she'd never dreamt that he'd actually died so close to her home. Maybe even *in* her home if Mr Jackman was wrong about the tunnels. But to be here for over ten years. Even now, Nova still had trouble wrapping her mind around the idea.

'Will you help me, Nova?' asked Mr Jackman. 'Please?'

'I —'

'What in the name of ruddy hell is going on here?' Dad's incredulous voice boomed out behind them, making Nova jump.

'Ah, Mr Clibbens,' began Mr Jackman as he headed up the stairs to the kitchen. 'I was just talking to your daughter about the history of this hotel.'

'At two o'clock in the morning? Have you lost your mind?' Dad said angrily. 'Nova, what's going on?'

'I just came downstairs to get myself a glass of milk,' Nova explained. 'And I saw Mr Jackman down here and we just got chatting.'

'At two o'clock in the morning?' Dad repeated.

'I'm sorry. It was all my fault,' said Mr Jackman. 'I should've insisted that Nova go straight back to bed.'

'And just what're you doing down in my wine cellar?' asked Dad.

'I must admit, I became intrigued with the idea of the tunnels you were talking about earlier, so I thought I'd have a look and see if maybe there was another entrance to them somewhere down there . . . somewhere.'

Dad's expression was dropping in temperature with every passing second. 'At two o'clock in the morning?'

'I'm afraid, when I get an idea in my head, I like to go with it.' Mr Jackman smiled apologetically.

'At two o'clock in the morning?'

Mr Jackman shrugged.

'And how did you get into the cellar in the first place? My wife always locks up last thing at night,' said Dad.

'I'm afraid I picked the lock,' said Mr Jackman. 'You know, you should open up the tunnels as a genuine historical attraction. I'm sure loads of people would love to explore the route smugglers took centuries ago – and you do own the land around the hotel, don't you?'

'I am not going to stand here discussing real estate at two o'clock in the morning,' said Dad, his tone hard as stone. 'Nova, go to bed. I want to have a word in private with Mr Jackman.'

'But, Dad, we can explain . . .'

Dad turned to look at Nova and the look alone was enough to quell everything else she wanted to say. For once, she didn't argue. She'd never seen her Dad quite so steamingly irate before, not even when the twins had smuggled a live snake into the hotel as their new pet and it'd got lost in one of the occupied guest bedrooms.

Nova headed out of the kitchen. At the door, she turned to see her dad standing in front of Mr Jackman. 'Dad . . .?' she began.

'Go to bed, Nova,' Dad repeated softly.

Nova did as she was told and headed back to her room. She could only hope that Dad would give Mr Jackman a chance to explain. But somehow, she doubted it.

27. Miss Dawn and Miss Eve

The early morning sunshine streamed through the hotel lounge windows, dancing on the table where Miss Dawn and Miss Eve sat playing gin rummy. Not for money, of course. Miss Dawn didn't hold with such things.

'Things aren't going too well for the Jackman family, are they?' smiled Miss Eve.

Miss Dawn studied her companion, before she leaned forward to pick up a card from the deck. 'How sad to only find happiness in the misfortunes of others.'

'I just meant that neither brother is distinguishing himself at the moment.'

'They'll be all right.' Miss Dawn carefully placed a card onto the discard pile.

'Oh, Miss Dawn, wake up. Liam may be ten years older but he's not ten years wiser. He's still full of rage and resentment, anger and animosity, hatred and hostility.'

'Spare me the alliteration, please.' Miss Dawn was distinctly unimpressed.

Miss Eve sat back. Miss Dawn rearranged every card in her hand at least once, deliberately not looking at Miss Eve.

'Don't pin your hopes on Liam,' Miss Eve said softly, picking up another card. 'He's lonely. And his loneliness is clouding his judgement.'

'When the time comes, he'll do the right thing,' Miss Dawn said confidently.

'Not a chance. He's going to mess up. I can see all the signs,' said Miss Eve.

'Signs can be misleading.'

'Signs can show you exactly which way the wind is blowing. And by the way – gin!' Miss Eve said smugly, laying her cards on the table.

'We'll see,' said Miss Dawn, laying her cards face down. 'We'll see!'

Miss Eve asked irritably, 'Don't you ever get tired of saying that?'

28. The Eavesdropper

'To be honest, I didn't think you'd remember,' said Andrew.

'Are you kidding? I've been looking forward to this all morning,' smiled Raye. 'I even had my breakfast extra early so we could have a longer walk – but don't let it go to your head!'

Andrew laughed. 'I won't.'

He and Raye exchanged a genuinely friendly smile. They'd been walking and talking together for almost an hour, although the time had flown by. They'd walked around the hotel grounds and through part of the copse. Now they stood a couple of metres away from the cliff edge, looking out over the bay. Andrew tilted his head to one side as he studied Raye's profile. She really was quite a stunner. If only Kieran and Raoul and some of his other friends could see her. And, more importantly, see him with her. Funny, but when Andrew first saw her, he hadn't thought she was anything much. But the closer he got and the longer he looked, the better she appeared!

After a few moments she turned. 'Do I have something nasty hanging off my nose?'

Andrew laughed, but it quickly faded. 'Raye, you're not . . . you're not what I expected,' he admitted.

'Oh please!' Liam said from beside them. 'How long have you been practising that line with that sincere look?'

'What were you expecting?' asked Raye, oblivious to the eavesdropper who'd been with them since they'd left the hotel.

'A bimbo airhead,' Liam provided.

'Someone who wasn't as witty and pretty and fun,' said Andrew.

'Pass me a bucket someone.' Liam stuck two fingers down his throat, as he glared at Andrew. What a shame neither Andrew nor Raye could see him. How he would've loved to scare the living daylights out of Mister Fake over there. And those lines he was coming out with, they were straight out of *Cheesy Chat-up Lines* – Volume One!

'Please, kind sir, you'll turn my head.' Raye raised her hands to her cheeks and pretended to simper.

'You'll turn my stomach,' Liam muttered.

'Maybe we could still keep in touch after I leave tomorrow?' asked Andrew.

'I'd like that,' said Raye.

'So would I.'

Liam watched them, unable to think of a single thing to say to make himself feel better. In fact, watching the two of them together was making him feel worse. Andrew and Raye had spoken about school and their friends and their exams and all the everyday, so-called mundane stuff that everyone took for granted. At that moment, Liam would've sold his soul to be alive for just one day like them. Did they have any idea how much he envied them? Of course not. They had no clue about him. They didn't want one either.

'We'd better turn back,' said Raye. 'Mum and Dad will be wondering where I am.'

'Maybe we could take another walk this afternoon?'

'Sorry, I've got to help out before dinner,' said Raye.

'After dinner then?'

'I'll try but I can't guarantee anything.'

'I really want to see you again before I leave tomorrow. You're really something special, Raye.'

'You're laying it on just a bit too thick there!' said Raye dryly.

'I'll spread it a bit thinner then,' smiled Andrew.

'I'd appreciate it!'

'So would I!' said Liam.

Andrew walked at Raye's side, both of them oblivious to Liam, who was walking on her other side.

'Raye, don't trust him,' Liam tried again. 'He's a moron. He's just setting you up.'

Raye stopped and looked around. 'You . . . did you hear something?'

'No,' Andrew replied.

Raye shook her head and smiled. 'Just the wind, I expect.'

She started walking again. Andrew fell into step beside her. Liam didn't. He watched them walk away from him. 'No, it wasn't the wind,' he called after them.

The wind had more of an effect on how things worked than Liam ever did. He rubbed both his hands over his face. What'd he ever done to deserve the existence he had now? When was this hellish ride he was on going to stop?

29. Nova

Nova chewed her bite of toasted bacon sandwich until it was no more than watery paste in her mouth, before she allowed herself to swallow. Eating this way took for ever but it made it slightly harder to bring it back up afterwards. Slightly. Food that was only moderately chewed was easier to coax upwards. But Nova had to eat like this because she didn't want to vomit up her food, knowing that Liam could be somewhere watching or listening or both. It was humiliating enough knowing that he knew.

Swallowing at last, Nova charily placed the last piece of bacon and toast in her mouth.

'Nova, are you OK?' Mum asked gently.

Nova looked up from her plate, where she'd been carefully putting her knife and fork together so that they lined up exactly. Mum was giving her a studied look.

'I'm fine, Mum.' Nova immediately let go of the knife and fork.

'It's just that . . . you're so particular with your food these days,' Mum continued. 'And Raye and the twins finished their breakfast ages ago.'

Nova shrugged. 'I'm just a slow eater.'

'No baked beans or tomatoes today?' asked Mum.

Nova's face began to burn. 'Didn't fancy them. Can I go now?'

'Are you going to finish your orange juice?'

Nova looked at the glass. 'Better not. I mean, no, I've had enough.'

'Off you go then,' said Mum, gathering up the empty breakfast plate.

Nova stood up and went off in search of Mr Jackman, oblivious to the searching look her mum gave her as she left.

Twenty minutes later she hadn't found Mr Jackman – but she had found the toilets on the second floor at the back of the hotel. She'd tried so hard to keep her break-fast down – deep breaths, trying to think of something else, closing her eyes as she walked past any of the toilets – but none of it did any good. It was as if there was a line from the toilet bowl to her stomach and the moment she ate, the line drew tight and taut and pulled at her until she had to give in and follow where it led. So here she was, back in her favourite toilet cubicle. And this time it was hard to throw up – and it hurt. She'd had no orange juice to smooth the way back up. The back of her throat felt like someone had taken a grater to it and her stomach was aching. Was her stomach empty? Without her usual colourful starter, Nova couldn't tell. She retched again and her whole head was seized by a vice-like spasm so intense that her hands immediately flew to her temples. Flushing the toilet, Nova put down the lid and sat down. She closed her eyes in despair. She really hadn't wanted to be sick this morning. But her little ploys and variations in her eating routine hadn't made the slightest bit of difference. With a sigh she unlocked the door and went out.

Liam was leaning against the wall, looking straight ahead. At Nova's gasp, he turned to face her. 'You OK?' Stupid question! Nova scowled at him. 'Yeah, all right. It was!' Liam agreed, reading her mind.

'What're you doing in here? If watching me heave is the highlight of your day, then you need to get a life!' Nova could've bitten her tongue off. 'Sorry. I didn't mean —'

'Watching you upchuck is not the be-all and end-all of

my existence, no,' Liam interrupted calmly. 'Would it do any good to tell you I think you're nuts?'

'No!'

'How about if I asked you to stop before you do some serious damage to yourself?'

'I'm trying. Now can we drop the subject?' Nova said brusquely.

Liam shook his head, but he did as she asked. 'There's something else that needs sorting out. You need to warn your sister about Andrew.'

'Who's Andrew? And why do I need to warn Raye about him?'

'He's one of the guests here,' said Liam. 'He and his parents arrived yesterday. But Andrew was on the phone betting one of his friends that he can get Raye to snog him before he leaves tomorrow and you need to tell her.'

'Why?'

'Because Andrew's a low-life creep. You don't want your sister kissing someone like that, do you?'

'I don't care who my sister goes around kissing,' Nova told him, rinsing out her mouth over one of the wash basins.

'But Andrew only wants to kiss her for a bet. I tried to warn her yesterday but she wouldn't listen.'

'You tried to warn Raye? Is that when she saw you?' said Nova.

'Only briefly. A few seconds. And she didn't believe a word. All I did was cheese her off, I think,' said Liam.

'So you didn't tell her you were a ghost?'

'Of course not.'

Nova wondered at the feeling of intense relief that flooded through her. Why had she suddenly felt so anxious when she'd heard that Liam had tried to talk to Raye? Nova dismissed her worries. She was just concerned about

Liam, that was all. Raye would freak if she thought there was a real, live ghost in the hotel.

'Nova, you have to do something. Once Andrew's got what he wants, he'll have a good laugh at Raye behind her back,' said Liam earnestly. 'Now, I know you wouldn't want that to happen.'

Nova straightened up. 'You're more bent out of shape about it than I am. Besides, I've got something more important to do. I've got to find Mr Jackman.'

'Raye needs our help.'

'So does Mr Jackman.'

'Never mind my— I mean, Mr Jackman,' said Liam.

'I know he's your brother so you can stop calling him Mr Jackman,' said Nova.

'You two did have a cosy little talk, didn't you?' Liam said bitterly.

'He only wants to help you. I can't understand why you're so dead against that,' said Nova, bewildered.

'Well, he can't help.'

'He can if you'll let him,' said Nova.

'He can't do anything any more. He's gone,' said Liam reluctantly.

'What d'you mean? What did you do to him?'

'You need to talk to your dad, not me,' snapped Liam. 'And after that you can help me give Andrew Stanley what's coming to him.'

30. Andrew

They were almost back at the hotel and Andrew was sorry. He'd enjoyed his walk with Raye far more than he'd thought possible. He risked a quick look at her as they continued their easy pace, then deliberately looked away. He tried to turn his mind back to the job in hand. How best to get a kiss? But the bet made him feel uneasy at best and guilty at worse. Still, a wager was a wager and he couldn't back out now. And even if he lied and said he had kissed her, Andrew would still know the truth. He'd still know he'd failed, and Andrew didn't like to fail.

'I really like you, Rainbow,' he said.

Raye turned to face him, a ready smile on her face. 'I know! I've got something for you.'

'Oh yes?'

Raye dug into her jacket pocket and removed a gift-wrapped package about fifteen centimetres square. 'Happy birthday! I didn't have time to go shopping but I thought you might like this.'

Andrew took the package from Raye's open hand. 'You didn't have to do this, you know.'

'That's why I did it!' smiled Raye. 'Well? Aren't you going to open it?'

Andrew tore off the wrapping paper – and stared.

'D'you like it?' Raye asked anxiously. 'I did it myself.'

'Raye, I love it.' Andrew couldn't take his eyes off the present.

'I thought you would,' Raye grinned.

It was a pencil drawing of Andrew's face. Raye was a gifted artist but for some reason she had trouble drawing faces unless it was of people she cared about. Landscapes and still-life pictures were a doddle. And so was the human body. But not faces. But she'd drawn Andrew's face with a slight, amused smile crinkling up his eyes and curving his lips. She'd been up most of the night doing it and it was definitely one of the best drawings she'd ever done.

Andrew finally looked up, his eyes strangely bright and almost sad.

'Happy birthday, Andrew,' said Raye again. And she kissed him.

31. Nova

'Dad, where's Mr Jackman? I've been looking for him everywhere,' Nova asked.

'Mr Jackman has left the building,' Dad announced.

'What d'you mean?'

'I mean I told him to leave and he had sense enough not to argue.'

'Dad, you didn't!' Nova said, aghast.

'Nova, I did.' Dad turned to answer the ringing phone, missing the best of Nova's scowl.

Nova ran to the kitchen, then into the lounge in search of Mum. When at last she found her, Mum was chatting with Lorna, one of the two regular hotel cleaners.

'Mum, d'you know what Dad did?' Nova interrupted. 'He chucked Mr Jackman out, that's what!'

'Sorry, Lorna,' Mum apologized. 'Nova's manners seem to have disappeared.'

'Mum, this is important. Mr Jackman has *gone*!'

'Quite right too!'

'What?' Nova couldn't believe her ears.

'You heard me,' said Mum evenly. 'Mr Jackman had no business creeping around our hotel in the early hours of the morning, he had no business keeping you up so late for a chat about nonsense and he certainly had no business being in our wine cellar.'

'But that's not fair. He was only trying to find another way into the tunnels,' Nova pleaded.

'That's no excuse and you know it − and so did Mr Jackman.'

'How long ago did he leave?'

'I don't know. First thing this morning, I guess. If I'd had my way, he would've been out on his ear about two seconds after your dad found him in the wine cellar, but your dad persuaded me to let him stay until this morning.'

So it was too late to go after him. What was Nova supposed to do now? She went out of the lounge to stand in the hallway. Dad was still on the phone, taking a booking.

'Are you ready to help me with Raye now?' asked Liam, appearing beside Nova.

'No!' Nova said with belligerence. 'And why didn't you come and tell me that Dad had kicked your brother out?'

'Who d'you think woke up your dad in the first place so he'd find you and Josh?' asked Liam.

'You did *what*?'

'It wasn't easy either. I had to make enough noise to wake . . . me . . . before your dad even opened one eye!'

'How could you?' Nova stormed at him. 'Josh is your own brother. He only wanted to find your body.'

'Who asked him to? I didn't.' Liam glared back. 'I reckoned he'd outworn his welcome and luckily I wasn't the only one who thought so.'

'What kind of brother are you?' Nova asked, aghast.

Liam's expression gave her frostbite. 'Nova, even I'm not exactly sure where my body is. And I don't see your dad letting Josh dig around the hotel grounds for the next couple of years trying to find me, do you?'

'That's not the point,' Nova began.

'That's exactly the point. I meant what I said about Josh not wasting his life on me. Two wasted lives in our family ought to be enough for anyone.'

'Two?'

'Yeah, me and my dad. I'm not going to let —' Liam suddenly shut up.

'What?'

Liam pointed behind Nova. She spun round to see Dad, Miss Dawn and Miss Eve all watching her with a great deal of interest and, on Dad's part, concern.

'Nova, if you're going to crack up, could you do it in a less public place?' Dad frowned.

'I'm not cracking up. I'm talking to . . . I mean, I'm working on a new play and I was just trying out my lines.'

Miss Dawn and Miss Eve exchanged a look. Nova surreptitiously beckoned to Liam, then pointed to the front door.

'Where're you going?' Dad called after her.

'For a walk,' Nova replied.

Out she went, looking round to see if Liam was following her, but he'd disappeared again. When she reached the bottom of the steps, he reappeared in front of her.

'I can't get used to you doing that!' Nova complained.

'One of the few perks I get,' Liam told her ruefully.

'Don't change the subject! You were telling me why you wanted to get rid of your brother so badly.'

'I've already told you. I'm not saying anything else. Now, are you going to help me stop Andrew from making a fool of your sister or not?'

For the life of her, Nova couldn't understand Liam's attitude. What was his problem? He kept going on about how much he hated being stuck at the hotel, but he wouldn't do a thing to get away from it. All his brother – and Nova for that matter – wanted to do was give him what he wanted, a proper burial so he could rest in peace. Move on or up or out or whatever it was that ghosts in his position did. So why was he so against it?

'You're getting worked up over nothing. Andrew doesn't stand a chance of succeeding,' Nova said at last, deciding to put Liam out of his obvious misery.

'What d'you mean?'

'With my dad around, Andrew won't get the chance to so much as pucker up.'

'Don't you believe it. I know what boys like Andrew are like. There's no way he's going to back out of a dare now.'

'And what are boys like Andrew like?' asked Nova curiously. 'A bit like you perhaps?'

'You're jealous of Raye. That's what this is all about, isn't it?' Liam said icily.

'And you're jealous of Andrew. What's the matter? Afraid Andrew will get to kiss Raye and you won't?'

'That has nothing to do with it,' Liam insisted furiously. 'I don't understand you at all. Raye's your sister.'

'So what?'

'So if Andrew wants to hurt and humiliate your sister, you've got no problem with that? She's got it coming to her. Is that it?'

Nova glared at Liam. 'I never said that.'

'It's obviously what you think, though.'

'Don't tell me what I do or don't think!'

'Don't take your sister for granted,' Liam said softly. 'That was my mistake with my brother. I thought we had all the time in the world and we had no time at all.'

'Fine! Right! OK! I'll go and tell her,' said Nova. 'Happy now?' She marched back into the hotel, leaving Liam behind.

Happy now . . . Liam shook his head. Happy now? He couldn't even remember what happy felt like.

32. Rainbow

Rainbow sprayed herself with more jasmine perfume – a Christmas present from her mum and dad – and smiled at herself in the mirror. Andrew had really liked his birthday present, and been surprised by it too. Rainbow could tell. And they'd made plans to go for another walk after dinner. He really was lovely. Rainbow smiled as she remembered how taken aback he'd been when she'd kissed him. It was only a friendly birthday kiss on the cheek, but the look on his face! Raye's smile faded. He didn't think she was too fast or forward, did he? No! He'd liked it, Raye was sure of that. What a shame he was leaving tomorrow, but maybe they could keep in touch? E-mail or text message each other regularly?

The single tap at her bedroom door brought Raye out of her daydream. The door opened immediately before Raye could even speak. And in walked Nova. Raye groaned. That's all she needed, Nova hanging around while she was trying to get to know Andrew better.

'Did I say you could come in?' snapped Raye, throwing her perfume bottle back down on her dressing table. It clattered onto its side and began to roll slowly forward. She pushed it back impatiently.

'No, but you didn't say I couldn't either,' Nova pointed out.

'Well, I'm telling you now. Out!'

'But I've got something important to tell you,' Nova protested.

'Out!'

'It's about one of the guests here,' Nova began. 'Andrew someone.'

'Andrew Stanley. What about him?'

Nova turned suddenly to glare over her left shoulder before turning back to Raye. 'Raye, just be careful, OK? I . . . he was overheard talking on the phone to one of his friends.'

'So?'

Once again, Nova turned to scowl over her shoulder. What on earth was she doing? 'Andrew made a bet that you'd kiss him before he left tomorrow,' she said when she turned back to Raye.

'He did what?'

'He wants to kiss you for a bet. I just thought you should know, that's all,' said Nova.

'And you heard him make this bet, did you?'

'Not exactly. Liam did,' Nova mumbled.

'So we're back to Liam again? This joke you and Liam and Mr Jackman cooked up between you was tired when you tried it yesterday.'

Nova turned her head as if she were listening to something or someone. But if she thought that by acting crazy, Raye was more likely to believe her, then she was way off.

'It's not a joke. And Liam's not lying,' said Nova urgently. 'He heard Andrew talking to one of his friends on his mobile. The friend's name is Kieran. Ask Andrew if you don't believe me.'

Raye's eyes narrowed, her expression freezing by degrees. 'I don't believe you, Nova. One of the best-looking boys to come to this place in months and you immediately try and ruin things between us.'

Nova's mouth fell open.

'He likes me and I like him and you're just jealous,' said Raye.

'I'm stopping you from making a fool of yourself,' said Nova.

''Course you are. No wonder you don't have many friends at school. You're spiteful, Nova Clibbens.'

Nova tried her best not to look hurt, but she failed miserably. 'I'm telling you the truth. I was trying to do you a favour.'

'Out of the goodness of your heart?'

'Because I'm your sister . . .'

'Worse luck. Trust me to get saddled with a waste of space like you,' said Raye.

'Thanks. Thanks a lot.' Nova barely got the words out before racing out of the room.

'Lying toe-rag!' Raye slammed her bedroom door shut behind Nova.

What'd got into Nova recently? Over the last few months she'd grown very strange – sulky and secretive. What was her problem? She was just jealous because Andrew really liked her. How sad was that?

Someone thudded at her door. Nova! Right, she'd asked for it and this time she was going to get it. Raye wrenched open the door – only to stare at the boy before her. Liam again. Raye's expression altered at once. 'Oh, sorry. I thought it was my sister,' she began uncertainly.

'Hi, I'm Liam. D'you remember? We met yesterday.' Liam held out his hand, his expression anxious, almost fearful.

'Yes, I remember.' Raye nodded, trying not to stare. Liam really was lush! She shook his hand, wondering why it was so cold.

Liam snatched back his hand. 'Your sister has just run off in tears,' he told her.

'Nova's crying?' Raye said, surprised.

'She's very upset.'

Raye tutted. 'She'll get over it.' The moment the words were out, she regretted them. Even to her ears they sounded cold and unfeeling.

'I doubt it,' said Liam seriously.

Raye looked at him, before lowering her eyes. 'I . . . we just had a bit of an argument, that's all.'

'Nova was telling you the truth about Andrew,' said Liam.

Raye felt a chill feather its way down her back. 'How d'you know what we were talking about? Were you listening at my door? And anyway, guests aren't allowed in this part of the hotel.'

'No, I wasn't listening at your door, but I couldn't help overhearing some of the stuff you said to her and I can guess what the two of you fell out about. But I was the one who encouraged Nova to tell you the truth. If you want to take it out on someone, you should take it out on me, not her.'

Raye wanted to deny that she was taking anything out on anyone but the words died on her lips. She'd only met Liam twice and both times they'd seemed to get off on the wrong foot. Her face begin to glow warm with embarrassment. 'Nova knows I was just joking when I said those things to her.'

'Some jokes aren't funny.'

There was nothing Raye could say to that so she didn't even try. With each second of the silence that stretched between them, Raye felt worse and worse. 'I'll make it up to her,' she said at last.

Liam regarded her, then smiled. 'I'm sure you will. And I didn't mean to interfere in your business. It's just that I hurt some-one very close to me once, and

I've always regretted it. And every day now I have to pay for it.'

'But Nova knows I don't mean anything by it,' Raye tried again.

'No, she doesn't,' Liam countered at once. 'She looks up to you and wants to be like you and every time you put her down, it knocks her confidence just that little bit more.'

'And she told you this, did she?' Raye frowned.

'She didn't have to,' said Liam. 'When I caught her deliberately making herself sick after breakfast this morning so she could look more like you, I got the message.'

'She did *what*?'

'And it wasn't the first time either.'

'I don't believe it. Nova's got more sense than that.' Raye shook her head.

'There are some things stronger than sense. Like the way Nova feels about you, and the way you make her feel when she's around you.'

'But . . .' Raye floundered to a bewildered stop. She couldn't take it in.

'You or someone in your family ought to know what's going on,' Liam said carefully. 'Nova's making herself ill by throwing up every time she eats anything bigger than a full stop.'

'How come you know all this and we don't?'

'I just happened to be around when she was doing it.'

'But . . . but why didn't she say something?' said Raye, dazed.

'You'll have to take that up with her. Anyway, like I said, I didn't mean to stick my nose into your business.'

At the sound of her perfume bottle thudding to the

floor, Raye's head whipped round. 'It's just my . . .' she began as she turned back.

But Liam had gone. Raye stepped out onto the landing looking left and right, but he was nowhere in sight.

33. Nova

Nova kicked at the sand beneath her feet. It arced up like a peacock's feathers before falling, some of it into her trainers. But it didn't stop her from kicking at the sand over and over again. She must've been mad to think that Raye might actually be grateful. At home, at school, it was always the same. Need someone to make fun of, look no further than Nova. Need someone to knock, to mock, to put down – Nova was available. It was like everyone looked at her and what they saw was someone dumpy, small, swotty, spotty – and that was all. Was everyone else right? Nova was desperate to change her image so that others would see her the way she truly wanted to be.

'You OK, Nova?'

Nova jumped, then snapped out, 'I wish I could just appear and disappear the way you do all the time!'

'No, you don't.' Liam shook his head.

Nova thought about it and decided he was right. 'I did what you asked me to do so please go away and leave me alone.'

'Your sister's really sorry for what she said,' Liam told her.

'Of course she is,' Nova said sarcastically.

'You should go back and talk to her. She's looking for you.'

'Why? So she can make me look like an even bigger fool?' asked Nova. 'Well, no thank you.'

'Nova, Raye really is sorry. I had a word with her and —'

'You did what?'

'I had a word with her and —'

'Who asked you to?' Nova said furiously. 'Why did you show yourself to her in the first place?'

'Because what she did to you annoyed me.' Liam frowned.

'But it's none of your business, is it? Just like you and Mr Jackman are none of my business . . .'

Liam got the point. 'Well, I'm sticking my nose in whether you like it or not.'

'Because you're burning to help me?'

'I want to help – yes!' Liam blustered.

'Why don't you be truthful for once?' Nova said scornfully. 'My sister's the one you're interested in, not me.'

Liam opened his mouth, only to snap it shut without saying a word. Nova took a deep breath, then a deeper one, but her blood was still boiling. 'Liam, please go away and leave me alone.'

Liam regarded Nova, perplexed frustration adding extra creases to his face. He slowly faded out, his expression, the way he was standing, everything about him letting Nova know that it was against his will. Only when he'd gone completely did Nova carry on walking along the beach, her head bent, her thoughts curling and coiling inside her head. Why did she want to be like Raye when her sister was so mean? Not to mention shallow. If Raye were a swimming pool, Nova would be able to walk from one side of her to the other without getting her toenails wet.

Nova sighed, knowing full well that it wasn't the way Raye was inside that she wanted to copy. It was what she looked like outside that counted. Raye made people's heads turn. And she knew it, but she couldn't care less, which made it even worse. And Nova had to admit, Raye wasn't mean to her all the time. Sometimes, she was asleep! But to be fair, she did stand up for Nova at school when one of the older girls had started picking on her. Raye had soon sorted that one out. And Nova had been so proud of her sister then. Until the resentment had set in that, once again, it was Raye riding to the rescue. And, once again, Nova was nowhere.

'Hi, Nova. I was hoping I'd see you down here.'

Nova's head snapped up. Joshua Jackman, Liam's brother, was standing in front of her and she was so lost in her own world, she hadn't even heard him approach. 'Mr Jackman! I thought you'd gone,' she said, relieved to see him.

'My dad is Mr Jackman. Call me Joshua.'

Nova wasn't sure about that. She wasn't used to calling old people in their twenties by their first names. She felt slightly uncomfortable about doing it. But he did say she could! 'OK.' She looked around. 'Does . . . anyone know you're here?'

'No. I dumped my stuff back at my dad's house and then headed straight back here,' said Joshua.

'I'm sorry Dad asked you to leave. That wasn't fair.'

'I'd have done exactly the same thing if I were him. I had no business being down in the cellar at that time of night.'

'And nothing . . . strange has happened to you while you've been on this beach, has it?'

'Strange like what?'

Nova shrugged.

Joshua regarded her speculatively. 'Liam wants me to go, doesn't he?'

Nova nodded.

'Is he here now?' asked Joshua.

Nova looked around. 'No. He was, but I told him to go. He . . . he won't be happy to see you're still here. He thinks you're wasting your time and your life searching for him.'

Joshua considered this for a few moments, deep creases furrowing the lines between his eyebrows. 'This is madness,' he said at last. 'I've been searching for my brother for so long. All over the country. Then I see him here, in a hotel dining room – and he's a ghost! I keep telling myself that I'll wake up in a minute and realize that I want to see him so much that I'm just imagining things.'

'I've seen him too, lots of times,' said Nova.

'But maybe you're part of my dream too. Or maybe I'm just losing my marbles.'

Nova wasn't sure what to say to that.

'He's really here, isn't he? At the hotel?' asked Joshua uncertainly.

Nova nodded. They stood in silence for a few moments. 'Do you have any other brothers or sisters?' asked Nova at last.

'No,' Joshua replied sombrely. 'Just Liam and me.'

'And your mum?'

'She died over fifteen years ago,' said Joshua.

Unsure what to say, unable to meet Joshua's gaze, Nova glanced out across the sea. Why was it so hard to talk about death and dying? What happened before and after death were easier to handle. Nova had listened to her parents and their friends discuss who was getting married or divorced or having a baby or moving house until their conversations rang in her ears for hours afterwards. Life stuff. All the everyday stuff that she and her friends and all the grown-ups around chatted about. And everyone loved to talk about ghosts and ghouls and things that went bump in the night. Nova suspected it was because not many people believed in actual ghosts – but they liked the thrill of being scared in a way that they could dismiss afterwards as not real.

But the subject of death, that was something else again.

Something to sweep under the carpet. Very taboo. Very hush-hush. Not pleasant to talk about. Not polite. Not nice. And look where it had got Liam and his brother. What had happened in their lives to make Liam a ghost stuck at Phoenix Manor and Joshua a slave to finding him? What was it that neither of them could let go?

'Where's your dad now, if you don't mind me asking?' said Nova.

'Where he's always been.' Joshua was unable to mask the bitterness narrowing his eyes and hardening his expression. 'At this time of day he's probably fast asleep. But his eyes will open at the same time as the local pub doors.'

'Where does he live?'

'The same place he's always lived. About half an hour away. Why?'

Nova was surprised. She had no idea Liam and Joshua's dad still lived so close. 'I just wondered. It was something Liam said.'

'What?'

'About two wasted lives in your family, which is why he doesn't want you to waste yours.'

Joshua turned away, but not before Nova saw the liquid sheen in his eyes. 'I need to find my brother,' he said forcefully. 'And I'm not leaving here until I do.'

'But how d'you intend to do that? The tunnels are blocked,' said Nova.

Joshua's eyes gleamed. 'Not necessarily. I've found another entrance, right here in the cliff wall.'

'How did you find it? I've been up and down this beach a hundred times and I've never seen an entrance to a tunnel.'

'I bet you've never been swimming in the sea around here, have you?' Joshua replied.

'No. Only paddling. The currents around here are too strong for me.'

'Well, I went for an early morning swim and I saw the entrance from about a kilo-metre out. Of course, with Miss Eve's help, I knew what to look for.'

'Oh, I see.'

'Liam's in one of those tunnels, I know he is,' said Joshua. 'I'm close. I can feel it. And no one, not even Liam, is going to stop me this time.'

34. Andrew and Raye

Raye checked both Andrew's room and the dining room. Dad said he hadn't left the hotel, so there was only one other place he could be. Raye stood in the doorway of the hotel lounge. Andrew was seated at a far table, his mobile phone pressed to his ear, his expression serious.

'Hi, Andrew.' Raye's voice was cool as she walked towards him.

Andrew immediately stood up. 'Kieran, I'll phone you back,' he said into his phone before pressing a button to disconnect the call. 'Hi, Raye. I was hoping I'd see you.'

'Well, here I am,' said Raye lightly. 'Were you just talking to someone called Kieran?'

'Yes, that's right. He's my best friend.'

'I see.'

'D'you want to join me?' Andrew indicated the seat next to his own. 'I need to talk to you.'

'OK.' Raye sat down; Andrew sat next to her and she shifted away from him slightly. It didn't go unnoticed.

'Is . . . is everything OK?' Andrew asked.

Raye looked at him, waiting for the right words to make it past the antagonism and disillusionment that churned inside her.

'Raye . . .?'

'Did you bet Kieran that you'd get to kiss me before you left tomorrow?' Raye said at last.

Andrew's mouth dropped open as he stared at her.

'Well? Is it true?' Raye persisted, unwilling to read the answer in Andrew's expression.

'Look, I can explain . . .'

'So it is true.' Raye couldn't remember when she'd felt so . . . so disappointed, not to mention disillusioned. Andrew was just being nice to her for a stupid bet and when Liam tried to warn her, she'd bitten his head off. And Nova . . . Raye groaned inwardly when she remembered all the things she'd said to her sister. She stood up.

Andrew jumped to his feet. 'Raye, I was just on the phone telling Kieran that the bet was off,' he rushed out.

'Of course you were,' said Raye, chips of ice flying from every word.

'It's true. I decided to call the whole thing off. It was a stupid thing to do anyway.'

'And I'm meant to believe that, am I?'

'It's *true*.'

Raye looked away, not wanting Andrew to see just how much he'd upset her. Her gaze fell onto the opposite seat, where her birthday present to him had been placed upright against a cushion. Raye's pencil drawing of Andrew's face.

Half the night spent working on it and agonizing over it and for what?

So Andrew could win his stupid bet. It took less than two strides to scoop up the picture and less than three seconds to dismantle the simple wooden frame she'd placed around it.

'Raye, no . . .'

'The drawing means something to you, does it?'

'Yes. Please don't,' Andrew pleaded.

'Keep it then. Keep it as a trophy to show your friends. D'you want me to write a message on the back, saying that I did kiss you? 'Cos I will. How much detail d'you want? Shall I say how long the kiss lasted and who had their eyes closed and who didn't? Anything to improve your sad, sorry little life.'

'Raye, I'm sorry.'

'Yeah, so am I.' Without another word, Raye turned and walked out of the room, leaving by the French windows which led straight out into the hotel gardens. She wanted to get away from Andrew and the hotel and her family and everyone and just be alone for a while. For a long while. She had to fight to keep her hands at her sides. She longed to wipe the tears from her eyes, but she wasn't going to give Andrew the satisfaction of knowing that he'd made her cry.

35. Jake and Jude

'All clear?' Jude whispered.

Jake peered down the stairs, looking left and right. The hall and, more importantly, the reception desk were deserted. 'All clear.' He gave the thumbs up.

He crept down the stairs, hiding behind each banister post in turn. He was Jake Clibbens, super-spy, the best secret agent in the universe. Jude slid down the banisters backwards, leaping off with a perfectly practised skill just before reaching the bottom to land on the bottom stair. Dad popped up from behind the reception desk.

'Jude, which part of "Don't slide down the banisters!" are you having trouble with, because I'd be happy to explain it to you,' Dad said, annoyed.

Jude turned an accusatory look on his twin brother.

'It's a trap,' Jake declared. 'Run!'

'Not so fast, you two.' Dad moved like greased lightning to appear in front of the stairs before the twins could get past him. 'What're you up to?'

'Nothing!' Jude said, with Jake nodding vigorously in agreement.

'Try again!'

'We're looking for the ghost,' Jake admitted.

'What ghost?' Dad frowned.

'Nova's ghost,' said Jake. 'The one she saw yesterday that made her scream.'

'She made that up,' said Dad. 'She just saw a spider and freaked – remember?'

Jude and Jake exchanged a look.

'Off you go and play outside,' said Dad. 'And stay out of mischief.'

'Where is everyone?' Jake asked, looking around.

'I saw Raye go into the lounge earlier,' Dad replied. 'And I have no idea where Nova is. She's like the Scarlet Pimpernel these days!'

'Who's that then?' asked Jude.

'Someone who used to help French aristocrats escape from the guillotine centuries ago,' Dad replied. 'But he was very elusive – which means very mysterious and hard to pin down – and the French authorities had trouble catching him.'

Jude and Jake turned to each other, their eyes agleam with the possibilities.

'Shall we play the Scarlet Pimpernel?' asked Jude.

'Yeah. Sounds cool!' said Jake.

'Er, just a minute, you two,' Dad said hastily. 'Remember what I said about staying out of trouble.'

'Don't worry,' Jake smiled.

'I'm your dad. That's my job!' Dad informed them.

The twins skipped off, grinning, leaving Dad to watch them, a loving yet rueful smile on his face.

'I wonder why Dad said Nova's ghost doesn't exist?' said Jake.

Jude looked at Jake curiously. 'Because he doesn't. There're no such things as ghosts.'

'Yes, there are. Nova's ghost exists. I've seen him,' Jake replied, surprised by Jude's response. And Jude didn't often surprise him.

'You heard Dad. Nova just made it up.'

'No, she didn't,' Jake argued. 'His name is Liam and he's about the same height as Dad and he wears jeans all the time.'

'What're you talking about?' Jude frowned.

'Liam. The ghost.'

'Stop winding me up. There's no such things as ghosts.' Jude's smile was hesitant as he regarded his twin.

Jake was just as stunned. He couldn't believe he could see Liam and Jude couldn't. There wasn't anything in the world that Jake and Jude couldn't do and hear and see together – until now, that is.

'You're just making it up, aren't you?' Jude said uncertainly.

Jake considered. 'Yeah, I'm just making it up,' he agreed at last, his fingers crossed behind his back.

36. Joshua Jackman

Joshua led the way along the beach away from the hotel. Nova looked up at the cliff face as she walked beside him.

'Are you sure what you saw was an entrance to one of the tunnels?' she said. 'It could've been just a big hole in the cliff that goes back for a bit and then stops.'

'You see that ridge up there?' Joshua pointed.

Nova nodded.

'The cave is just up from that. That's why you can't see it from the ground. It looks like a small, oval depression in the cliff face, but I've been up there and it's narrow for about a metre but then it opens out into a tunnel high enough to stand up in.'

Nova stared at him. 'Have you been along it? Did you see . . . anything?'

Joshua shook his head. 'It was too dark and I didn't have a torch or a compass on me. But I do now.'

'So you're going back into it now?'

'I've waited almost eleven years to find my brother. I'm not waiting any longer,' Joshua told her.

'But you can't just go in there. Don't you need all kinds of proper equipment?'

Joshua held up the rucksack he was carrying in his hand. 'I've got everything I need in here: compass, torch, spare batteries, rock hammer, rope, water. I don't need anything else.'

'Let me come with you,' Nova began.

Joshua shook his head. 'No way! You stay out here.'

'But the tunnels aren't safe. Liam said so.'

'All the more reason for you to stay put,' Joshua pointed

out. 'Don't worry. I've done this before. I know what I'm doing. Besides, I'm hoping Liam will show me the way – somehow.'

'What if something goes wrong?' Nova said desperately.

'Which is why I need your help,' said Joshua. 'I want someone I know and trust to be here in case I get into trouble. Give me an hour exactly. If I'm not out by then, you can go and get help.'

Nova was growing less and less enthusiastic about the whole plan. What had seemed fine in theory now seemed mad and, worse than that, dangerous.

'So will you help me?' asked Joshua.

Nova nodded reluctantly. What choice did she have? 'How're you going to get up there?' she asked, eyeing the ridge. It looked a lot further up than it had five minutes ago.

'Like this!' Joshua put on his rucksack and immediately began to climb up the cliff face, seeking out hand- and footholds with careful skill.

'Shouldn't you have a rope around you or something?' Nova called.

'No time,' Joshua replied.

Nova looked up and down the beach but they were alone. There was no one to help her talk Joshua down.

He was already halfway to the ridge. How did he intend to get round it? One false move and he'd plunge down. And he'd probably break every bone in his body – or worse.

'If you fall you could kill yourself,' Nova realized aloud.

'Either way, I'll see my brother again,' came Joshua's flip reply.

Joshua was almost at the ridge now. Terrified, Nova watched as he tried to swing out to grasp a handhold on the underside of it. Joshua had to swing his body out so

162

that his entire weight was now supported only by his hands gripping scant handholds on the underside of the ridge. If he were to slip now . . .

Nova's palms were sweaty and, much as she longed to look away, she just couldn't. 'No!' She clapped her hands over her mouth as Joshua lost his grip with one hand. He scrambled to find another handhold, his legs and body still swinging freely under him. Nova's heart leapt into her throat and stayed there. She could hardly breathe as she watched him.

'Liam, where are you? Liam, please,' Nova whispered. 'We need your help. Please.' She didn't dare speak over a whisper in case she made Joshua lose his concentration. 'Liam, your brother needs your help. Please.'

Joshua was now at the edge of the ridge. He tried to swing one leg up onto it but he didn't swing high or hard enough. Even from where Nova was standing, she could see he was getting tired. He swung his leg up again, his foot just making the ridge. He pulled himself up using his arms and first one leg, then the other. Only when his whole body had disappeared out of sight did Nova breathe such a huge sigh of relief that she felt giddy from it. But it didn't last long. She glanced down at her watch. Joshua was about to go into a tunnel in the cliffs that would more than likely collapse down on him at any second. He'd asked Nova to give him an hour before calling for help but what if something happened to him before then? What if waiting that long actually cost Joshua his life? What should she do? She looked up and down the beach again. She was still alone. 'Joshua?' she shouted.

No reply.

'*Joshua?*' Nova yelled so hard she immediately started coughing afterwards.

Still nothing.

Nova went over to the cliff face. Maybe she should go up after him? Tentatively she began to climb. 'Nice and easy . . .' she muttered. 'Slow and steady . . .'

She was less than four metres off the ground when she realized she didn't have the physical strength to go any further. Her arms were aching already and her heart was pounding and perspiration kept running down into her eyes. She climbed down just as carefully, yelping when she caught her knee on a jagged piece of rock. She jumped down the last metre, wincing on impact.

'*Joshua?*' Nova tried again.

Panic rose up inside her like a tidal wave. Where was he? Why didn't he answer? What should she do now?

'Liam? Liam, where are you? I need your help,' she cried out.

But her only answer was the sound of the waves lapping up on the pebble-strewn beach.

37. Andrew and Raye

'Raye, wait. Please wait.'

Andrew was running after her. Raye could hear his footsteps crunching with quick regularity on the gravel. She carried on walking, quickly wiping her tear-stained cheeks. She turned off the gravel to cut across the garden. The dry autumn grass crunched beneath her feet as she tried to put as much distance between herself and Andrew as she could without actually running away.

'Raye, please.' Andrew ran in front of her, blocking her path. 'Listen. I was on the phone cancelling the stupid bet. I swear I was. It was a moronic thing to do in the first place, I realize that. I'm really sorry.'

'Why did you do it?' Raye asked.

'I don't know. It was just me, mouthing off. Showing off to my best mate. I'm sorry,' said Andrew.

'You're just sorry you got caught. Nova tried to warn me and I said some really horrible things to her—'

'Nova?'

'My sister.'

Raye hadn't spoken to anyone about Nova making herself sick after each meal. She'd dismissed both Liam's and Nova's accusations as ludicrous. But Nova had been right about Andrew. Suppose Liam was right too? Raye didn't even know if what he'd said about Nova throwing up after every meal was true – and that in itself made her feel at fault. She *should* know. Nova was her sister, for heaven's sake. It shouldn't take a stranger to tell her that something was wrong with her sister. Liam had to be wrong, he just had to be. But Raye couldn't do anything about his assertion until she'd personally spoken to Nova.

But she had no idea where Nova was or what she was doing. They used to hang out together, but not any more. When had that stopped? Raye took a good look at Andrew and knew the answer. Nova was too much of a rugrat to be seen with and Raye had made sure she knew that. Raye was nearly sixteen, a grown-up, one step away from an adult. Nova ruined her street cred. So Nova had been ditched, without a backwards glance. For people like Andrew. She didn't want what Liam had said to be true, but the fluttering wings of guilt in her stomach told their own story.

'Raye, I do want us to be friends.' Andrew brought Raye out of her reverie.

'Then tell me the truth.'

'About what?'

'About everything. About yourself. No lies and no lines this time.'

'I don't understand.' Andrew frowned.

Raye thought for a moment. 'Do you have brothers or sisters?'

'No. I'm an only child.'

'Spoilt?'

Andrew looked startled at the question. Then he unexpectedly smiled. 'Yeah, I guess so.'

'Your mum was a bit concerned about you yesterday. What was that about?'

Andrew shrugged. 'I broke my leg early last year and it took a while to heal. It gave Mum a chance to fuss over me and she hasn't quite managed to stop yet.'

'Oh, I see. How did you break your leg?'

'Showing off!' Andrew admitted. 'I jumped down from the wall bars in PE and landed awkwardly.'

'That must've been painful,' said Raye with sympathy.

166

Silence.

'I did better than the boy I landed on,' said Andrew.

Astounded, Raye stared at him. 'Is this a wind-up?'

'No. I wish it was. I broke my leg. But Julian was knocked unconscious. It was only meant to be a joke, but it went wrong.'

Andrew started walking again. Raye fell into step with him. 'What happened to . . . Julian?'

'He was unconscious for two days and he had to wear a neck brace for ages. We were both lucky that I didn't break his neck.'

After a moment's hesitation, Raye put her hand on his arm. Just that. Nothing more. But it was enough to make Andrew turn back to her, a strange defiance laced with regret twisting his face. 'You have no idea what it was like,' he said with a trace of bitterness.

'I can imagine,' said Raye. 'You must've been so scared.'

'Not for me.'

'I didn't mean that,' she hastened to reassure him. 'But you must've been worried out of your mind about Julian. Is he all right now?'

'Oh yeah, he's fine. Thank goodness.'

'And what happened to you?'

'I lost some of my friends. Invites to parties and days out dried up, that sort of thing. I was suspended from school – but then I was lucky they didn't boot me out altogether. I was the lucky one.'

'It must've been tough for you though.'

'I got over it. I got older,' said Andrew.

'And wiser?'

'Not as much as I should've.'

Raye nodded at that. They'd reached the hotel lounge again, without even realizing it. Raye suddenly felt as if she had the whole world on her plate waiting for her to deal with it, and she had no idea what to do, or even where to start. She faced Andrew and said seriously, 'I thought we were friends, Andrew. I imagined us swapping e-mail addresses and mobile numbers just so we could keep in touch. But I don't think that's going to happen now.'

'It was just meant to be a joke, Raye,' said Andrew unhappily .

'Some jokes aren't funny,' Raye shot back at him. How strange that she should use the very words Liam had used when he told her about Nova.

'Aren't you going to let me off the hook?' Andrew pleaded. 'I cancelled the bet. I promise I did.'

A slight cough to Raye's left had her head whipping round. They weren't alone. Liam was standing in a corner of the room, watching.

'Who're you?' Andrew frowned. 'I didn't see you when we came in here.'

'That's because you weren't looking,' Liam said easily. 'You were too busy trying to wriggle off the hook you put yourself on.'

'What did you say?' said Andrew incredulously.

'You heard me.'

'Who d'you—?'

'Liam, I want to ask your advice on something,' interrupted Raye.

'I'm listening.'

'Andrew here made a bet . . . but hang on, you already know this, don't you? You're the one who told Nova to tell me.'

Liam nodded. Andrew's eyes narrowed.

'Andrew says he cancelled the bet and wants me to forgive him. What d'you think I should do?'

'Tell him to get lost,' Liam said immediately.

'Who asked you?' Andrew flared up.

'Raye did – about five seconds ago. Or don't you have any short-term memory either?'

'Either? What d'you mean?' asked Andrew belligerently.

'Well, you don't have any class, that's for sure,' Liam told him.

'Why you . . .' Andrew took a step towards him.

'Just a minute, you two.' Raye moved to stand between the two of them. She turned to look at Liam. He looked straight back at her. 'You believe in speaking your mind, don't you?'

'Always have,' Liam replied. 'Sorry.'

'No. I like that in my friends,' said Raye.

'I'm glad you realize I am your friend,' Liam said softly. 'Because I do like you, Raye . . .'

'Let's see how you like this,' said Andrew angrily. He sidestepped round Raye to take a swing at Liam. Raye turned to him, trying to push him away. Liam ducked back, but not far enough. Andrew's fist reached his chin – and swung right through it. With a surprised gasp, Andrew tried to steady himself, but his centre of gravity had shifted and he carried on pitching forward. Liam side-stepped out of the way as he crashed to the ground like a felled tree.

'Andrew, that's enough,' said Raye.

'You . . . my fist went straight through you . . .' Andrew gasped.

'You wish!'

'Liam, please,' said Raye. 'Could you leave now?'

'I'm not leaving you with him.' Liam folded his arms across his chest.

'I'm telling you, I hit him, but my hand went right through him,' Andrew insisted.

Liam's head turned sharply towards the hotel reception and beyond.

'I hit you.' Andrew wasn't going to let it drop.

'You couldn't hit the front of this hotel from a metre away with a dinner plate,' Liam scoffed. But once again, his head turned towards the hotel reception. 'I've got to go,' he announced. 'Someone's calling me. Raye, will you be all right?'

'Of course,' Raye assured him.

With one last smile, Liam ran off before either Raye or Andrew could say another word.

'Raye, who was that loser?' Andrew said with belligerence.

'A friend of mine. And someone who tells me the truth,' said Raye pointedly.

Slow, burning red crept across Andrew's cheeks. Raye followed Liam out to the reception area. But apart from Dad and Miss Dawn it was empty.

'Dad, where's Liam?'

'Who?'

'Liam. The boy who just came out of the lounge.'

'You're the first person to come out of there in over ten minutes,' said Dad, returning to the mass of papers in front of him.

Raye shook her head as she had another look around. Dad never noticed anything unless it was directly related to the hotel. A marching band could stride through the foyer and out the back and if they didn't stop to book in first, Dad would never know they were there.

'I saw him, dear,' said Miss Dawn. 'But he's gone now.'

'Which way did he go?' asked Raye eagerly.

Miss Dawn shrugged. 'To the beach would be my guess. He's good-looking, isn't he?'

'Is he?' said Raye. 'I hadn't noticed.'

'Of course you hadn't, my dear,' said Miss Dawn with a definite twinkle in her eyes.

Raye's cheeks flamed. She went back into the lounge before the air around her head caught fire.

'Ah! How romantic!' she heard Miss Dawn sigh from behind her.

But as Raye regarded Andrew, she was feeling anything but romantic.

38. Brothers

'Nova, did you call me?'

Nova swung round, faint from relief when she saw Liam. 'Yes! Yes, I did. I've been calling you for ages.'

'I was in the middle of doing something, you know,' Liam said with frost. 'Something important.'

'So is this! Up there! Quick! Joshua's looking for you.'

Liam looked up immediately.

'He found a tunnel and thinks it may lead to where you are. But I've been calling and calling him and he hasn't answered,' Nova said, on the verge of tears.

'Why didn't you stop him?'

'How? Tie him to a boulder?' Nova tried to defend herself.

'Stay here. I'll find him,' said Liam grimly.

It took all of Liam's powers of concentration to think himself into the tunnels. He hadn't done so since the cave-in . . . Usually, all he had to do was think of himself at a place and he faded out of his current location and appeared at his new destination. And more often than not, he could move faster than a blink if he really wanted to. He called it tuning. Like tuning a radio station away from one channel and immediately to another. But thinking himself into the tunnels was proving difficult. He suspected that the cave-in was what had killed him but he'd never had the nerve to check and make sure. So since then he hadn't been in the tunnels. Not once. The thought of walking through them to be confronted by his own body didn't appeal in the least. But now he had to find his brother.

Liam closed his eyes and forced himself to think of the tunnels, to imagine himself inside. Nothing happened. Maybe if he picked a specific spot. He'd been through the cliff entrance before. You had to crawl on your hands and knees for a couple of metres but after that the tunnel opened out so that you could stand up. If he could just think himself into the part of the tunnel where it broadened out. Liam forced himself to concentrate on the tunnel and nothing else. He cleared his mind, then filled it with the image of the exact place he wanted to be. He knew the moment it worked. Even with his eyes closed he could feel the darkness. He opened his eyes and looked around, but he couldn't see his brother.

What was Joshua thinking of, coming into the tunnels like this? If he was so convinced that Liam's body was in there, didn't that tell him something, like how unsafe the tunnels were in the first place?

'Joshua?' Liam's eyes quickly became used to the gloom. The walls, the very air, were tinged with a bluish light which made everything around him very clear but very cold. Liam felt an iciness creep over his body that he hadn't felt in a long, long time. Everything inside him screamed for him to get out of there. Now!

But he couldn't.

He looked around again. Joshua was nowhere to be seen. Liam walked further along the tunnel.

'Joshua?' he called, even though he knew he wasn't in a state where his brother was likely to hear him.

Liam closed his eyes and thought himself another fifty metres along the tunnel. Then another. And another. With each reappearance, the tunnels sloped steeply downwards. Liam remembered that, from the cliff face, the tunnels sloped downwards for quite a while before there was a sharp incline towards the hotel gardens.

There was still no sign of Joshua. But the icy dread biting at Liam when he first entered the tunnels was now threatening to swallow him whole. It was like nothing he had ever experienced before – sick, blinding panic combined with a fear that gnawed at him from deep within. 'Joshua, for God's sake . . .'

Liam couldn't take any more. He was about to fade out and think himself back onto the beach when he heard a faint thudding sound. Just ahead, the tunnel bent sharply to the left. Liam remembered that the rise upwards happened just after this particular bend. At least, he thought it did. It'd been a long time.

It took all his powers of concentration just to stay put. Something about the tunnels, or in the tunnels, was zapping his strength. He could feel himself getting weaker. Maybe he should just get out while he still could. Being a ghost was bad enough. Being a ghost forced to wander up and down the tunnels and nowhere else because he couldn't think himself out would be an absolute nightmare.

There it was again – the thud-thudding. Liam moved forward tentatively. He stopped abruptly, taking a deep breath, then another. 'Get it together,' he told himself fiercely.

After all, there was nothing in the tunnels that could hurt him any more. Only his brother. Liam turned the corner to see Joshua sitting down with his back against the tunnel wall. His knees were drawn up as he stared straight ahead. His torch was still on and lay with his rucksack on the floor beside him. Joshua's left fist thumped slowly and steadily on the ground.

'Josh, what're you doing?' Liam squatted down to ask.

Joshua didn't move, didn't blink. Liam tried to touch his brother's arm, but his hand moved straight through it as if Josh were the ghost and not Liam. He tried to force himself to focus so that he could materialize, but it just wouldn't work. In the tunnel his concentration scattered like thistledown before a high wind. One thing at a time. What was Josh doing? Focus on that. Liam glanced down at Josh's hand. In that moment, he realized why Josh was thumping the ground. Pure frustration. Nothing more, nothing less.

'Josh, you have to turn back,' said Liam, hoping against hope that something of what he said would get through.

But Josh didn't move.

Liam looked around desperately. Further ahead, the tunnel was completely blocked from floor to ceiling. He stood up, horror like an alarm bell clanging in his mind. He stared at the rocks and rubble blocking the path. Instinctively he knew what was underneath the debris. Like a rabbit caught in a car's headlights, he could do nothing but stare.

Joshua jumped to his feet and moved towards the rubble. He took the rock hammer out of his rucksack and began hacking away at it like a man possessed. Years of anger and bitterness erupted out of him as he pounded at the barrier. Above Joshua's head, some of the rubble began to shift. Dust began to rain down from the tunnel ceiling. Joshua ran his hands over his hair to shake it off, then carried on digging at the base of the pile of rubble.

Liam sprang forward as more rubble was dislodged from further up the mound. 'Josh, don't do this. It's not safe. You're going to cause a rock slide,' he said desperately.

Joshua carried on digging.

'Josh, no.' Liam desperately tried to drag Joshua's arm away from the rubble. He made contact. His body was solid as he snatched Joshua's rock hammer out of his hand.

Joshua stared at him, stunned. 'NO!' he yelled, pulling away. 'You're not real. You're just a wish in my head, but

I'm not going to stop. Liam's here, I know he is.' He turned back to the rubble and started pulling rocks and stones and earth behind him in a frenzy.

Dropping the hammer, Liam tried to pull harder at Joshua's arm, but already he was dematerializing. Joshua dived to pick up the hammer before Liam could stop him and started hacking at the rock fall with renewed vigour.

'Stop it. You'll bring the whole lot down on your stupid head,' Liam shouted.

The rain of dust above them was getting heavier. Then came an ominous cracking sound. Liam remembered it. How could he have forgotten? That cracking sound was the last sound he had heard before he died . . . Joshua started hacking at the pile of rubble even harder than before, using his other hand to pull away the loose scree his hammer dislodged. Liam could see blood on Joshua's fingers where the jagged bits of rock had torn at his flesh. The cracking, rumbling noise was getting louder.

'JOSHUA!' Liam grabbed Joshua's arm and pulled him backwards. But not fast enough. A crack like the lash of a whip echoed around them as the pile of debris slid down like a rocky avalanche. Liam managed to pull most of Joshua's body out of the way, but not all. Joshua screamed in agony as his legs below the knees were pinned under a mass of rocky debris at least three-quarters of a metre high. Liam tried to pull him backwards, but Joshua screamed even harder and then his head and body flopped like a rag doll's.

'JOSHUA!' Liam cried out.

But it was no good. Joshua was pinned like a butterfly to a collector's card.

'Help! HELP ME!' Liam yelled.

But he and his brother were quite alone.

'Please God, no. Please, please . . .' Liam begged.

176

Gently, he lowered his brother's head to the ground. He had to get help and fast. It might already be too late. Where was Nova? Still on the beach? She was the only one who could see him no matter what. He couldn't risk going back to the hotel, only to remain invisible.

'Hang on, Joshua,' Liam pleaded. He tried to fade out and return to the beach, but he stayed right where he was. Frustrated he slammed his fist into the tunnel wall beside him. It didn't hurt, but his hand didn't pass through either. He had to calm down. But how, with his brother lying unconscious at his feet? Liam turned his head away, closed his eyes and forced himself to concentrate.

'Liam? Thank goodness. Did you find your brother?' asked Nova.

Liam opened his eyes. He was back on the beach with Nova right in front of him. 'Josh is trapped. Get help. He's hurt.'

'What's happened?' asked Nova.

Liam turned to her with such a burning expression on his face that he almost seemed to glow with it. 'Go and get help – NOW!' he yelled.

Without another word, Nova turned and ran.

39. Help

Andrew and Raye sat opposite each other. They'd been talking for the last ten minutes but they weren't back on the easy, friendly footing they were on before.

'Rainbow, haven't you ever done something you've regretted afterwards?' Andrew asked.

'No,' Raye lied.

'Then I feel sorry for you,' said Andrew, standing up. 'I really like you, but if you don't know how to forgive then maybe you're not half the girl you like to think you are.'

Raye sprang to her feet. 'Now wait just a —'

But before she could let fly with her indignation, Nova tumbled through open French windows, gasping for breath.

'Nova, what's the matter?' Raye ran over to her.

'It's Joshua. Mr Jackman,' Nova gasped, struggling back up onto her feet as she dragged air back into her lungs. 'He needs our help. He's in a cave . . . down at the beach and he's trapped. He needs our help.'

'Slow down,' said Raye. 'Where is Mr Jackman?'

'In a cave above the ridge near the old, broken boat,' Nova explained in a rush. 'Oh, please hurry. Get Dad to phone for an ambulance. I have to go back.'

'I'll come with you,' Andrew told Nova at once.

'Raye, get help. Quick,' Nova urged.

As Raye ran from the room to tell her dad, Andrew and Nova raced back to the beach.

Liam knelt down on the ground beside his brother. Joshua's breathing was erratic and shallow and his skin had lost almost all of its colour. Liam tried to touch his brother's forehead but his hand passed right though Joshua's head. 'Joshua, hang on. Help is on the way,' he whispered.

Joshua's eyelids fluttered open. He looked straight at Liam, but Liam knew he couldn't be seen. He was no longer solid. The tunnel effect again.

'Liam . . . you . . .' Joshua struggled to speak as the words fell out on a mere sigh.

'Can . . . can you see me?' asked Liam.

Joshua nodded. The movement of his head was only slight but it was enough. 'Real . . .? Not imagining . . .?'

'No, you're not imagining me,' Liam smiled. 'You didn't imagine me in the dining room either. I really was there.'

'. . . was so afraid . . .' Joshua's eyes closed.

'Josh, wake up. Don't fall asleep,' urged Liam.

Joshua opened his eyes reluctantly.

'Stay with me, Joshua,' said Liam.

'T-that's what I'm t-trying to . . . do . . .'

Liam froze at those words. He stared at Joshua in horror. 'You stupid fool!' he snapped. 'You may be older than me now but I'm still your older brother so listen up. I don't want you here, Josh. I'm dead. You're not. I wasn't a very good brother.' Liam paused and thought for a moment. 'I wasn't a very good son either. But I'd never forgive myself if something happened to you because of me. Don't you understand that? I couldn't bear it. I just couldn't.'

'But I . . .' Joshua began softly.

'But nothing! You don't owe me anything, Josh. And certainly not your life. I don't want it. And it isn't yours to give to me anyway.'

'. . . miss you,' Joshua breathed.

'I miss you too, you idiot,' Liam replied angrily. 'But if you want to do something for me, go out and have a life. And make the most of it – for both of us.'

'Dad's fault . . . shouldn't have quarrelled . . . with you . . .'

'Haven't you been listening to a single word I just said?' Liam raged. 'It wasn't Dad's fault. And it wasn't your fault – and it wasn't even my fault. It was an accident. I was unlucky, that's all.'

Liam stopped abruptly.

It wasn't Dad's fault . . .

Where had that come from? Liam had spent so long, maybe for ever, believing exactly that. Blaming Dad, blaming Josh too, if he was honest. But he didn't any more. His death was just one of those things. But life went on.

'Tell Dad it wasn't his fault,' Liam said slowly. 'Tell him, the whole point of life is not how you die, but how you live. Tell Dad I love him very much – and I'm sorry.'

'Liam, I . . .' Joshua closed his eyes and his head lolled to one side.

'Joshua? JOSHUA . . .' Liam yelled. 'Wake up. Wake up. WAKE UP . . .'

40. Andrew and Liam

'Andrew, you can't go up there. It's too dangerous.'

But Andrew was already searching the cliff face for likely handholds. Much as he wanted to just get going, he knew he had to take his time and work out each move carefully – or there'd be two people going to the hospital, not one.

Nova grabbed his shirt and pulled him back. 'You can't do this. For all we know, there's another ton of rubble waiting to rain down on the next person brainless enough to go in there.'

'Mr Jackman needs help and I can't do anything from down here,' Andrew argued.

'You could get hurt too,' said Nova unhappily.

'I won't. I'll be careful. Besides, I'm a trained first aider!'

'This isn't funny.'

'I'm not laughing. Mr Jackman might be in shock or worse and with no one to help him he won't stand a chance.'

'But Liam's in—'

'What about Liam?' Andrew said quickly.

Nova shook her head. 'Nothing.'

Andrew studied Nova. What wasn't she telling him? 'What's Liam got to do with this?'

'Nothing,' Nova insisted. 'Can't we wait for an ambulance and the coastguard?'

'By the time they arrive and get Mr Jackman out, it may be too late,' said Andrew. 'Nova, I'm not being a hero. Believe me, if there were some other way to do this, I'd be doing it.'

And wasn't that the truth. He didn't even like heights much. Without another word, he started up the cliff face. If he paused to think about the stupidity of what he was trying to do, he'd probably bottle out.

'What d'you want me to do?' Nova cried out from below him.

'Pray,' Andrew called back.

He breathed deeply to fill his lungs and steady his nerves. Keep climbing, he told himself. He'd be OK if he just thought of this as a climbing wall like the one at his local sports centre back home. He'd be fine if he took his time – and didn't look down. OK, now he'd reached the underside of the ridge, but how was he going to get onto it to reach the tunnel entrance beyond? He could try to swing along beneath it, but Andrew doubted that his arms were strong enough to take his entire weight for anything longer than a few seconds. There was only one other option. He'd have to climb past the ridge, then hopefully make his way round and then down onto it. He carried on climbing, getting higher and higher, searching all the time for a way to move across the cliff face so he'd be over the ridge.

'Where're you going?' Nova shouted from below. 'The ridge is to your right.'

'I know. Shut up!' Andrew called back, immediately sorry he'd answered at all when he lost concentration and slipped half a metre. Below him, Nova let out a strangled scream. 'Focus!' Andrew hissed to himself.

He had to do this. He edged his slow, careful way along to the cliff face, then worked his way down until he was about two metres above the ridge. Letting himself drop was one of the hardest things he'd ever had to do. Would the ridge take his weight? Would he even land on it properly? He forced himself to get on with it and let go before

182

he froze completely. The ridge shook slightly on impact but that was all. And there before him was the tunnel entrance, concealed partly by the ridge and partly by gorse bushes.

Andrew ducked down and crawled in. It grew darker and darker as he went further in. He hadn't expected that. What if he got lost too? After a couple of metres the tunnel grew larger and Andrew was able to stand up, but the light coming from outside struggled to reach this far inside the tunnel. As far as Andrew could see, the tunnel carried on straight ahead. Taking a deep breath, he put his arms out in front of him and started walking.

One minute blended seamlessly into ten, until Andrew lost all track of the time he'd spent underground. He had no idea where he was and was beginning to wonder what on earth he was doing. After following the slope down-wards for several minutes, he was now having to make his way upwards and it was hard work, made especially diffi-cult by the fact that it was in total, inky darkness.

'MR JACKMAN? MR JACKMAN?' Andrew knew full well that he was not just shouting for Mr Jackman's sake but for his own as well. Nothing but the sound of his own anxious, shallow breathing was getting to him. The ground was beginning to level out now, but each step grew harder to take.

Deciding enough was enough, Andrew was about to turn round and head back to the beach, when something caught his eye – a strange, sickly yellow light up ahead. He stood still, wondering what he should do next. Taking a deep breath, he made his way towards the light. If it was nothing, he'd head straight out of this place before he became hopelessly lost – if he wasn't already.

A minute later Andrew was not just walking but run-ning. He scooped up the torch on his way past, taking a few more steps before he reached Joshua Jackman, who was still out cold. Andrew kneeled down, playing the light over Joshua's face before flashing it around. And what he saw made him wish he hadn't. The mound of rocky debris before him stretched from floor to ceiling and looked as if it might slide and cover both him and Joshua at any second.

Andrew placed an ear close to Joshua's mouth and nose. Joshua was still breathing but it was shallow and erratic. He took hold of his wrist and felt for a pulse. Joshua's skin was cool and clammy and the pulse was so weak it was almost impossible to feel. Some soil and rocks from the mound before them slid down over Joshua's chest. Andrew brushed them off, forcing himself to bank down the panic firing up inside. He knew you should never move an unconscious person until paramedics or someone who knew what they were doing could check them over first – unless the unconscious person's life was in grave danger. Well, if this didn't qualify, Andrew didn't know what did. He couldn't leave Joshua. Any moment now, the pile of rocks and dirt would slide down to cover him completely. Somehow he had to free Joshua's legs – just enough to pull him clear.

Andrew carefully removed the dirt and rocks from Joshua's body, moving slowly so that he didn't cause a landslide. When he got to the rocks on Joshua's left leg, another pair of hands started removing the rocks from Joshua's right. Startled, Andrew fell backwards in surprise. 'You!'

'I thought you could use some help,' Liam told him grimly.

'Where did you come from?' asked Andrew.

'I came in after you,' said Liam. 'We can chat later. That lot is going to go at any second.'

Andrew agreed with a quick nod. Together they worked to free Joshua's legs. The rumble of rocks being dislodged made them work even faster.

'We need to pull him clear,' said Liam, standing up.

'One of his feet is still trapped,' Andrew pointed out.

'The rest of his body will be in the same state if we don't move him now,' said Liam.

Each holding Joshua under an arm, Andrew and Liam tugged at his body to free him.

'Come on! Pull!' Liam shouted as the bank of rocks and earth before them began to slide . . .

41. Joshua

'Wake up . . . Joshua, please wake up. Wake up.'

Joshua opened his eyes slowly. His head felt as if it were stuffed with cotton wool, but that was nothing compared to the fireworks shooting up and down both his legs. He groaned.

'Joshua? Thank God you're all right . . .'

'Dad?' Joshua turned his head to see his dad smiling down at him from the bedside. Joshua blinked wearily. Where was Liam? He'd expected to see Liam.

'You're going to be all right, son,' Joshua's dad smiled.

Joshua looked at his dad through half-closed eyes. His dad looked so tired, old before his time. Myriad silver strands now overwhelmed what was once chestnut-brown hair. What had once been a lean, wiry frame was now simply too thin. His white shirt and navy-blue trousers hung on him like extra-large clothes on an extra-small hanger.

'Thank God I didn't lose you too. I wouldn't have been able to stand that. Not you too . . .'

Joshua's gaze moved up to his dad's eyes, one brown, one blue. He froze in astounded disbelief to see the shimmer of tears.

'What happened? How . . .?' Joshua couldn't say any more. His throat felt as if he'd swallowed a ton of gravel.

'A boy called Andrew saved your life. Your legs were trapped but he managed to pull you clear. Apparently you stopped breathing but he gave you mouth to mouth as well. They're keeping him in overnight for observation.'

Joshua closed his eyes. He was so tired.

'Josh, I've got something to tell you.'

Josh forced himself to open his eyes at the solemn note in his dad's voice.

'They found a body buried under the rubble in the tunnel. They think it might be Liam's body . . .'

Shock, like a lightning jolt, shook Joshua's body. Even though he'd suspected as much, expected as much, it was still a blow to hear it like that.

'Where is he . . .?'

'They've brought the body to the hospital for confirmation.' Joshua's dad's voice cracked as he spoke. 'Liam . . . my boy . . .'

Joshua closed his eyes against the pain and grief on his dad's face. He knew his face held the same. But at least he'd found Liam. At least Liam could have some peace now. They all could.

'When you come out of hospital, I'll look after you,' said his dad. 'You will come home, won't you, Joshua? Just until you're better?'

Joshua turned his head away. He needed time to think. He hadn't lived at home since he was eighteen and had barely spoken to his father in all those years. But Liam said . . .

Had Liam said . . .?

Or was it just a hallucination? Or wishful thinking? Or just a strange dream when he was unconscious in the tunnel? Or maybe . . . just maybe it had been true and he really had seen his brother?

'My legs hurt.' Joshua winced. The fireworks going off in his legs were getting worse. He opened his eyes, just in time to catch the acute disappointment on his dad's face.

'I'll go and get a nurse. Maybe they can give you something for the pain.'

'Dad?' Joshua began.

His dad turned back to face him.

'When can I go home with you?' Joshua whispered.

His dad stared in disbelief. Joshua tried to smile but it came out pained and crooked. But it didn't matter. His dad took Joshua's hand in both of his. Joshua closed his eyes, fatigue finally overtaking him – so he missed his dad wiping away the single tear that now ran down his left cheek.

42. Sunday

Nova lay on her bed staring up at the ceiling. The morning light streaming through her window was rich and warm, but Nova turned away from it. Mum had already called her down for breakfast but the last thing Nova wanted to do was eat. If anything happened to Joshua Jackman, she'd never forgive herself. Josh was stable in hospital but his right ankle was fractured and his left leg was broken in two places. He was extremely lucky it hadn't been worse, a lot worse. Nova didn't even like to think about it.

What had started off as a fun game, a great adventure, had turned into something Nova never, ever wanted to experience again. She dreaded to think what would have happened if Andrew hadn't been on hand to help out before the ambulance arrived. He was the one who'd risked his life to climb up to the tunnel to help Joshua. And even though the paramedics had laid into Andrew for risking his own life, they'd freely admitted that if Andrew hadn't been there . . . And Andrew had been the one to insist that Liam was still trapped in the tunnels somewhere. After an extensive search, a body had finally been found. But when Nova had eavesdropped on the paramedics' conversation, she'd learned that the body was at least ten years old. She knew then that it was Liam's body. The paramedics reckoned it would take a number of days at least to identify the body properly, but Nova knew.

Mum and Dad had torn a strip off her for a solid hour once Joshua had been taken to hospital. As far as they were concerned she should have come back immediately to raise the alarm. And the guests had spoken of nothing else all evening until Nova couldn't stand it any more and had escaped to her room before dinner. She'd been there ever since.

And the very worst thing of all was that she hadn't seen Liam once in all that time. Not once. She knew he was furious with her. He had every right to be. He'd told her more than once that he didn't want her or his brother hunting for his body. But Nova hadn't listened. She'd convinced herself she was doing something . . . noble. The fact that she now knew better was of little comfort. Joshua was in hospital and Mum and Dad were furious and, worse still, very disappointed in her 'lack of judgement', as they put it.

A faint tap at the door made Nova sit up. 'Come in.'

To Nova's surprise, it wasn't Mum. It was Raye.

'Can I come in?'

Nova shrugged. Raye entered the room, carefully closing the door behind her. She looked around the room as if she'd never seen it before. Curious, Nova watched her, wondering why her sister was so ill at ease.

'How're you doing?'

'OK, I guess,' Nova replied.

'Nova, I want to ask you something,' Raye said, looking at her for the first time.

'Go on then.'

'Are you bulimic?'

No beating about the bush then. Just straight for the jugular. The blood drained from Nova's face. Her body went from ice-cold to burning hot in a split second. 'I think there are more important things going on around here at the moment,' she said.

'This is just as important as anything else. Are you deliberately making yourself vomit after everything you eat?'

'Who told you that?' Nova sprang off the bed to confront her sister.

'Is it true?' asked Raye, standing her ground.

'You're the one who always argues with Mum about food – not me,' Nova reminded her.

'Liam said that —'

'Liam?'

'One of the guests here.'

'I know who he is. And he's not a guest. He's a ghost,' said Nova grimly. 'It hasn't been confirmed yet but it was his body they found in the tunnels yesterday.'

Raye frowned. 'What're you talking about?'

'Liam's a ghost.'

'Don't be ridiculous. I'm being serious.'

Nova regarded her. 'I should've guessed you wouldn't believe me,' she said at last.

'Look, don't try to change the subject. I want to know if you're bulimic.'

'Why?'

Raye's eyebrows shot up. 'Because I want to know.'

'Why?' Nova repeated.

Raye shook her head at Nova, unable to believe the question. Nova walked over to her window. She looked out over the gardens and beyond, silently cursing Liam where two minutes earlier she'd been feeling guilty about him. He had no right to go telling everyone about her. No right at all. It was no one's business – not even Liam's.

'I should know,' Raye tried.

'What possible difference could it make to you, one way or the other?'

'I'm your sister —'

'By accident, not by choice. I'm just a waste of space. Isn't that what you said?'

'I didn't mean it.'

'Yes you did.' Nova's tone was matter of fact. 'When you're not insulting me, you completely ignore me. We may have the same parents but we're not sisters – not what I'd call sisters. You don't talk to me or share things with me. I might as well not exist for all you care.'

'That's not true.'

Nova turned her head to look over her shoulder at Raye. 'Isn't it? Be honest, Raye. Just for once, be honest.'

'If I didn't care, I wouldn't be in here asking if you're being stupid enough to make yourself sick,' Raye flared up. 'Since Liam told me that yesterday, I haven't been able to concentrate on anything else.'

'Am I meant to say sorry?'

'You're meant to tell me the truth,' said Raye. 'Are you bulimic or not?'

'Not.' Nova turned round. 'Now you can go away back to Andrew – or whoever it is you're sighing over this week – and leave me in peace.'

Raye considered Nova, a strange look on her face which dissolved into intense sadness.

'What is it?' Nova asked.

'You really hate me, don't you?'

'Of course I don't hate you,' Nova sighed. 'This isn't about you.'

'Isn't it?'

'No. This has nothing to do with you.'

'Then why do it, Nova?'

'And I've already told you —'

'D'you know what you're doing to yourself?' Raye interrupted. 'To your body?'

'You sound like Liam.' Nova turned back to the window.

'Nova, listen to me. I could help you —'

'With what?'

'Your hair. Some make-up. I could . . .' Raye trailed off at the look on her sister's face.

'So you're saying there is something wrong with me?'

'I'm not saying that at all.'

'Then why do I need make-up? And what's wrong with my hair?'

'Nothing,' Raye floundered. 'I'm just saying I could help you make them better.'

'Even if I wanted to wear make-up, which I don't, Mum wouldn't let me,' Nova pointed out. She turned her back towards Raye, wishing her sister would leave.

'I'm just trying to help.'

'Go away, Raye. I want to be left alone,' said Nova.

'Mum sent me to get you for breakfast,' Raye told her.

'There's no point in eating it,' Nova said without turning round. 'It'd only come up again.'

The silence in the room was deafening. Even when Nova heard her bedroom door open and close, she still didn't turn round. She had a lot of thinking to do. One thing was certain, she couldn't go on the way she was. One way or another, something had to change.

43. Realization

'I don't know what to do,' said Raye unhappily. 'She won't talk to me. She won't even look at me.'

'You're going to have to force her to listen —'

'How can I?' Raye interrupted. 'Nova doesn't want to listen to anything I say and I can't honestly say I blame her.'

Focusing hard on remaining solid, Liam took Raye's hand in his. He struggled to find something meaningful to say. Something that would make Raye feel better. She'd come into the lounge looking distraught and obviously seeking someone to talk to. It'd taken a while to calm her down enough to get her to talk to him, but at last the reason for her distress had coming pouring out.

Nova.

'I didn't want any of this to happen. I care about Nova, I really do,' sniffed Raye. And without warning, she burst into tears. 'I'm sorry,' she sobbed, embarrassed but unable to stop. 'It takes a lot to make me cry.'

'Don't apologize,' Liam said gently.

They sat next to each other on one of the sofas in the lounge. Awkwardly, Liam put his arm around Raye. She instantly turned into his shoulder, her tears flowing faster. Liam hugged her, feeling as if his insides were being flipped over – except that he didn't have any insides. Not any more. Once again, he wondered why he was still stuck at the hotel when his body had been found and taken to the local hospital. He'd thought that once he was found, that'd be that and he could move on. But nothing had changed. He had tried to walk away from the hotel, but the same thing still happened. He'd collapsed unconscious, or whatever the ghost equivalent was, and woken up back at the hotel again. Maybe finding his body had nothing to do with anything. Maybe Liam really was going to be stuck at Phoenix Manor for the rest of eternity.

'This has been one of the worst weekends of my life,' Raye sniffed, moving away from Liam in an effort to pull herself together. 'What with Andrew —'

'I was wrong about Andrew,' Liam interrupted. 'He's not the entire jerk I thought he was.'

'I'm glad, because I really like him,' said Raye.

Liam clenched his fists and turned away so that Raye wouldn't see the look on his face.

'Liam, what am I going to do?'

'About Andrew?'

'No. About Nova.'

Liam sighed and sat back in his chair. He couldn't remain solid for much longer. It was taking all his concentration to stop himself from fading right before Raye's eyes. 'What d'you want to do?' he asked.

'Tell Mum and Dad,' Raye admitted. 'But that might make things worse instead of better.'

'You can't just leave Nova to get on with it,' said Liam.

'I know. I know.' Raye shook her head. 'I need to work out what to do for the best.'

Liam nodded but said nothing else. How strange! In just two short days his whole existence had come to revolve around Nova and her family. None of them knew about him before. He existed around the edges of their lives – with them but not of them. He'd convinced himself that he was fine, that he was OK being by himself. He'd watched them getting on with their lives while he had none. Their contentment in each other highlighted his own sadness, their togetherness had forced him to admit just how alone he was. And that was bad enough. But now that Nova knew what he was and, strangely enough, he seemed to be able to make himself more solid more often because of it, his existence was surprisingly worse, not better. He grabbed a bit of life here and a bit of life there – but that was all he was allowed to have. And snatches of life hurt almost more than no life at all. Like just now, when he'd hugged Raye as she wept all over him. He'd have done anything, anything at all, to keep that one moment for ever. To have her company, to laugh and cry with her. To be real and needed by someone. When he was alive, in his arrogance he'd thought it would go on for ever. Now he realized he'd wasted so much time blaming his dad for something that was not his fault. Dad was hurting just as much as Liam was over Liam's mum's death. But in his grief, Dad had turned away and Liam had hated him for it.

Even thinking about Joshua gave him no peace. He couldn't even get to the hospital to make sure his brother was OK. It was too far away. He'd heard Nova's dad on the phone and although Joshua had broken some bones, he was going to be OK. But hearing it wasn't the same as being with his brother and seeing for himself. With a bitter start, Liam realized that just as Dad had turned away from him, so he'd turned away from his little brother. Maybe that was why Joshua was so determined to find Liam again, to turn the clock back.

Liam sighed. If only. If only he could have his time over again . . . But it was a pointless wish. It was never going to happen. But at least Joshua and even his dad could get on with their lives. They could move forward. Liam couldn't. He was stuck, watching the rest of the world go on without him. Stuck like a mosquito in amber. And he couldn't bear it any more. He just couldn't.

Liam stood up. 'I thought I'd go for a walk on the cliff top. I like to look out over the sea. Maybe you could join me?'

'I'd love to,' smiled Raye tentatively. 'If you don't mind my company.'

'I'd like nothing better. I'll meet you outside the hotel in fifteen minutes. I just have something I need to do first.'

'No problem. I need to wash my face anyway. See you in a minute,' said Raye.

Liam turned and headed out of the room. He was close to fading out. He couldn't, he *wouldn't* allow himself to do that in front of Raye. She believed in him. He couldn't lose that. He ran the last couple of metres out of the lounge, looking around quickly before he let himself go. He was safe. There was only Miss Dawn deep in conversation with Raye's mum at the reception desk. But as he began to fade out, Miss Dawn turned to look directly at him.

She had the saddest look on her face he'd ever seen. And she wasn't sad for herself. Liam instinctively realized that she was deeply sad for him. Before he disappeared altogether he had the strangest feeling that, in some way he didn't begin to understand, she was desperately worried.

44. Liam

'Well?'

Nova put her hand over the mouthpiece. 'Just a minute!' she hissed at Liam.

They were in the tiny private study that Mum and Dad used as their office. It was the only place where they could use a phone undisturbed.

'I'm sorry,' said the voice at the other end of the phone, 'but we can only give out that kind of information to members of the immediate family.'

'I just want to know how he's doing,' Nova pleaded.

Liam was almost jigging up and down in front of her. He moved to get his ear as close to the phone as possible.

'I'm sorry,' the male nurse told Nova. 'It's against hospital policy.'

Nova sighed. 'Thanks anyway.' She put down the phone. 'Well, I tried.'

No way was that the end of it. Liam wasn't going to stop at the first hurdle. He just had to think. Focus and think. 'I'm not giving up now,' he said, his lips set.

Then he had a brilliant idea. If he could just persuade Nova to . . .

'I'm not going to the hospital to find out how your brother is doing, so forget it,' said Nova hastily.

'Did I ask you to?' Liam snapped, because that was just what he was going to ask her to do. 'And I'd have thought you'd be only too glad to help me, as this is all your fault in the first place.'

Nova dredged up the filthiest look she had and let Liam have it, full force. Head high, she went to march past him.

'I'm sorry,' Liam told her.

Nova carried on walking. Liam ran round her to stand in her way. He wasn't surprised she was annoyed. What was the matter with him? Why did he always need someone to blame?

'I'm really sorry. I shouldn't have said that,' said Liam.

'If that's what you really believe, why not?' Nova said frostily.

'Of course I don't believe it. It's not anyone's fault. And I'm sorry. I . . . I'm just not sure which way is up at the moment. OK?'

'OK,' Nova said at last. 'But there was no need to bite my head off. I am doing my best.'

'Yes, I know. Thank you.'

'Not that my best has got us very far,' she sighed.

'Hmm!' Liam agreed, his tone morose, his head bent. Suddenly he looked at Nova, his eyes lit up. 'My dad! Phone my dad.'

Nova caught on immediately. 'Will your dad tell me how Mr— I mean, Joshua is doing?'

'I'll tell you what to say,' said Liam.

Nova moved back to the phone. 'D'you know what his number is?'

Liam considered. 'Probably the same as when I lived there with him. He's in the same house we've always lived in, so why would he change it? And if he has, we'll phone directory enquiries.'

Nova keyed in the number Liam gave her. Her mouth was dry, her throat tight as she waited to see if anyone picked up the phone at the other end.

'Hello?'

'Hello? Mr Jackman?' said Nova breathlessly.

'Yes . . .?'

'Ask him about Joshua,' Liam whispered.

'Mr Jackman, I'm a . . . friend of your son, Joshua. I was just phoning to find out how he's doing.'

Liam moved to stand on the other side of the phone so that he could also hear the conversation.

'He's stable in hospital. I'm just on my way to see him now,' said Mr Jackman.

A jolt like lightning shot through Liam. His dad's voice. His dad was at the other end of that phone line. How was he? Did he look the same? Had he changed? Was he missing Liam – as much as Liam was missing him? Liam closed his eyes, feeling his throat get tighter and his eyes begin to well up. How stupid to cry at the sound of his dad's voice. He hadn't cried like that before. Why start now?

'Joshua's going to be all right, isn't he?' asked Nova.

'His legs will take a while to heal but luckily he didn't have to wait too long for help to arrive,' said Mr Jackman. 'Who is this?'

'My name is Nova. Nova Clibbens from the Phoenix Manor Hotel.'

'I understand my son was staying there for a while,' said Mr Jackman.

'That's right.' Nova was about to add more but then she thought better of it.

'You were one of the ones who found him, weren't you?'

'I suppose so. And I was on the beach when the ambulance arrived.' Nova didn't want to take credit where she deserved none. 'I didn't do much.'

'Thank you. I'm afraid they're just small, very inadequate words, but thank you so much,' said Mr Jackman. 'I won't forget it.'

'That's OK,' said Nova, feeling distinctly uncomfortable.

Liam smiled at her. He knew what she was going

through, but the last thing she needed now was to blame herself for what had happened to his brother.

'When Joshua gets out of hospital, you're more than welcome to visit him if you want to.'

'Thank you,' said Nova. 'But I thought he lived in Manchester.'

'My son will be staying with me for a while,' said Mr Jackman firmly. 'I'll be looking after him.'

Liam straightened up and turned away, but not before Nova saw the odd expression on his face. He looked . . . hurt.

'Well, thanks for letting me know about Joshua,' said Nova. 'Please tell him that I hope he gets better soon.'

After the goodbyes had been said Nova slowly put down the phone. She walked round Liam to look directly at him. 'What's the matter?'

'Nothing.'

'Your brother's going to be fine.'

'I heard,' said Liam. 'And he's going to recuperate at Dad's.'

'That's good news, at any rate,' said Nova.

Liam didn't answer.

'Isn't it?' prompted Nova, puzzled.

Liam still didn't answer.

'I thought that's what you wanted, for Joshua to get on with his life and maybe get back together with your dad?'

'It was . . . it is.'

'Then why the face?'

'I don't know what you mean.'

'Rubbish! Your face is longer than a physics exam. Aren't you happy for them?'

'Yeah, it's great that they've got together again. But what about me?' Liam suddenly flared up. 'Where does that leave me? I can't think myself into Dad's house any more than I can visit Josh in hospital. I can't get further than a mile in any direction.'

'You can still stay here—' Nova began.

'By myself. Watching you and your family and your guests get on with their lives. Watching all of you grow up, move out, move on – while I'm still stuck here like . . . like bad wallpaper.'

What could Nova say to that? She stared, stricken, at Liam, obviously feeling bad for him. Liam glared at her, hating that sympathetic look on her face. He didn't want her pity. How dare she?

'Or are you going to starve yourself to death so you can be with me for all time?' Liam asked viciously.

'That's . . . that's horrible,' Nova gasped.

'Is it? You're the one throwing up your food. You're the one who has a choice in this and you're choosing to die—'

'No, I'm not!' Nova yelled at him. 'I want to be thin. I want to look like Rainbow. I don't want to die. That's a terrible thing to say.'

'What does it matter if you're thin or fat?' asked Liam. 'There are worse things in this world to be, you know.'

'You don't understand—'

'No, I don't. And I don't want to. On a scale of one to ten, your problems don't even make the chart,' said Liam. 'I'm alone. This time tomorrow I'll be alone and this time next year and this time in the next century, I'll probably still be stuck here.'

'That's not my fault.'

'I never said it was.'

'Then why're you taking it out on me? If you really want to move on, then do something about it. Find a way. Let me help you.'

'I don't want your help.'

'Oh, that's right. You don't need anyone's help, do you? You want to stay here whingeing about your life but you won't help yourself and you won't let anyone else help you either.'

'In case you haven't noticed, I haven't got a life to whine about,' said Liam.

'I'm serious, Liam. If you won't help yourself then you've got no one else to blame for where you are now,' said Nova.

'And the same goes for you,' Liam told her succinctly.

Nova stared at him. Liam could tell that she understood immediately what he was talking about and she didn't like it one little bit. 'You know something,' he said softly. 'Maybe I should've left you and Joshua and Andrew to it. Maybe I should've let you get yourselves killed. Then at least I would've had some company.'

'You don't mean that,' Nova said, aghast.

'Don't I? I just spent the last decade by myself, Nova. I don't intend to do the same for the rest of eternity.'

'What're you going to do?' asked Nova, a frisson of fear chilling her entire body.

'I can't be by myself again, Nova. I just can't,' said Liam. 'And if that means doing something that's going to make you hate me – and make me hate myself – then so be it.'

'What're you talking about?' The alarm bells pealing inside her were deafening.

Liam didn't say a word as he slowly began to fade out.

'Answer me,' Nova ordered desperately. 'Liam, where're you going?'

'I've got to meet someone.'

'Who?'

'No one you know.'

'Liam . . .? Come back. Liam . . .?'

Liam could hear her voice echoing after him, but he didn't go back. He was so desperately tired of being lonely. He was just so desperately tired. He had meant every word of what he'd just said – and it scared him.

But being alone scared him even more.

45. Confession

'Isn't it terrible about the man trapped in one of the tunnels around here?' said Mrs Cooper, the elderly woman at the reception desk. 'The guard on our train told us all about it.'

'Yes, it was terrible,' Dad agreed. 'Thank goodness he was found in time.'

'And I understand a body was found in the tunnels. A body that's centuries old.' Mr Cooper's blue eyes gleamed.

'I'm not sure it's centuries old. They did find a body and it's been taken away for further analysis,' Dad informed them. 'But most people round here think it's the body of a boy who disappeared over ten years ago.'

'Is there any chance that we might have a quick look in the tunnels?' asked Mrs Cooper hopefully.

'You're the seventh person today to ask me that.' Dad's smile took the edge off his words. 'I'm afraid I couldn't possibly let anyone into the tunnels while they're so unsafe.'

'What a shame!' Mrs Cooper was extremely disappointed.

'Do you plan to open them once they have been made safe?' asked Mr Cooper.

'I'm not sure. Maybe,' said Dad truthfully. 'Anyway, you said you'd like a room for how many days?'

'Dad, where's Raye?' asked Nova.

'Nova, I'm trying to book these people in.' Dad smiled through gritted teeth.

'This is important,' said Nova. 'I have to talk to her.'

Nova had spent the last twenty minutes sitting in the hotel lounge trying to make up her mind what she should do next. Now she'd finally decided to talk to Raye. She'd tell her sister the truth about her bingeing and vomiting – and the reasons behind it – and if Raye decided to tell Mum and Dad then so be it. And Nova was going to tell Raye about Liam – all about him. She'd sit Raye down and make her listen and she wouldn't stop until Raye believed her. In his current mood, there was no telling what Liam might do and Nova felt totally out of her depth. But Liam really liked Raye. If he was going to listen to anyone, it would be her sister.

'Raye said she was going for a walk,' said Dad, less than impressed with Nova's interruption.

'Where?'

'I'm so sorry. I'll only be a moment,' Dad apologized to the elderly man and woman waiting to check in.

'Take your time, dear,' the elderly woman smiled.

'She went to the cliffs. Or the beach,' Dad said to Nova impatiently. 'She said she was meeting a friend there.'

'Who? Is Andrew out of hospital then?'

'I'm not sure. Maybe. Now if you don't mind . . .'

'Why is she going for a walk?' asked Nova.

'Because it's a lovely day? Because there's an R in the month? Take it up with your sister. OK?' said Dad, adding to himself, 'I'll be glad when school starts again!'

With a deep frown turning down every line in her face, Nova headed into the kitchen.

'Hello, love,' said Mum, placing a huge roasting tray filled with marinated chicken portions in the oven. 'Come for a snack?'

'No, I . . . Mum, can I talk to you?' said Nova.

Mum shut the oven door and sat down at the table. To Nova's surprise, she instantly had her mum's full attention.

Mum's expression was watchful as she indicated the chair opposite her. Nova sat down.

'What is it, Mum?' asked Nova.

'I should be asking you that. I've thought for some time that maybe you had something to tell me,' said Mum gently.

'Like what?'

'I don't know, Nova,' said Mum. 'But something's going on with you, isn't it?'

Nova nodded.

'Is it school?' Mum asked at last when Nova didn't continue.

Nova shook her head.

'Are you being bullied?'

'No, nothing like that,' said Nova.

'Then I'll shut up and let you tell me,' smiled Mum.

'I was really going to talk to Raye about this first,' Nova began.

'Anything you can tell Raye, you can tell me,' said Mum quietly. 'But I'm glad to see you two are friends again. You both had me worried there for a while.'

'Why?'

'Well, it was like you weren't sisters and you weren't friends. Like you didn't even know each other any more . . . So what is it you want to tell me?'

'You won't like it,' Nova sighed.

'I rather thought I wouldn't,' said Mum.

'It's just that . . .' The alarm bells that had been pealing in Nova's head a while ago now sounded as loud as cannon fire. Why was that phrase so familiar – 'like you didn't even know each other any more . . .'? Where had she just heard something similar? Like a light being switched on in her head, Nova suddenly remembered. She sprang up from the table. 'Raye's meeting Liam . . .' she said, appalled.

Mum sat back in her chair. 'Is that what you wanted to tell me? Raye's gone for a walk with her latest boyfriend?'

'No, I . . . Mum, I've got to go,' said Nova, already on the way to the door.

'But what about our talk?'

'We'll talk later, I promise.'

'Nova . . .?'

'I promise, Mum,' Nova said earnestly. 'But I've got to find Raye before it's too late.'

'Before what's too late? Nova?'

But Nova was gone.

46. The Final Test

Liam and Raye walked along the cliff top in a comfortable silence. Liam had listened to Raye chat about life at the hotel for the last ten minutes and it'd felt great to have a proper conversation again. The strange thing was, now he was outside, he didn't feel even close to fading out. He supposed it was because he was still too keyed up after his talk with Nova. Or maybe it was simply that he wanted to be here with Raye more than anything else in the world.

'I'm sorry I didn't believe you about Nova. You were right all along,' Raye said unexpectedly. 'She is . . . ill at the moment.'

'I don't think she sees it as an illness,' said Liam.

'But it is – right? I mean, she's deliberately making herself sick.'

'Did she tell you that?' Liam asked, surprised.

'Yes . . . no . . . not in so many words, but I could tell,' said Raye. 'I feel like it's all my fault.'

'It's not your fault, it's not Nova's fault. It's just one of those things you all have to get on and deal with.'

'We used to be close, you know – Nova and me. I didn't realize how far we'd grown apart until I asked her about her . . . bulimia. She wouldn't look at me and I stood in her bedroom realizing that I didn't really know my sister any more. Does that make sense?'

Liam nodded.

'It was so strange. It was like looking at a stranger. I feel closer to you at the moment than I do to my own sister – if you see what I mean.' Raye's cheeks took on a reddish

209

tinge as she looked away, embarrassed. 'Am I talking too much?'

'No, not at all,' Liam hurried to reassure her. 'Besides, I like to listen to you.'

'You're the first one who does!' Raye smiled.

Liam returned her smile and looked out over the sea towards the horizon. This was the happiest he'd been in a long, long time. If only he could bottle this feeling so that he could keep it for ever. If only he could bottle Raye and keep her with him for ever. That would be true heaven.

'It is beautiful, isn't it?' said Raye.

Liam nodded. 'Yes, it is,' he agreed.

They stood side by side on the cliff top, looking out across the gently rippling sea. They were only about ten metres away from the edge. There were wooden barricades further along the cliff edge, where the ground sloped more sharply, but here there was nothing but a warning sign.

'D'you like it here?' asked Liam, moving slowly closer towards the edge.

'At the hotel?'

'Yeah, and the beach and the cliffs and gardens.'

Raye considered. 'Yes, I do actually. But don't tell my parents that, will you?'

'Don't worry, I won't. Do you like it enough to stay . . . for ever?'

'For ever?' Raye said, surprised. 'No one stays anywhere for ever, do they? We all move on at some time – that's just the way life works. What about you? Where's your home?'

'Near here.'

'How come I haven't seen you around before this weekend?'

'I kept to myself,' said Liam. 'And you may not have noticed me, but I certainly noticed you.'

'You did?'

'Of course,' Liam smiled. 'I noticed you from the first day you moved in. You were wearing a red jumper and black jeans and you were arguing with your mum about which room would be your bedroom.'

'You saw all that?' Raye asked, astounded. 'How come you didn't introduce yourself to us? To me? I could've really used a friend when we first moved in.'

'If I could have, I would have. Believe me,' said Liam. 'Were you very lonely?'

Raye nodded and looked away, suddenly self-conscious. 'It took me a long time to settle in.'

'But you got used to it?'

'More than that. I love it here now. It's my home,' smiled Raye. 'Don't you feel the same way about where you live, then?'

'I guess so,' said Liam.

They were now only a metre away from the cliff edge. Liam took another step and stopped. Raye moved to stand beside him.

'Raye, have you ever wanted something so much that you'd do anything to get it? Anything at all?'

'Depends what you mean by anything,' said Raye lightly.

Liam turned to her. 'I suppose it does.' He peered over the edge of the cliff. 'Ever climbed down there?'

'Are you kidding?' Raye scoffed. 'Do I look like a mountain goat?'

'Never been tempted?'

'Nope!'

'Very wise,' Liam smiled. 'But I've got something to show you.'

'What?'

'You have to stand right in front of me or you won't see it properly,' said Liam.

Raye looked at the remaining forty or so centimetres between Liam and the edge of the cliff. 'I'm not sure about that . . .'

'I'll tell you what,' said Liam seriously. 'I promise that if you fall, I'll follow you down.'

'That'll be a great comfort as I break every bone in my body,' Raye said dryly.

'I mean it. I won't let you go alone.'

'So what d'you want to show me?'

'Stand in front of me and then you'll see it.'

Cautiously, Raye moved to stand in front of him, peering gingerly over the cliff top. 'So what am I looking at?'

Liam sidestepped to stand behind and slightly to the side of Raye. 'Look over to the right, about five hundred metres away – just above that ridge,' he said. 'There's a cave just above that ridge . . .'

'That's the one Mr Jackman was trapped in, isn't it?'

Liam nodded. Raye shuddered.

'What about it?'

'I used to use the cave down there as an escape route,' said Liam.

Raye turned to face Liam. 'An escape from what?'

'Life.'

Raye wasn't quite sure what to make of that. 'And did you escape?'

Silence. Raye waited for Liam to answer. The intensity of his expression almost scared her as his eyes burned into hers. But then his expression cleared and his body relaxed as he sighed deeply. 'We'd better be getting back,' he said wearily. 'I'd never forgive myself if anything happened to you.'

'But you didn't answer my question. Did you —?' Before Raye could say another word, someone else interrupted her.

'*Raye, get away from him!*' Nova screamed out from down on the beach.

'What on earth . . .?' Raye turned. 'Nova? What're you doing?'

'Get away from him. He's a ghost. *He's trying to kill you!*' Nova yelled frantically.

'What's she on about?' Raye turned her head to ask Liam.

But Liam's arms were moving towards her, his hands outstretched.

'No!' Raye backed away from him, afraid of what he was about to do. But she stepped off into nothing. Her arms shot out towards Liam, but it was too late. She plummeted downwards.

'RAYE!' Nova screamed.

Raye scrambled desperately for the cliff face. She grabbed hold of an old, thick root, trailing outwards from the cliff face, and gripped it as her hands slid down it. The rough stem scored her skin but she just managed to hold on. Her feet dug against the cliff face, searching for a foothold. She found a tenuous one of sorts in another old root, short and sharp but better than nothing.

Liam fell to the ground and stretched out both hands. 'Raye, reach up and grab hold of my hands.'

'*Raye, don't!*' Nova shrieked out from below her.

Raye screamed as the root she was holding onto cracked and groaned and gave slightly under her weight.

'Raye, whatever you do, don't take his hand!' Nova cried out.

Rainbow looked up at Liam above her. His eyes caught hers and they regarded each other silently. Raye knew in that moment that everything Nova had said was true. She also knew that she was seconds away from falling to her death.

'Rainbow, take my hand. Trust me.' Liam lowered himself even further down until his hand was just centimetres above her own.

'I can't!' Raye screamed. She was terrified of what might happen if she didn't let him help her up, but she was equally terrified of what might happen if she did.

'Take my hand, Rainbow,' Liam ordered, adding with a dry smile, 'I won't let you down!'

'Raye, don't do it!' Nova screamed.

'Please. Trust me,' Liam said softly.

And in that moment it was as if all sound in the world had suddenly stopped. There was just Liam and Rainbow and the silence between them. Raye looked at Liam as he smiled down at her. His silly joke and the words 'trust me' were all she could think of at that moment.

Trust me . . .

Rainbow felt the branch beneath her feet creak and crack and give just a little more. And the root she was holding onto was giving out. She closed her eyes momentarily, then took a deep breath. It was now or never. She reached out and jumped to grab hold of Liam's hand. The root beneath her feet cracked one last time before falling away from the cliff face. Rainbow was left dangling with just Liam's grip between her and a deadly fall.

Immediately Liam tried to haul Rainbow up. He caught hold of her hand with both of his and the strain was evident on his face. But he was doing it. Rainbow pushed herself upwards, her feet braced against the cliff face as Liam struggled to drag her to level ground.

'Liam, don't let her fall!' Nova cried out. 'Please don't let her fall.'

'. . . not . . . going to happen,' Liam grunted, pulling Raye up all the while, until at last he hauled her over the cliff edge and they both lay gasping for breath on the ground.

'I . . . I wasn't going to push you. I was trying to pull you away from the edge,' Liam said when he'd barely got back his breath. 'I wasn't going to do it. I promise.'

Raye looked over at him, still breathing heavily. 'You thought about it, though, didn't you?'

'Only for a second,' Liam admitted.

'Sometimes a second can last a lifetime.'

'And sometimes a lifetime can pass in a second.'

'That's a bit too deep for me right now,' said Raye, still trying to catch her breath. 'But thanks for saving my life, Liam.'

'And thanks for saving mine. Do something for me, Raye. Tell Nova I said . . . eat something!' said Liam.

'Why don't you tell her yourself?' asked Raye, turning her head to face him, only to sit bolt upright and stare.

'I can't.' Liam grinned at her as he slowly faded from view. 'I'm not going to be here for much longer.'

'Wait. Where're you going?' asked Raye urgently.

'No idea! I'm not doing this! Isn't it wonderful?'

Nova ran puffing towards them, having raced all the way up the cliff steps. She stood in front of Raye and Liam as they both got to their feet.

'Liam's leaving us,' Raye said, her voice uneven. 'For good . . .'

Nova turned to Liam, her eyes huge with dismay. 'Aren't you coming back?'

'I don't know, but . . . but I don't think so.'

'But . . . but why're you leaving now? They found your body yesterday. How come you didn't disappear then?' asked Nova.

'Because I was wrong. Leaving this place had nothing

215

to do with my body being found,' said Liam slowly, still gradually fading from sight. 'It was about what was going on up here –' he tapped his forehead – 'and in here –' he placed a hand over his heart.

'I don't understand,' said Nova.

'Nova —'

'And I don't want to understand – not if it means you'll leave,' Nova admitted in a rush. 'I don't want you to go, Liam.'

'I'll miss you too, Nova,' smiled Liam. 'But it's time for me to move on. At last.'

'But you're the first person to take any notice of me around here.'

'I might've been the first,' said Liam, looking at Raye. 'But I won't be the last. You need to let your family know how you're feeling. Don't bottle things up inside. That was my mistake.'

Liam looked up at the sky, suddenly raising his arms upwards as if he wanted to pull it down and around him. He spun around slowly, his arms still outstretched. When did everything get so *bright*? It was as if he'd spent his entire death with sunglasses on and now they were off and the world was bright and alive and so wonderful. Liam breathed in deeply, feeling he must surely explode with the bliss fizzing inside him. When Raye had fallen over the cliff edge, all he'd wanted to do was reach her and get her to safety. He'd offered up all kinds of silent prayers – like never complaining about being stuck in Phoenix Manor again, just as long as Raye didn't die. How strange that things should work out this way. He turned to Nova, his smile fading slightly when he saw the look on her face. He tried to wipe a tear from her cheek but his finger passed right through it. He bent his head and kissed her. His lips made contact, skin against skin, but when he tried to touch her cheek again, his fingers moved through her as if through mist or a breeze.

'Enjoy your life, Nova. It's very precious,' Liam said softly.

'Raye, do something,' Nova appealed to her sister.

'Don't go . . .' Raye had no idea where the words came from but they spilled out anyway.

Liam's smile was made of pure happiness. 'I have to. I *want* to.'

Raye could hardly see Liam now. He was just a blur through the unexpected tears in her eyes.

'I can't believe I'm outta here at last!' Liam shouted joyfully. 'Raye, you've got a very special sister there. Look after her.'

'I will,' Raye whispered.

'Be happy, Nova,' the last vestige of Liam's image told her. 'And don't be a div-brain all your life. Eat!'

'Wait, Liam. I just want to say . . . goodbye . . .' But she was too late.

He'd gone.

47. Miss Dawn and Miss Eve

Miss Dawn and Miss Eve stood on the front steps of the hotel, watching Nova and Raye walk towards the hotel, arm in arm.

'There you go!' said Miss Dawn smugly. 'He didn't drop her. I knew he'd do the right thing.'

'No, you didn't.'

Miss Dawn laughed. 'All right then, I *hoped* he'd do the right thing. It was always his choice, though.'

'Admit it. He had you worried, didn't he?'

'He certainly did!' Miss Dawn agreed.

'I don't understand him at all,' said Miss Eve. 'If he'd dropped her, he would've had a companion for life – I mean for eternity.'

Miss Dawn shook her head. 'No, he wouldn't. Knowing Raye, she would probably never have spoken to him again. I think she would've hated him for ever. And she wouldn't have been bound to the hotel the way he is. Being stuck at the hotel was his problem to solve, not hers. He would've lost her for good.'

Miss Dawn watched Raye and Nova smile at each other as they carried on walking.

'What about Nova? Is she cured?' asked Miss Eve.

'Of course not. But she's not so alone any more. She's got her family to help her now.'

Miss Eve sighed. 'I'm going to miss Liam. I liked him.'

'Why, Miss Eve, I do believe you're getting soft in your old age,' teased Miss Dawn.

'Never! Come on, old woman. It's time for us to pack up and move on.'

'But we will come back once Mr Clibbens opens the tunnels, won't we?' asked Miss Dawn.

'If we must,' sighed Miss Eve.

'Oh, definitely. They're going to be the biggest tourist attraction for miles around. We can't miss at least one trip through them.'

'What we will miss is our train, if you don't hurry up,' Miss Eve complained.

Miss Dawn watched Nova and Raye for a while longer. 'Good luck to both of you,' she whispered. 'And try not to miss Liam too much.'

'Will you please get a move on?' snapped Miss Eve. 'Nova and Raye won't be that unhappy. They have each other now.'

'I do so love a happy ending!' sighed Miss Dawn.

'I don't!' Miss Eve grumbled. 'So tell me, will they ever see Liam again?'

Miss Dawn turned to Miss Eve and smiled silkily, saying, 'Now that would be telling!'

And the two old women turned round and went back into the hotel.

AUTHOR	CLASS
NARAYAN, R.K.	F

TITLE

The grandmother's tale: three novellas

The Grandmother's Tale

Three Novellas

The
Grandmother's
Tale

Three Novellas

R K Narayan

HEINEMANN : LONDON

First published in Great Britain 1993
by William Heinemann Ltd
an imprint of Reed Consumer Books Ltd
Michelin House, 81 Fulham Road, London SW3 6RB
and Auckland, Melbourne, Singapore and Toronto

A CIP catalogue record for this book
is available at the British Library

ISBN 0 434 49618 9

Typeset by Falcon Graphic Art Ltd
Printed in Great Britain
by Clays Ltd, St Ives plc

Contents

The Grandmother's Tale

The Grandmother's Tale

I was brought up by my grandmother in Madras from my third year while my mother lived in Bangalore with a fourth child on hand after me. My grandmother took me away to Madras in order to give relief to an over-burdened daughter.

My grandmother Ammani was a busy person. She performed a variety of tasks all through the day, cooking and running the house for her two sons, gardening, counselling neighbours and the tenants living in the rear portion of the vast house stretching away in several segments, settling disputes, studying horoscopes and arranging matrimonial alliances. At the end of the day she settled down on a swing – a broad plank suspended by chains from the ceiling; lightly propelling it with her feet back and forth, chewing betel, she was completely relaxed at that hour. She held me at her side and taught me songs, prayers, numbers and the alphabet till suppertime.

I mention 'suppertime', but there was no fixed suppertime. My uncles returned home late in the evening. The senior uncle conducted a night school for slum children.

(Some of them, later in life, attained eminence as pundits in the Tamil language and literature.) The junior uncle worked in the harbour as a stevedore's assistant and came home at uncertain hours. Suppertime could not be based on their home-coming but on my performance. My grandmother fed me only when I completed my lessons to her satisfaction. I had to repeat the multiplication table up to twenty but I always fumbled and stuttered after twelve and needed prodding and goading to attain the peak; I had to recite Sanskrit verse and slokas in praise of Goddess Saraswathi and a couple of other gods, and hymns in Tamil; identify six ragas when granny hummed the tunes or, conversely, mention the songs when she named the ragas; and then solve arithmetic problems such as, 'If a boy wants four mangoes costing one anna per mango, how much money will he have to take?' I wanted to blurt out, 'Boys don't have to buy, they can obtain a fruit with a well-aimed stone at a mango tree.' I brooded, blinked without a word, afraid I might offend her if I mentioned the stone technique for obtaining a fruit. She watched me and then, tapping my skull, gently remarked, 'Never seen a bigger dunce . . . ' It was all very taxing, I felt hungry and sleepy. To keep me awake, she kept handy a bowl of cold water and sprinkled it on my eyelids from time to time.

I could not understand why she bothered so much to make me learned. She also taught me some folk songs which now, I realize, were irrelevant, such as the one about a drunkard sleeping indifferently while his child in the crib was crying and the mother was boiling the milk. The most unnecessary lesson however, in my memory as I realize it now, was a Sanskrit lyric, not in praise of God, but defining the perfect woman – it said the perfect woman must work like a slave, advise like a Mantri (Minister), look like Goddess Lakshmi, be patient like Mother Earth and courtesan-like in the bed chamber – this I had to recite on certain days of the week. After the lessons she released me and served food. When I was six years old I was ceremoniously escorted to the Lutheran Mission School nearby and admitted in the 'Infant Standard'.

Later I grew up in Mysore with my parents, visiting my grandmother in Madras once a year during the holidays. After completing my college course, I frequently visited Madras to try my luck there as a freelance author.

My junior uncle, no longer a stevedore's assistant but an automobile salesman for a German make, set out every morning to contact his 'prospects' and demonstrate the special virtues of his car. He took me out with him, saying 'If you want to be a writer, don't mope at home listening to grandmother's tales. You must be up and doing; your B.A. degree will lead you nowhere if you do not contact "prospects". Come out with me and watch . . . ' He drove me about, stopped here and there, met all sorts of persons and delivered his sales talk, making sure that I followed his performance intelligently. I avoided his company in the evenings, since he wined and dined with his 'prospects' to clinch a sale. During his morning rounds, however, I went out with him to be introduced to men, who, he thought, were in the writing line. He left me in their company to discuss with them my literary aspirations. Most of them were printers, established in the highways and byways of the city, or publishers of almanacs, diaries, lottery tickets and race-cards, who were looking for proofreaders on a daily wage of ten rupees.

My uncle urged me to accept any offer that came: 'You must make a start and go up. Do you know what I was earning when I worked at the harbour? Less than twenty-five a month, in addition to occasional tips from clearing agents. That is how I learnt my job. Then I moved on to a job at a bookshop in Mount Road, cycling up in the morning, carrying my lunch, and selling books till seven in the evening. It was hard work, but I was learning a job. Today do you know what I get? One thousand for every car I sell, in addition to expenses for entertaining the prospects. You will have to learn your job while earning, whatever the wages might be. That is how you should proceed.'

After brooding over these suggestions, I began to ignore his advice and stayed at home, much to his annoyance: 'Well, if you do not want to prosper, I will just say G.T.H.

(go to hell). I have better things to do ... ' (However, he relented subsequently after the publication of my first three novels, my first three in England.) In 1940, when I started a quarterly journal 'Indian Thought' in Mysore, he took it upon himself to help its circulation, applying his sales talk at high pressure. Carrying a sample copy of 'Indian Thought' from door to door, he booked one thousand subscribers in Madras city alone in the first year. Unfortunately, 'Indian Thought' ceased publication in the second year since I could not continue it single-handed.

Although ageing, my grandmother was still active and concerned herself with other people's affairs, her domestic drudgery now mitigated by the presence of two daughters-in-law in the house. She sat as usual on the swing in the evenings, invited me to sit beside her, and narrated to me stories of her early days – rather of her mother's early life and adventures, as heard by her from her mother when she, Ammani, was about ten years old.

Day after day, I sat up with her listening to her account, and at night developed it as a cogent narrative. As far as possible, I have tried to retain the flavour of her speech, though the manner of her narrative could not be reproduced as it proceeded in several directions back and forth and got mixed up with asides and irrelevancies. I have managed to keep her own words here and there, but this is mainly a story-writer's version of a hearsay biography of a great-grandmother. She was seven when she was married, her husband being just ten years old. Those were the days of child marriages, generally speaking. Only widowers re-married late in life. It is not possible to fix the historical background by any clue or internal evidence. My grandmother could not be specific about the time since she was unborn at the beginning of her mother's story. One has to assume an arbitrary period – that is the later period of the East India Company, before the Sepoy Mutiny. My grandmother could not specify the location of their beginning. It might be anywhere in the Southern Peninsula. She just mentioned it as 'that village', which conjures up a familiar pattern: a hundred houses scattered in four or five narrow streets, with pillared verandas and pyols, massive front doors, inner courtyards, situated at the bend of a river or its tributary, mounds of garbage here and there, cattle everywhere, a temple tower looming over it all; the temple hall and corridor serving as a meeting ground for the entire population, and an annual festival attracting a big crowd from nearby hamlets – an occasion when a golden replica of the deity in the inner shrine was carried in a procession with pipes and drums around the village.

'What god was he?' I could not resist my curiosity; my grandmother knew as much as I did, but ventured a guess.

'Could be Ranganatha, the aspect of Vishnu, in repose in a state of yoga lying on the coils of the thousand-headed Adisesha. The god was in a trance, and watched and protected our village. They were married in that temple – my father and mother. Don't interrupt me with questions, as I have also only heard about these events. My mother told me that she was playing in the street with her friends one evening when her father came up and said, "You are going to be married next week."

' "Why?" she asked and did not get an answer. Her father ignored her questions and went away. Her play-mates stopped their game, surrounded and teased her. "Hey, bride! Hey, bride!"

' "Wait! You will also be brides soon!" she retorted. She rushed back home to her mother, crying, "Whatever happens, I am not going to marry. My friends are making fun of me!" '

Her mother soothed her and explained patiently that she was old enough to marry, something that could not be avoided by any human being, an occasion when she would be showered with gifts and new clothes and gold ornaments. The girl, however, was not impressed. She sulked and wept in a corner of their home. After fixing the date of the wedding they kept her strictly indoors and did not allow her to go out and play. Her playmates visited her and whispered their sympathies.

*

On an auspicious day she was clad in a saree, decked in jewellery, and taken to the pillared hall of the temple where had gathered guests and relations and priests: a piper and drummer were creating enough noise to drown the uproar of the priests and chanting mantras and the babble of the guests. She was garlanded and made to sit beside a boy whom she had often noticed tossing a rubber ball in an adjoining street whenever she went out to buy a pencil, ribbon or sweets in a little shop. She felt shy to look at him now, sitting too close to him on a plank. The smoke from the holy fire smarted her eyes and also created a smoke-screen blurring her vision whenever she stole a glance in his direction. At the auspicious hour the piper, drummer and the chanting priests combined to create the maximum din as Viswa approached the girl, seated on her father's lap, and tied the yellow thread around her neck, and they became man and wife from that moment.

In a week all celebration, feasting and exchange of ceremonial visits between the bride and bridegroom parties ceased. Viswanath the bridegroom went back to his school run by a pedagogue on a brick platform under a banyan tree on the riverside. He was ragged by his class-fellows for getting married. He denied it and became violent till the pedagogue intervened and brought his cane down on the back of the teasing member.

The boy said between sobs, 'He is lying. I was at the temple with my father and ate, along with the others, a big feast with four kinds of sweets. Viswanath wore new clothes, a gold chain and a big garland around his neck. If I am lying, let him take off his shirt and show us the sacred thread . . . ' He bared his chest and held up his sacred thread to demonstrate that he had only a bachelor's three-strand thread. The teacher was old, suffered from a sore throat, and could not control his class of twenty-five children when a babble broke out on the subject of Viswa's marriage. A few cried, 'Shame, shame,' which was the usual form of greeting in their society.

The teacher tapped his cane on the floor and cried over the tumult, 'Why shame? I was married when I was like Viswa. I have four sons and two daughters and grandchildren. My wife looks after those at home still, and runs the family; and they will also all marry soon. There is no shame in marriage. It's all arranged by that god in the temple. Who are we to say anything against his will? My wife was also small when we married . . . '

The girl's life changed after her marriage. She could not go out freely, or join her friends playing in the street. She could not meet her husband, except on special occasions such as the New Year and other festival days when Viswa was invited to visit his wife's home with his parents. On those occasions the girl was kept aloof in a separate room and would be escorted to his presence by young women who would giggle and urge the young couple to talk and say something to each other and leave them alone for a little time. The couple felt embarrassed and shy and tongue-tied but took that opportunity to study each other's features. When they got a chance, the very first sentence the girl uttered was, 'There is a black patch under your ear.' She made bold to touch his face with her fore-finger. Apart from holding each other's right hand before the holy fire during their wedding ceremony this was their first touch. He found that her finger was soft and she found the skin under his left ear rough but pleasant. When she removed her finger she asked 'What is this patch?' She thrust her finger again to trace that black patch under his left ear. 'Oh, that!' he said, pressing down her finger on the black patch. 'It's a lucky sign, my mother says.'

'Does it hurt?' she asked solicitously.

'No. They say it's lucky to have that mark,' he said.

'How much luck?' she asked and continued, 'Will you become a king?'

'Yes, that's what they say.' And before they could develop this subject, others opened the door and came in, not wanting to leave the couple alone too long.

After that they discovered an interest in each other's company. But it was not easy to meet. It was impossible for the girl to go out, unless chaperoned by an elder of the family. Even such outings were limited to a visit to the temple on a Friday evening or to a relation on ceremonial occasions. Viswa wished he could be told when and where he could see her. Occasionally he found an excuse to visit her home on the pretext of wanting to meet his father-in-law on some business but it did not always work as the man would be in his coconut grove far away. Viswa did not possess the hardihood to step into the house to catch a glimpse of his young wife. She kept herself in the deepest recess of their house for fear of being considered too forward, and he would turn back disappointed. But he soon found a way. He spied and discovered that she was more accessible at their backyard, where she washed clothes at the well. There was only a short wall separating their backyard from a lane, which proved a more convenient approach since he could avoid a neighbour always lounging on the pyol and asking, 'Ay! Visiting your wife? Insist upon a good tiffin . . . ' It made him self-conscious. He would simper and murmur and hasten his steps only to be met by his mother-in-law at the door. Now the backyard could be approached without anyone accosting him, but the lane was dirty and garbage-ridden; he did not mind it. On his way back from school if he took a diversion, he could approach the lane and the short wall. He placed a couple of bricks close to the wall, stood on the pile with his head showing up a few inches above it. It was a sound strategy though her back was turned to him, while she drew water from the well and filled a bucket and soaked her clothes. He watched her for a few moments and cried, 'Hey!'

When she did not hear his call he clapped his hands, and she turned and stared at him. He said, 'Hey, I am here.'

Looking back watchfully into their house she asked, 'Why?'

'To see you,' he said.

'Come by the front door,' she said.

And he said promptly, 'I can't. It's no good. How are you? I came to ask,' he said rather timidly.

'Why should you ask?' she questioned. He had no immediate answer. He just blinked. She laughed at him and said, 'You are tall today.'

'Yes,' he said. 'Is your name Balambal? It is too long.'

'Call me Bala,' she said, picked up her bucket and suddenly retreated into the house.

He waited, hoping she would come back. But the back door shut with a bang, and he jumped off muttering, 'She is funny. I should not have married her. But what could I do? I was never asked whether I wanted to marry or not . . .'

He ran down the lane and sought the company of his friend Ramu, who lived in a house next to the temple and who knew when the poojas at the temple were performed and when they would distribute the offerings – sweet rice and coconut pieces. If one stuck to Ramu one need not starve for snacks. He could take Viswa to see the god at the appropriate moment when the evening service was in progress and wait. After waving camphor flames and sounding cymbals and bells, the offerings would be distributed. Piously standing on the threshold of the sanctum Ramu would whisper, 'Viswa, shut your eyes and pray, otherwise they will not give you anything to eat!'

At the next session Viswa was more successful. Standing on the pile of bricks, he told her: 'On Tuesday evening I went to the temple.'

'Did you pray? What for?' she asked. Seeing his silence, she said, 'Why go to temple if you don't pray?'

'I don't know any prayer.'

'What did you learn at home?'

He realized she was a heckler and tried to ward off the attack. 'I know some prayer, not all.'

'Recite some,' she said.

'No, I won't,' he said resolutely.

'You will be sent to hell if you don't say your prayers.'

'How do you know?' he asked.

'My mother has told me. She makes us all pray in the evenings in the pooja room.'

'Bah!' he said. 'What do you get to eat after the prayers? At the temple if you shut your eyes and prostrate before the god, they give you wonderful things to eat. For that you must come with me and Ramu . . . '

'Who is Ramu?'

'My friend,' Viswa said and jumped off the pile of bricks as there were portents of the girl's mother appearing on the scene. He was now satisfied that he had been able to establish a line of communication with Bala although the surroundings were filthy, and he had to tread warily lest he should put his foot on excreta, the lane serving as a public convenience.

They could not meet normally as husband and wife. Bala, being only ten years old, must attain puberty and then go through an elaborate nuptial ceremony, before she could join her husband.

Viswa had other plans. One afternoon he stood on the brick-pile and beckoned her. She looked up and frantically signalled to him to go away. 'I have to talk to you,' he said desperately and ducked and crouched while her mother appeared at the door for a moment.

After she had gone in, he heard a soft voice calling, 'Hey, speak.'

His head bobbed up again over the wall and he just said: 'I am going away. Keep it a secret . . . '

'Where are you going?'

'I don't know. Far away.'

'Why?'

He had no answer. He merely said, 'Even Ramu doesn't know.'

'Who are you going with?'

'I don't know, but I am joining some pilgrims beyond the river.'

'Won't you tell me why you are going away?'

'No, I can't . . . I have to go away – that is all.'

'Can't you mention a place where you are going?'

'I don't know . . .'

She began to laugh. 'Oh! Oh! You are going to "I don't know" place. Is it?'

He felt irked by her levity and said, 'I don't know, really. They were a group of pilgrims singing a bhajan about Pandaripura or some such place . . . over and over again.'

'Are you sure?'

'You won't see me for a long time . . .'

'But when will you come back?'

'Later . . .' he said and vanished as he noticed her mother coming again, and that was the last the girl saw of him for a long time to come.

She remained indifferent for a week or ten days and then began secretly to worry. She thought at first Viswa was playing a joke and would re-appear over the wall sooner or later. She wanted to tell her mother, but was afraid she might begin to investigate how she came to know Viswa had disappeared, and then proceed to raise the wall to keep him off. She suffered silently, toyed with the idea of seeking Ramu's help, but she had never seen him. Others at home did not bother. Her father was, as ever, interested only in his coconut garden, the price of coconut, coconut pests and so on. He left home at dawn after breakfasting on rice soaked over-night in cold water, packed a lunch and returned home at night tired and weary, leaving domestic matters to his wife's care.

Bala's mother noticed her brooding silence and gloom and asked one day, 'What is ailing you?'

Bala burst into tears 'He . . . he . . . is gone,' she said.

'Who?'

Bala replied, 'He . . . he . . . ' since a wife could not utter a husband's name.

When Bala's father returned home from the garden the lady told him, 'Viswa has disappeared.'

He took it lightly and said, 'Must be playing with his friends somewhere. Where could he go? How do you know he has disappeared?'

'I have not seen him for a long time. He used to come up to see you, but as you were always away, he would turn back from the door.'

'Poor boy! You should have called him in. Young people are shy!'

'Bala also shut herself in whenever he came . . . '

'She is also young and shy. I must take him with me to the garden some time.'

The lady persuaded the man to stay away from the coconut garden, and next morning they went over to

Viswa's house. 'After all they are our *sambhandis* (relations through matrimonial alliance) and we must pay them courtesy visits at least once in a while.'

Viswa's parents lived in what was named Chariot Nook (where the temple chariot was stationed in a shed).

After a formal welcome and the courtesy of unrolling a mat for the visitors, both Viswa's father and Bala's asked simultaneously, 'Where is Viswa?' When they realized no one knew the answer, Viswa's parents said, 'We thought he was in your house. We were planning to come and see him.'

Next they visited the schoolmaster, who said he had not seen Viswa for more than ten days.

It became a sensation in the village. Well-wishers of the family and others crowded in, speculating, sympathizing, and suggesting the next step, vociferous and excited and talking simultaneously. A little fellow in the crowd said, 'I saw him with a group crossing the river . . . '

'When?'

'I don't remember.'

'Didn't you talk to him?'

'Yes, he said he was going to Delhi.' There was ironic laughter at this.

'Delhi is thousands of miles away . . . '

'More . . . '

'I hear sepoys are killing white officers.'

'Who told you?'

'Someone from the town . . . '

'Who cares who kills whom while we are bothered about Viswa?'

Someone suddenly questioned Viswa's father. 'Are you in the habit of beating him?'

'Sometimes you can't help it.'

Viswa's mother said, 'Whenever his teacher came and reported something, you lost your head,' and burst into tears. 'Teachers are an awful lot, you must pay no attention to what they say.'

'But unless the teacher is strict young fellows can never be tamed.'

Viswa's mother said, sobbing, 'You thrashed him when that awful man came and said something.'

'He had thrown cowdung on the master when he was not looking.'

'You slapped him,' said the mother.

'I only patted his cheek.'

Everyone nursed a secret fear that Viswa had drowned in the river. Then the whole company trooped out, stood before the god in the temple hall, prayed and promised offerings if Viswa came back alive. If Bala could have opened her mouth to announce what she knew, it would have been a relief to everyone, but she remained dumb.

As time passed Bala found existence a sore trial. She was no longer the little girl with a pigtail, dressed in a cotton skirt and jacket. Now she had reached maturity – rather stocky with no pretensions to any special beauty except the natural charm of full-blown womanhood, she could not pass down the *agraharam* street without people staring at her, whispering comments at her back. Sometimes some friend of the family would stop her on her way to the temple and ask, 'Any news? Do you hope he will come back?' She found it a strain to be inventing answers. She snapped at her questioners sometimes, but it made things worse. 'Where is he?' people persisted in demanding.

She said one day, 'In Kashmir, making a lot of money, and has sent a message to say he will be back soon.'

'Who brought you the message?' She invented a name. Next time when they questioned her again about the messenger she just said, 'He has gone there as a priest in some temple . . . ' She soon tired of it all, and showed herself outside home as little as possible, but for a visit to the temple on Tuesday and Friday evening. She would gaze on the image in the sanctum when the camphor flame was waved to the ringing of the bells and pray, 'Oh Lord. I don't even know whether my husband is alive. If he is alive help me to reach him. If he is dead, please let me die of cholera quickly.' Other women looked at her strangely and asked among themselves, 'Why is her mother not coming with her? There must be some reason. They are not on talking terms. She must be hiding something. He is no more but they are keeping it a secret. Instead of shaving her head and wearing white, she oils and combs her hair and decks flowers! And comes to the temple with *kumkum* on her brow pretending to be a Sumangali. A widow who pretends to be otherwise pollutes the temple precinct and its holiness is lost. She should be prohibited from entering the temple unless she shaves her head and observes the rules. Her mother must be a brazen woman to allow her out like this. We should talk to the priest.'

The priest of the temple visited them one afternoon. Bala's mother was all excitement at the honour, unrolled a mat, seated him, offered him some fruits and milk and made a lot of fuss. The priest accepted it all and looked around cautiously and asked in a hushed voice, 'Where is your daughter?' Bala generally retired to a backroom when there was a visitor; but tried to listen to their talk. The priest was saying: 'I remember Bala as a child, in fact I remember her wedding.' He paused and asked, 'Where is her husband, that boy who married her? I notice Bala at the temple some evenings.'

Her mother was upset and not able to maintain the conversation. The priest said: 'You know the old proverb "You may seal the mouth of a furnace, but you cannot shut the mouth of gossip." Till you get some proof to say he is living it is better that you don't send Bala to the temple. Its sanctity must be preserved – which is my duty, otherwise as a priest of the temple my family will face God's wrath.'

At this point of their talk Bala rushed out like a storm, her face flushed, 'You people think I am a widow? I am not. He is alive like you. I'll not rest until I come back with him some day, and shame you all . . . ' She threw a word of cheer to her mother and flounced out of the house.

Bala's mother tried to follow her down the street but Bala was too fast for her. People stood and stared at the mother–daughter chase. Bala halted. When her mother came up she whispered, 'Go back home . . . People are watching us. Keep well, I will come back. Remember that the priest is waiting there in our house . . . ' Mother was in a dilemma. She hesitated as Bala raced forward.

Bala dashed for a moment into the temple and prostrated before the image, rose and hurried away before the priest or others should arrive and notice her. She rushed past all the gaping men and women, past all the rows of houses to Chariot Nook, to Viswa's house and knocked. Her mother-in-law opened the door and was aghast. 'Bala! You look like Kali . . . what is the matter? Come in first . . . You should stay with us . . . '

'Yes, when I come with my husband.' She took a pinch of vermilion from a little bowl on a stool and pressed it on her brow, fell prostrate at her mother-in-law's feet, touched them reverently, sprang back and was off even as the lady was saying, 'Your father-in-law will come back

23

soon, wait . . . ' Before her sentence was completed, Bala was gone.

Up to this point, my grandmother remembered her mother's narration. Beyond this, her information was hazy. She just said, 'Bala must have gone to the village cart stand in the field beyond the last street, where travellers and bullock carts assembled.' Bala must have paid for a seat in a carriage, travelled all night and reached a nearby town. Even in her hurry before leaving home, she did not forget to pack a small bag with a change of clothes, some money she had saved out of her birthday and other gifts, a few gold ornaments, and above all a knife in case she had to protect her honour and end her life. At the town she stayed in a choultry where an assortment of travellers and pilgrims was lodged. Her mind harped on a single word: 'Pandaripur'. She made constant enquiries of everyone she came across and set forth in that direction. After many false starts and retracing her steps, she got on the right track and joined travellers going on foot or by other modes of transport available, and reached Poona about a year later.

My grandmother's account had many gaps from this point onward. What Bala did after this, how she managed. What happened to her mother, where was her father all the while? What happened to Viswa's parents? Above all, why she went to Poona to search for her husband? What were the steps that led her steps to Poona? These were questions that never got an answer. My grandmother only snapped, 'Why do you ask me? Am I a wizard to see the past? If you interrupt me like this, I'll never be able to complete the story, I can only tell you what I have heard from my mother. I just listened without interrupting her as you do now. If you don't shut your mouth and keep only your ears open, I'll never tell you anything more. You can't expect me to know everything. If you want all sorts of useless information about the past I cannot help you. Not my business. Whenever my mother felt like it, she would gather us around and tell her story – so that we might realize how strong and bold she was at one time. She would boast. "You only see me as a cook at home feeding you and pampering your father's whims and moods, but at one time I could do other things which you, petted and spoilt children, could never even imagine . . . " she would remark from time to time.'

By the time Bala reached Poona she had exhausted all her gold and cash and was left with nothing. She felt terrified and lonely. People looked strangely different and spoke a language she did not understand. She reached a public rest house, a charity institution where *roti* was distributed, and held out her hand along with the others, swallowed whatever she got in order to survive. She made the rest house the central point and wandered about studying the faces of passers-by, hoping to spot Viswa. She feared that if he had grown a beard she would not be able to recognize him. All that she could remember was the head peeping over the wall, also the black patch under his left ear which he boasted would make him king – perhaps he was now the king of this town. She thought in her desperation of stopping some kindly soul to ask: 'Who is the king here?' But they might take her to be a madcap and stone her.

The bazaars were attractive and she passed her time looking at the display of goods. She was afraid to move about after dusk for fear of being mistaken for a loose woman soliciting custom. She returned to the rest house and stayed there. One day she was noticed by an elderly lady who asked in Marathi, 'Who are you? I see you here every day. Where are you from? What is the matter?' Of course Bala could not understand her language, but felt it was all sympathy from a stranger and was moved to tears.

The old woman took her hand and led her out of the rest house, to a home nearby where there was a family. Men, women and children, who kept gazing on her like a strange specimen, surrounded her and joked and laughed. To their questions, all that she could answer was to take her fingers to the *thali* around her neck. They understood she was a married woman. When they questioned her further, she burst involuntarily into tears and uncontrollably into Tamil. She made up in gesticulation whatever she felt to be lacking in her Tamil explanation. She said, 'My fate ... ' She etched with her forefinger on her brow: 'It's written here that I must struggle and suffer. How I have survived these months which I have lost count of, God alone knows. Here I have come, to this strange city and I have to behave like a deaf-mute, neither understanding what you say nor making myself understood.'

They listened to her lamentation sympathetically, without understanding a word, only realizing that it was a deeply-felt utterance. Someone in the crowd, recognizing the sound of the language, asked, 'Madarasi?'

'Must be so, she doesn't cover her head,' said another. Bala could guess the nature of the query and nodded affirmatively.

'I can take you to a man who came here many years ago. He may understand you.' He beckoned her to follow him. She indicated that she wanted a drink of water, feeling her throat parched and dry after her harangue.

A boy was deputed to guide her. She followed him blindly, not knowing or caring where she was going. The boy took her through the main street, past the bazaars and crowds, but proved too fast, running ahead. It was difficult to keep pace with him. She was panting with the effort. 'Where are you taking me?' she asked again and again, but

27

he only grinned and indicated some destination. Finally she found herself under an archway with a path leading to a big house. Leaving her there, the boy turned round and ran off before she could question him, perhaps feeling too shy to be seen with a woman.

She was puzzled, there was no one in sight. Beyond the archway and gate there was a garden. Presently a gardener appeared above a cluster of plants. He looked at her for a moment and stooped down again to resume his digging. Not knowing what to do next, she sat down on a sentry platform beside the arch, felt drowsy and shut her eyes. She woke up when she heard the sound of a horse trotting. She saw the rider pass under the arch and dismount in front of the house, helped by an attendant. He had thrown a brief glance at her in passing. He was dressed in breeches and embroidered vest and crowned with a turban – very much a man of these parts. Rather lean and of medium height. Could this be the man from the Tamil Land? Seemed unlikely. She did not know what should be her next step. She continued to sit there. A little later, she noticed him again coming out on his horse. She was all attention now, staring at him when he passed under the arch. She noticed his moustache curving up to his ears. He threw at her another brief glance and passed. She decided to sit through and wait indefinitely, hoping to find some identification mark next time. She invoked the god in their village temple and prayed: 'Guide me, Oh

28

Lord, I don't know what to do . . . ' A couple of hours later the horse and the rider appeared, and once again he threw at her the briefest glance and passed.

An attendant in livery approached her from the house. He asked, 'Who are you? Master has seen you sitting here. Go away, don't sit here. Otherwise he will be angry and call the Kotwal. Go away . . . ' She shook her head and sat immobile.

'Go away . . . ' He gestured her to go. He kept saying, 'Kotwal, Kotwal, he will come and take you to prison . . . ' She would not move. The servant looked intimidated by her manner and backed away. Ten minutes later he reappeared and asked her to follow him. She felt nervous, wondering what sort of a man she was going to encounter. The front steps seemed endless and she felt weak at the knees and crossed the threshold expecting the worst.

The man lounging in a couch watched her enter. She could not understand whether this was the beginning or the end of her troubles. She tried to study his face. There was not even a remote resemblance between the head she last saw over the wall and this man. He had no turban on and he was bald on top though his whiskers reached up to his earlobes. Gazing at his face she wondered what would happen if she made a dash for his whisker and lifted it to look for the black patch below his left ear: this might prove conclusive and the end of her quest. While

29

she toyed with the idea, he thundered in Marathi, 'Who are you? Why do you sit at my gate?'

She said, 'They said that you speak Tamil . . . ' Shaking his head, he took out his purse, held out some money and tried to wave her off. She refused the money. He summoned a servant to show her out. She sat down on the floor and refused to move.

'They said you are from the South. Keep me here. I have nowhere to go . . . I am an orphan. I will be your servant, cook for you and serve you. Only grant me a shelter.'

He gave an order to the servant, suddenly got up, went upstairs and shut himself in a room. She began to doubt her wisdom in depending upon the urchin who guided her. So far this man had shown no sign of understanding Tamil in which she was addressing him. He had no identifiable feature except the greenish colour of his eyes, something that did not alter with years. She felt it might be wiser to sneak away quietly.

The servant fetched two Kotwals who stood over her and commanded her to get up. She felt she was making a hideous mistake in accosting a stranger and they were likely to think she was a characterless blackmailer.

As the Kotwals were trying to move her physically, she screamed in Tamil, 'Don't touch me. I will reduce you to ashes . . . ' (Thodade unnai Posikiduven) She looked fierce and the Kotwals, though fiercer in a grotesque uniform and headgear, shrank back.

While this was going on a woman entered, nearing middle age and authoritative. She scowled at the men and cried, 'What are you doing? Leave her alone.' They tried to explain, but she dismissed them instantly. She helped Bala to rise to her feet, seated her in a chair and asked: 'Who are you? I heard you speak. Do you not understand our language?' Bala shook her head.

The other woman asked in Tamil: 'Who are you?'

At this point, Bala had the shrewdness to conceal her purpose and just said: 'I came with some pilgrims to fulfil a vow at Pandaripura, got stranded, separated from a group.' And spun a story, which fell on sympathetic ears. 'You are fortunate to live in a home like this, so comfortable and beautiful with its garden . . . ' said Bala.

'Yes, we love plants . . . ' She pointed upstairs. 'He is a keen gardener himself . . . When my father lived, he had no time left. All his hours he spent in his shop and came home late at night. After my husband joined us, my father got some relief . . . '

Bala refrained from asking any question for fear of betraying her purpose but allowed the other to ramble on, gathering much information. She was on the point of asking his name but checked herself as the woman referred to him only as 'He' or 'Bhatji'.

Suddenly she cried, 'Oh, how thoughtless of me to be sitting and talking like this without even asking if you are hungry . . . Come in with me.' She got up and led her to the kitchen. She lifted the lid of some vessels, bustled about, picked up a plate, set it on a little platform, put up a sitting plank and said, 'Sit down and eat. I have something still left. We are both poor eaters. He is so busy outside in the shop and visiting the palace, he seldom eats at home – only at night. I make something for myself. I don't like to spend too much time cooking. I also sit in the shop part of the day, especially when he has to go on his rounds. He is an expert in judging diamonds and all gems. His advice and appraisal is sought by everyone in this city. We have a large collection of precious stones, apart from getting our supply from the mines in this country, we also import – he has to go to Bombay sometimes when ships arrive at the port.'

She fed Bala, which revived her, since she had had nothing to eat after a couple of free *rotis* and a tumbler of water in the morning. She became loquacious and spirited. She washed the dishes at the backyard well and restored them to the kitchen shelf. The lady took her round the house and the garden. 'My father built this in those days when we could engage many servants who kept the house clean, but now we have only ten. He always rests upstairs. Shall we go up and see the rooms there?'

Bala said, 'Later, let us not disturb him now.'

'Come, I'll show you your room. You should stay with

us. Have you left your box in the rest house? Let us go and fetch it.'

Bala said, 'I came only with a small bag, but that was stolen on the way. Robbers set upon us and took away everything.'

'My first glimpse of Bhatji was when he came into our shop one morning, long ago,' said Surma. 'My father was concentrating, with his eye-glass stuck on one eye, on selecting diamonds for a party. I was minding something else, bent over a desk. He was standing at the entrance, how long I could not say. When I looked up he was there. There were people passing in and out of the shop, he was unnoticed. When the shop was clear of the crowd, he was still there at the doorway. I asked, "What do you want? Who are you?" There was something about his person that touched my heart. He was lanky and looked famished. My first impulse was to rush to his help in some way, but I held myself back – I was a young woman of eighteen years, he might be of my age . . . or a little more. Somehow I felt attracted to this lean boy with hair falling on his nape untended, covering his forehead and unshaven face. It must have been months and years since a barber came near him. "Father!" I called suddenly. "Here is a boy waiting since the morning." It was a propitious moment since father instead of losing his temper, as was his habit whenever anyone stepped into the shop without any business (he was suspicious of youngsters particularly), somehow took off the eye-glass, and asked mildly, "What do you want?" He answered promptly, "I want to work . . . " in Marathi and then gave an account of himself. How he had started from a southern village, travelled up and about, visiting other parts of the country, working his way . . . "How did you learn our language?" "I was in Bombay and learnt it."'

Father took to him kindly. He asked him to step in and questioned him in detail. Father enjoyed the narration of the boy's adventures in other cities and his descriptions fascinated him. That a village boy from far off south should have had the courage to go out as far as Delhi (which was beyond father's dreams) and survived seemed to my father a great achievement. He engaged him immediately as a handyman, gave him a room above our shop and arranged for his food and other comforts. Very soon he became my father's right-hand man, doing a variety of jobs in and out of the office and shop. He relieved father of a lot of strain and understood not only the nature of the trade but a lot about gems, their qualities and value. Father was impressed with the boy's intelligence and the ease with which he could be trained. Within six months he left a lot of responsibilities to him, trusting him absolutely. At the earliest opportunity my father set a barber on him and made him presentable with his head shaved in the front, leaving an elegant little tuft on his top. Later, after we married, I induced him to grow whiskers so that he might have a weighty appearance.

'My father did not approve of our proposal to marry at first. He threatened to throw him out not only from our shop but from this country itself and ordered me not to talk to him and confined me at home. I had a miserable time. We eloped to Nasik and married in the temple of Triambaka – a sort of marriage, quiet and private. Eventually, father reconciled himself to the situation. When he died the gem business and the house fell to my share.'

Surma constantly expressed her admiration and love for Viswanath: 'When I saw him first, he was so young and timid; now he manages our business and is often called to the court and high places for consultations and supply of gems.'

The story-writer asked at this point: 'Were they the only ones in that house?'

'Yes, must be so,' said my grandmother.

'What happened to the rest of the family – there must surely have been other members of the family!'

'Why do you ask me? How do I know?' said my grandmother. 'I can only tell the story as I heard it. I was not there as you know. This is about my father and mother, who were still apart though living under the same roof . . . '

I asked the next question, which bothered me as a

story-writer: 'Did Surma Bai have no children?'

'I don't care if she had or had not or where they were, how is it our concern?'

'But you say they were living together for fifteen years!'

'What a question! How can I answer it? You must ask them. Anyway it is none of our business. My mother mentioned Surma, and only Surma and not a word about anyone else. If you want me to go on with the story you must not interrupt me. I forget where I was, I am only telling you what I know!' She stopped her narration at this point and left in a huff and went off to supervise her daughters-in-law in the kitchen.

Bala's opportune moment came when Surma said one evening, 'I am joining some friends who perform Bhajans (group singing) at the Krishna temple on Fridays. I will come back after it is over. You won't mind being alone?'

'Not at all,' said Bala. 'I'll look after the house and take care of everything . . . '

'He is in his room, he may come down if he wants anything.'

'I'll take care of him, do not worry about him,' said Bala reassuringly and saw her off in her tonga at the gate. The moment the tonga was out of sight she ran back into the house, shutting the front door, ran upstairs and entered Viswa's room. He was reclining on a comfortable couch reading a book. She shut the door behind her softly. He did not look up. He pretended to be absorbed in the book. She stood silently before him for a few moments, and then said, 'What is the book that grips you so completely that you do not notice anyone entering your room?'

'What are you blabbering? Get out! You have no business to come up here!'

'Oh, stop that tone. Don't pretend. It's not good for you.'

'Are you threatening me? I'll call the guard and throw you out.'

'By all means. I know the guards. I am not what I was on the first day. I can speak to them myself. In fact I am closer to them than you. Call them and see what happens.'

'Oh!' Viswa groaned. 'Go away, don't bother me.'

She said, 'We must end this drama and how we are going to do it, I can't say now. But leave it at that . . . '

He pretended not to understand her language. But she said, 'Your whiskers do not hide your face. If you lift the left one slightly, as you did the other day while washing your face, the black is still there, which proved correct my guess and also what you said years ago, when you peeped over the wall, that it was lucky and would make you a king. You are lucky, rich and favoured at the court . . . I have waited long enough.' She fingered her *thali* and said, 'This can't lie. You knotted it in the presence of God.'

He protested again, 'No, no, I don't know what you are saying,' but she was hammering her point relentlessly.

Ultimately he was overwhelmed. 'Be patient for some more time. Be as you are, Surma is a rare creature. We must not upset her.'

'I will wait, but not forever . . . '

By the time Surma came back from the bhajan she found nothing unusual. Bala was at her post in the kitchen. Viswa was in the garden trimming a jasmine plant. Once again Viswa and Bala had resumed their aloofness. Bala was in no hurry. Now that she had established her stand, she just left him alone until the next bhajan day when Surma was away.

She said: 'This can't go on much longer. We must go back.'

'Go back where?'' he asked in consternation.

'To our village, of course,' she said calmly.

'Impossible!' he cried. 'After all these years! I can't. I can't give up my trade!'

'You may take your share and continue the business anywhere,' she said calmly. She knew his weak point now, she could exploit it fully. Any excitement or anger would spoil her plan. She was very clear in her mind about how she should carry out her scheme. She had worked out the details of the campaign with care, timing it in minute detail. He knew it was going to be useless to oppose her.

He pleaded, 'I'll tell her the truth and you may continue here as my wife, and not as a domestic.'

'I want to get back to our own place and live there. I have set a time limit; beyond that I won't stay, I'll go back.'

'Certainly, I will make any arrangement you want and send an escort to take you back home safely.'

'You will be the escort, I'll not go with anyone else.'

'Then stay here,' he said.

At this stage, they had to stop the discussion, since they heard Surma return home. He was nervous to be alone with Bala and was terrified of her tactics.

'I can't live without Surma,' he kept wailing.

'You will have to learn to live with your wife.'

'Surma is also my wife.'

'I know she is not. I know in this country it is not so easy. You have kept her, or rather she has kept you . . . '

He realized in due course that there was no escape. He said, 'Give me time. I'll see how we can manage it.'

'I've given you all the time . . . years and years. The trouble and the risk I have undergone to search you out, God alone is the witness! I am not going to allow it to go to waste. I am taking you back even if you kill me. I have set the date of our departure – not later than the next full moon.'

At their next meeting he said: 'I can't survive without Surma, she must also come with us. I don't know how to tell her.'

'Try to persuade her to stay back. We will have to

tell her the facts. After all you are going back to our legitimate home, to your real wife.'

'No, I can't. You don't know her nature. She will commit suicide . . . '

'I will commit suicide if you are not coming away. Which of us shall it be?'

He felt desperate and said, 'I can't live without her. Let her also come with us. We shall go away. Show some consideration to my feelings also.'

'Very well, if she won't agree to go with us?'

'Please don't drive me mad. Who asked you to come all the way and torment me like this?' At this point she lost her patience and left him.

Surma asked him later: 'You look rather tired and pale, shall I call the physician?' She lost no time in calling a physician who said, 'He is disturbed in mind. He must take medicine and rest. Something is troubling his mind.'

Surma became agitated: 'I have never seen him so sick at any time. What could it be! He was all right.' She put him to bed and stayed by his side, leaving all household work to Bala; Viswa tossed and groaned in bed. Bala carried food to his bedside upstairs. She made it unnecessary for Surma to come down except for her bath and food and pooja and then went up and sat by his side silently. The physician had given him some potion which acted as a sedative and put him to sleep.

Bala assumed an air of extreme gloom to match Surma's mood in sympathy. A week later she said, 'Bhatji looks better. You should not fall sick moping at home. We will leave a guard at his side and go out for a little fresh air. Let us visit the temple and offer pooja to Vitobha and stroll along the lake. You will feel refreshed.'

'No, I can't leave him alone.'

Four days later Bala repeated her suggestion, and added, 'Ask him, he may like you to go out for your own good. I am sure he will have as much concern for your welfare.'

Surma eventually agreed. Bala said, 'You must think of the shop too. You must not leave it to Guru's care completely.'

'Guru is a good man,' Surma said. 'He brings the accounts and reports every day, very dependable.'

'Even then,' Bala persisted. 'You must go there or Bhatji can go as soon as possible. It'll also refresh him . . . '

'True, he is worrying about the shop silently. I do not know what to do . . . I have never been in this predicament before . . . '

When Guru came the next evening, they went out in the tonga, leaving him in charge of Viswa. They visited the temple first and then on to the lake. Strolling round the lake, which reflected the setting sun, Bala cried, 'Oh, see how beautiful! See those birds diving in.'

'I wish I could enjoy the scene and the breeze but my mind is troubled. How I wish Bhatji were well. If he was his normal self, riding his horse, sitting in the shop with his diamonds and customers, I could sit here and watch the lake with a free mind.'

'He will benefit if he could travel and go for a change. We could leave for three or four months on a tour, the shop to be looked after by Guru and his son. That will make a new man of Bhatji.'

'Where can we go?'

'We may go south, so many temples we could visit – especially I have in mind Gunasekaram where prayer to that god is specific for the kind of depression afflicting Bhatji. There are special poojas and offerings to be made to the god called Vaitheeswaran, the cure is miraculous after a visit . . . '

'We can't, so far away and so long it'll take!'

Bala did not continue, but left the subject at that. But she repeated the suggestion whenever she found the chance. Surma thought it over and discussed the matter with Viswa and worked out the details and made preparations earnestly and settled for the journey after consulting their astrologer and physician.

'I remember,' said Ammani, 'my mother mention that they were carried in two palanquins and had a retinue of bearers who took over in relays at different stages, and many torch-bearers and lancemen to protect them from robbers and wild animals when they crossed jungles in the mountain ghats. Arrangements for the journey were made by Surma, and Viswa, having influence at the court, also got the Peshwa's support. I am sure the Peshwa sent word to his vassals and subordinates along the route to protect and help the party. On the day fixed, Bala and party began their journey and arrived about a month later in Bangalore and camped in the rest house on a tank bund. I think from the description I had it is the same tank known as the Sampangi today.'*

They camped for three days. All three were very happy: Bala, because she was on the way home, Viswa because they had succeeded in persuading Surma to undertake the tour, and Surma because Viswa already looked better and eagerly anticipated the visit to the temples – he did not wish to think of the future beyond.

On the fourth day they wound up the camp, packed up and were ready to start onward. Bala however had made up her mind differently. From the rest house one set of steps led up to the highway where the palanquins were waiting. All other members of the party, the bearers and guards, Surma and Viswa, went up the steps. Bala

*Actually, at present, it is the Nehru Stadium, the tank having been drained.

however lagged behind, suddenly turned right about and went down the steps leading to the water's edge. At first they did not notice her. When they reached the road Surma asked, while climbing into their palanquin, 'Where is Bala?'

Viswa said: 'She seems to be taking her own time. Let us start. We should reach the next stage before nightfall. She will follow.' The bearers lifted the palanquin containing Surma and Viswa. Viswa hesitated and said, 'Stop! I see that she is going down the steps. Why? Probably a last minute wash? She is stepping down into the water.'

Surma said: 'It looks strange to me ... Oh, God, she has stepped into the water ... Oh, stop!' she said in alarm when she heard Bala's scream:

'I'm drowning ... Viswa come for a moment!'

Viswa jumped off the palanquin and reached the water's edge. By that time Bala stood neck-deep in water. Viswa shrieked in alarm: 'What are you doing?'

She replied, with water lapping her chin, 'I am not coming with you.'

'Are you mad? Why this scene?' He made a move to go down and pull her up.

She said, 'If you take another step, I'll go down. Stay where you are and listen. No, don't come near, you can hear me where you are.'

'All right, I won't come forward. Don't stand in the water. Come up and speak.'

44

'I won't come up until you turn Surma back to Poona.'

Surma had meanwhile come down and was standing behind Viswa: 'What! What have I done to you that you should say this?'

'You have been like a goddess to me, but I can't go home with you. Our village will not accept you. I am Viswa's wife. You see this thali was knotted by him. He is my husband, I can't share him with you.'

Surma was shocked. 'We were such good friends! Let me also drown with you.'

At this Viswa held her back firmly. Bala said: 'Viswa, take her with you and leave me alone. I am already shivering and will die of cold if you don't make up your mind quickly whether you want me or Surma. Send her back honourably home. Let the palanquins be turned around with her if you want to save me.'

They pleaded, appealed, and shed tears but the palanquins and the entourage had to turn around and head for Poona before Bala would come out. She did not want any of Surma's entourage to stay back.

'Ammani,' I (this writer) said, 'I can't find any excuse for the way your mother manoeuvred to get rid of the other woman. Your mother was too deep and devious for the poor lady, who had shown so much trust in Bala whom she had sheltered and nourished when she was in desperate straits, not to mention the years she cared for and protected Viswa who had after all strayed his way to Poona and was literally a tramp at the start . . . '

'Don't talk ill of your ancestors. Not right. He was not a tramp but a respected merchant and official at the Peshwa's court,' Ammani retorted.

'He had only been a lowly clerk in her father's shop, remember . . . '

'What of it? Whatever it is, he rose high because of his mettle.'

'And mainly through Surma's support – he should have remembered it at the time he yielded to your mother's coercive tactics.'

'What else could a poor woman like her do to recover her husband? Only a woman can understand it. To a woman, her husband is everything. She can't lose him. Remember in what condition Bala had left home and what trials she must have gone through to reach Poona and how much misery she faced before she could reach him? Everything is justified, all means are justified in her case. Did not Savitri conquer Yama himself and trap him into promising her a boon? And the boon she asked for was to have children and he gave her his blessing that she would have children. After accepting the boon, she asked how it would be possible when he, as the god of Death was carrying away her husband's life, leaving his inert body in the forest, and then Yama had to yield back Satyavan's life. You could not imagine a greater woman than Savitri for austerity and purity of mind . . . '

'Still, I am unable to accept your mother's tactics – she could have adopted some other method . . . '

'Such as?' she said, suppressing her irritation.

'She could have revealed that she was his wife on the first day itself.'

'Surma would have bundled her off or got rid of her in some manner.'

'Would not Viswa have protected her?'

'No, he was completely under her spell at that time.'

'Was it necessary to drag the poor woman with false promises up to Bangalore? Could they not have managed it some other way?'

'Such as?' she asked again.

'I don't know. I'd have thought of more honourable ways . . . '

'You cannot manipulate people in real life as you do in a story,' she said.

As my remarks incensed her, she refused to continue her story and abruptly got up with the excuse, 'I have better things to do at this time than to talk to an argumentative fellow.'

For nearly a week she ignored me while I followed her about with my notebook. She ignored me until I pleaded, 'You must please complete the story. I want to hear it fully. You know why?'

'Why?'

'Otherwise I will be born a donkey in my next janma.'

'How do you know?'

'The other day I attended a Ramayana discourse. A man got up in the middle of the narrative and tried to go out of the assembly but the pundit interrupted himself to announce, "It's said in the Shastras that anyone who walks out in the middle of a discourse will be a donkey in his next birth", and the man who was preparing to leave plumped back in his seat when he heard it. And so please . . .'

'Tomorrow evening, I'm going to be busy today.'

Next evening after she had pottered around her garden and had her evening cold bath and said her prayers, she summoned me to the hall, took her seat on the swing, and continued her story.

At Bangalore the parting of ways was harrowing. Surma, always so assured, positive, and a leader, broke down and humbled herself to the extent of saying, 'Let me only go with you. I have surrendered Viswa to you, only let me be near you. I have loved you as a friend. I'll come with you and promise to return to Poona after visiting the temples. Please show me this consideration. I accept with all my heart that he is your husband, I'll never ever talk to him again or look at him even. But let me be with you . . . Viswa, talk to her please . . .'

Viswa turned to Bala and said, 'Let her come with us. She will visit the temples and go back. I promise.'

Bala stood thinking for a while and wept a little, then controlled herself and said firmly to Surma, 'No, it won't be possible, in our place we will be hounded out. I'll advise Viswa to go with you, anywhere, back to Poona or forward. Only leave me alone. You have got to choose.'

It was pathetic and humiliating with their retinue and palanquin-bearers watching the scene. Bala put her arms around Surma, rested her head on her shoulder and then, sobbing, bowed down and prostrated at her feet, got up and moved away from her towards the tank again, whereupon Surma cried desperately, 'Don't! Don't! I am leaving. May God bless you both.' She hurried up her retinue and got into her palanquin and left while Bala stood on the last step of the tank and watched: and Viswa stood dumbstruck, not knowing what to do. That was the last they saw of Surma. She was not heard of again: whether she went back home to Poona or ended her misery by walking into the next available tank on the way, no one knew.

Viswa would have frantically raced behind the palanquins, but for the check of Bala's silent stare. They stayed in the same rest house for three more days waiting for travellers going south. Meanwhile, Bala summoned a barber and persuaded Viswa to shave off his whiskers, saying, 'In our part of the country you will be taken for a ghoul and children will run away screaming at the sight of you.' She stood away from him after the shave and observed, 'Now I can recognize you better. The patch under the ear is intact. I am doubly assured now – the same features I knew, I used to see over the backyard wall, only filled up with age. Whatever made you hide such a fine face behind a wilderness of hair?'

'At the Peshwa's Court it was customary and considered necessary . . . '

At this point Ammani interrupted herself to warn me: 'Don't ask me how long they took to reach their village. All I can say is ultimately they did reach their village, the river was there and the temple stood as solid as ever, but the old priest whose remarks had driven Bala out of her home and to whom she vowed to prove that her husband was alive was not there. The temple had a new priest who did not remember the old families. All the same the very first thing Bala did was to enter the temple and stand before the god with her husband, praying for continued grace. She ordered an elaborate ritual of prayers and offerings and distributed food and fruits and cash to a large gathering of men, women, and children. Viswa had left the place thirty years, and Bala about twenty years, before. Most of the landmarks were gone, also the people.

Bala went back to her old house in Fourth Street and found some strangers living in it, who said, 'We bought this house from an old woman, who went to live her last days in Kasi after her husband's death. Their only daughter had run away from home and was not heard of again . . . '

Viswa searched for his old house but could not locate it. That neighbourhood had been demolished and Viswa could not find anyone to answer his questions, except a man grazing his cow, who just said, 'Ask someone else. I know nothing.' Viswa tried here and there, but could get no news of his parents or relatives. The village seemed to have been deserted by all the old families. Bala's main purpose to visit the temple and offer Pooja to Ranganatha accomplished, she saw no reason for staying in the village. They decided to move to a nearby town where Viswa could establish himself as a gem merchant and start a new life.

At this point I could not get my grandmother to specify which town it was. If I pried further, she only said, 'I was not born then, remember.'

'What was that town. Could it be Trichy?'

'Maybe,' she said.

'Or Kumbakonam?'

'Maybe,' she said again.

'Or Tanjore?'

'Why not?' she said mischievously.

'Or Nagapattinam?'

'I was not born. How could I know? I tell you again and again – but you question me as if I could see the past.'

'From your village, the nearby town must have been within fifty or a hundred miles.'

'You are again becoming argumentative.'

'Have you not heard your mother mention any special landmark like a river or a temple?'

'She only mentioned that the river Kaveri was flowing and that it was a place with several temples: she mentioned that every evening she could visit a temple, a different one each day of the week.'

'Let us take it as Kumbakonam. Where did your marriage take place?'

'On a hill temple, not far from where we lived.'

'It must be Swami Malai in Kumbakonam. Were you so ignorant as not to notice where you were being married?'

'I was eleven and followed my parents.'

'Extraordinary!' I said, which offended her and she threatened to stop her narration. But I pleaded with her to continue. I realized that she knew it was Kumbakonam but was only teasing me.

Viswanath established himself as a gem expert in Kumbakonam. He acquired a house not far from the river. He sat in a small room in the front portion of his house and kept his wares in a small bureau, four feet high, half glazed. (The heirloom is still with the family; when I was young I was given that little bureau for keeping my school books and odds and ends. I had inscribed in chalk on the narrow top panel of this bureau 'R.K. Narayanaswami B.A.B.L. Engine Driver'. My full name with all the honours I aspired to. I wonder if one can detect any trace of that announcement now. I have not seen the heirloom for many years.) Viswa's reputation spread as an expert appraiser of gems. People brought him diamonds for evaluation and to check for flaws. Through an eye-glass he examined the stone and gave his verdict before they were handed over to the goldsmith for setting.

Bala turned out to be a model wife in the orthodox sense, all trace of her adventurous spirit or independence completely suppressed. One could hardly connect her with the young woman who had tramped all alone across hundreds of miles in search of her husband and succeeded in bringing him back home – dominating, devious and aggressive till she had attained her object. Now she was docile and never spoke to her husband in the presence of other people. Her tone was gentle and subdued. It was a transformation. She wore an eighteen cubit length of silk saree in the orthodox style, instead of the twelve cubit cotton wrap favoured in Poona. She wore diamond ear rings and decked herself in a heavy gold necklace and bangles, applied turmeric on her cheeks, and a large vermilion mark on her forehead. She rose at five in the morning, walked to the river, bathed and washed her sarees, took them home for drying, filled a pitcher and carried it home, also drew several pails of water from the well in their backyard to fill a cauldron for domestic purposes. She circumambulated the sacred

Tulasi plant in the backyard and then sat down in the pooja room with lamps lit and chanted mantras.

By the time Viswa woke up at six she had lit the kitchen fire and prepared his morning porridge or any other thing he needed for breakfast. She cooked for him twice a day; he went out on his work and they had their vegetables from a woman who brought them to their door in a basket for selection. In the evening she went to the temples with offerings and oil for the lamps in the shrines.

Their first born came two years later – a daughter, and then another daughter, and another daughter – 'that is myself,' said my grandmother. The fourth was a son.

The next twenty years, roughly, were years of prosperity. Viswa's business flourished. In proper time, he found bridegrooms for his daughters and sent his son Swaminathan to study in Madras at the Medical College; he was in the first batch of Indians to qualify for the medical profession.

Viswa was past sixty when he found himself isolated. His daughters were married and gone. 'I was the youngest and last to leave home,' said Ammani. 'My husband, your grandfather, was a sub-magistrate and posted to work in different villages of our district, here, there and everywhere, until we came to rest in Madras after his retirement. We bought this house in which we find ourselves now, he also acquired a number of other houses in this street, and bungalows in the western area on Kelly's Road, agricultural lands somewhere, and a garden, and all his time was taken up in managing his estates.' (The garden, known as 'Walker Thottam', supplied vegetables to the wholesale market at Kotawal Chavadi in George Town in 'cart loads' according to Ammani.)

'You said he was started on less than fifty rupees. How did you manage to buy so many houses and lands?' I asked.

'We did not actually have to depend upon his pay . . . '

'Oh, I understand. I will not question you further.'

'Even if you asked, I wouldn't be able to explain how a magistrate earned – money just poured in I think. We had a brougham and horse, a coachman and so much of everything. My own family consisted of three daughters and two sons. The eldest daughter was married and died in Madurai and my family was reduced to four. Your mother was my second daughter . . .

'I always felt that the kind of wealth your grandfather amassed was illusory, because within six months of your grandfather's death, by a court decree all his property was lost through a foolish business venture of his in steel. His trusted partner declared insolvency and fled to Pondicherry and your grandfather's properties were attached and auctioned to make good a bank loan; something to do with the notorious Arbuthnot Bank crash. Even this house was nearly gone but for the help of a neighbour,

55

who loaned us five thousand rupees to redeem it at the last moment. Our creditors had already stuck notices of auction on our door, and by the beat of tom-toms and loud announcements were inviting bidders. Crowds gathered at our door. You were due to be delivered in a couple of weeks, but the bustle, crowd, and tom-tom beats, while we were cowering inside the house, were nerve-racking and affected your mother, who had come for her confinement and was in a delicate state of pregnancy; she became panic-stricken and got labour pains in that excitement. Your birth was rather premature. Only this house was saved of all your grandfather's property – thanks, as I mentioned, to the last minute help of our neighbour Mr Pillai who lived in Number Two, Vellala Street.'

(One morning, two years ago I had a desire to revisit Number One, Vellala Street in Puraswalkam, where all of us were born in one particular room. We habitually considered the house as the focal point of the entire family scattered in other districts, visiting it from time to time. My friend Ram (of *The Hindu*) was also curious to see the house and the environs as I described it in *My Days*. We drove down to Vellala Street in Purasawalkam, but found no trace of the old house. It was totally demolished, cleared and converted into a vacant plot on which the idea was to build an air-conditioned multi-storeyed hotel. Among the debris we found the old massive main-door lying, with 'One' still etched on it. Ram made an offer for it on the spot and immediately transported it to his house, where he has mounted it as a show-piece.)

To go back to the main theme. Changes were coming in Viswa's life. His son Dr Swaminathan was selected for the District Medical Officer's post at Kolar in Mysore State.

When Dr Swaminathan left for Kolar, Viswa and Bala lived as a couple as at the beginning of their life. They missed their children and found life dull. Viswa, now nearing seventy, worked less, finding it tedious to continue his gem business. He felt irritated when customers came for advice and discouraged them. Gradually he stopped all business although his little bureau had a stock of precious stones.

Bala had become rather tired and engaged a cook, a woman, who brought along with her a twelve-year-old daughter. Bala found their company diverting. The woman, who had been destitute, now felt she had found a home and worked hard, relieving Bala of a lot of drudgery. Gradually, Bala preferred to lounge in bed, hardly stirring out, leaving the management of the house to the woman and her daughter. Viswa too, stationed himself all day in an easy-chair on the veranda overlooking the street. Bala often implored him to go out and meet his cronies in the neighbourhood who used to gather in the temple corridor, sit around and chat after a darshan of the god.

But now he never went out, secretly worried about Bala's declining health. He sent for the Vaid, who came every other day, studied her pulse and prescribed a medicine, a concoction of rare herbs, he claimed. Viswa wrote a letter to his son expressing anxiety, but official work kept Swaminathan busy. He could come only four weeks later. When he found his mother's condition serious, he struggled hard to retrieve her but with all the medicines and needles in his bag, he could not save her.

'When the obsequies were over, my brother and sisters returned to their respective places. My husband was a magistrate in Tindivanam. I had two daughters at that time and we also left.'

Viswanath was persuaded to go to Kolar with his son. The house was practically locked up, with one or two rooms left open for the woman, with her daughter, to live there as a caretaker on a monthly salary.

Viswanath's life entered yet another phase: he had to live in Kolar with his son, whose family consisted of his wife and a daughter and a son, both under ten. At first Viswa had protested and resisted, but the doctor persuaded him to wind up his establishment in Kumbakonam.

At Kolar Doctor Swaminathan lived in a bungalow set in a spacious compound. He enjoyed an early-morning walk in the compound and then inspected the kitchen garden in the backyard, and from the veranda watched the birds and trees, watched his two grandchildren going off to a nearby mission school, and his son leaving for the hospital in the morning. He turned in at noon for his bath, and then said his prayers in the pooja room. His daughter-in-law, although reserved and formal, looked after his comforts and needs hour to hour. He had a room and he enjoyed his siesta after lunch. In spite of all the comfort and security he missed Bala and felt a vacuity at times. 'No one can take her place,' he often told himself. Sometimes he thought of Surma too but the intensity of feeling was gone, it was just a faded memory revived with effort, without any pangs of recollection. His son, the doctor, was a busy man having to attend the Government Hospital, as well as administer medical services in the whole district and he had to be away on 'circuits' frequently.

Viswa felt proud of his son, especially at the beginning when he brought his salary home and handed over the cash, about four hundred rupees, in a net bag. Viswa carried it in after counting the amount, and called his daughter-in-law, 'Lakshmi, come and take charge of this cash. Count it properly and spend it wisely. You must also build up savings. I want nothing of this. I have no use for this cash. I have my own. This is all yours, keep it safely.' This was a routine statement every month. He awaited the salary day month after month and the routine continued.

He was happy as long as it continued, but when the practice was gradually given up for practical reasons, and Swami began to hand his monthly salary directly to his wife, Viswa became resentful secretly, but tried to overcome it, hoping next time or the next time, Swami would resume the courtesy of recognizing his presence when he brought home the salary. This was probably a temporary aberration or an absent-minded lapse. He bore it for three months. At the end of it, he said to himself: 'I'll intercept him tomorrow evening when he comes with the salary, I will not leave the veranda until he arrives; test whether he'll hand me the bag or still give it to his wife.' Brooding over it he had magnified the situation and imparted an undue significance to it.

Next pay day Swaminathan did not come in the evening but at noon suddenly, and was in a great hurry. Swaminathan did not enter the house but called from outside, 'Lakshmi.' When she emerged from the kitchen, he held out the salary bag from the veranda. 'I can't come in now ... People are waiting. We are off to a nearby village where rat-falls are reported.' He rushed back to the medical team waiting at the gate in a horse carriage. They were to go out and investigate a possible outbreak of bubonic plague and inoculate the population.

Viswa, who had been gathering coriander leaves in the kitchen garden, came in with a sprig for seasoning the lunch items. Lakshmi presented to him the money bag.

'What is this?'

'Salary. He brought it now.'

Viswa glared at her, and asked, 'Why at this hour? Why did he not call me?'

'He was in a hurry, people waiting at the gate . . . '

'Oh!' he said. 'He is a big man, is he?' and ignored the bag, dropped the coriander on the floor, marched off to his room and bolted the door, came out at lunchtime, ate in grim silence, retired to his room again, sat on his bed and brooded: 'He is becoming really indifferent. This morning he left without a word to me. All of them are behaving callously. Children go out and come in as they please. They don't notice me at all. Lakshmi thinks her duty done after feeding me as she would feed a dog, without a word. The last three days Swami never spoke to me more than three sentences. They think I am an orphan depending on their favours. This is the curse of old age. I will teach them a lesson . . . '

He briskly made up a bundle of clothes, stuffed them in a small jute bag, wore his long grey shirt, seized his staff and started out. 'Lakshmi,' he called. She came out and was taken aback at the sight of him. He just said, 'I am off . . . ' as he had said to Bala over the wall before absconding years ago. That tendency seemed to be ingrained in his blood.

'Where?' she asked timidly.

'Never mind where – did your husband tell me where he was going? That is all.' He briskly got down the steps and was out, leaving the lady staring after him speechlessly. The children had gone out to school. He found his way to the railway station, waited for a train, got into it, changed trains and ultimately reached Kumbakonam and was back in his home in Salai Street, surprising the caretaker and her daughter.

My grandmother's actual words: 'That was a disastrous step he took. What mad rage drove him to that extent no one could say. The caretaker and her daughter were not the kind he should have associated with. They were evil-minded, coming from a nearby village notorious for its evil practices such as fostering family intrigue, creating mischief and practising black magic. When my father knocked, they were rather surprised but welcomed him with a great show of joy. They fussed over him. They consulted him on what he liked to eat, and cooked and fried things, and bought choice vegetables and fruits to feed him. Washed his feet whenever he came in after a short visit outside. They treated him like a prince, till he must have begun to think, "My son and wife treated me like a tramp and hanger-on, not a day did anyone ask what I liked. They always restricted my eating with the excuse, 'You should not eat this or that at your age.' My son thought that as a doctor, he was Brihaspathi himself! They denied me all delicacies, whereas this woman and her daughter know what I want . . . " '

The house was filled all the time with the smell of frying – chips, bondas, pakodas, and sweets. Viswa was a very contented man now. He had a sturdy constitution which withstood all the gluttony he was indulging in.

One fine day Ammani's family heard that he had married the caretaker's daughter in a quiet, simple ceremony conducted by the woman who managed to get a priest from her village. It was a culmination of his rage against his son. He could think of no better way to assert his independence. He was seventy-five and the girl was seventeen. He married her convinced that it would be the best way to shock and spite his family, all of whom seemed hostile to him.

Now the woman had him under her control. In course of time, she took further steps to consolidate her position. She began to suggest that they were no longer mere care-takers of the house, but his family, and that the young wife and her mother should be made the owners of the house through a deed of transfer. She found a pleader who prepared a document and presented it to Viswa for his signature. At this point, he still had some sense left. He hesitated and delayed while his mother-in-law kept up her pressure, through persuasion, bullying, and even starving him. He dodged the issue with some excuse or other, and began to wonder if he should not have continued in Kolar. He was losing his cheer, his second wife nagged him to sign the document. They had their eyes on his stock of precious stones, which he always kept with him although he did no business now; he also had enough cash left but took care to keep it with a banking friend, drawing just the amount he needed at a time. This irked his mother-in-law, who had aimed high, and now goaded her daughter to sulk and nag him at night. He dodged her by taking his bed-roll to the pyol on the excuse that he found the room too stuffy; thus evading his wife's pillow talk. He avoided her all through the day too, while the mother-in-law murmured asides and remarks. He was beginning to brood and plan a return to Kolar. The thought of his son was exhilarating and Kolar seemed a paradise and haven of peace.

The woman was shrewd and began to guess from his mood that he might slip away. She told her daughter, 'I have to go to our village on some important work and will be back tomorrow, keep a watch on your husband. Keep him in and shut the front door . . . '

At their village the woman consulted the local wiseacre, explaining the difficulties her son-in-law was creating. The wiseacre's income was through his claims to magic, black or white, the exorcising of spirits, and making potions, and amulets. He said, 'You must tell me frankly what you want. Don't hide anything.'

She explained that while she wanted her son-in-law to be friendly and amenable, he was becoming tough and hostile. She said tearfully, 'Out of compassion for the fellow in dotage, I agreed to give him my daughter so tender and young. But he is becoming indifferent and ill-treats her. You must help me.'

The wiseacre pretended to note down points and said, 'Come next week and bring two sovereigns . . . I'll have to acquire some ingredients and herbs, which will cost you something. I won't charge you for my service, that's my guru's command.'

The woman went home thinking, 'Only a week more . . . '

When she came back to the village a week later the wiseacre gave her a packet. 'There are two pills in it. Give them both to him with his food. They are tasteless and will dissolve and when the pills get into his system, he'll follow his wife like a lamb and treat you as his guru.'

The woman went back home gloating over the possibilities ahead, with the packet tucked in her saree at the waist. On the following Friday she prepared a special feast, explaining that this Friday was particularly sacred for some reason. She was secretive about the pills and did not mention it even to her daughter, but planned to get him to sign the document next day after the pill was completely assimilated in his system, with the document ready at hand. Viswa, a confirmed glutton these days, was pleased and seemed relaxed, bantered with his wife and mother-in-law in anticipation of the feast, saying, 'This indeed is a pleasant surprise for me. What a lot of trouble you take!' The fragrance of delicacies emanating from the kitchen was overpowering. When the time came for lunch, the woman spread two long banana leaves side by side saying that the couple must dine together today, and heaped the leaves with item after item – the high point of the feast being almond and milk payasam in a silver bowl for him and in a brass cup for his wife. Before serving it, the woman managed to dissolve the two pills in the silver bowl.

My grandmother concluded, 'That was the end. My husband was a sub-magistrate at Nagapattinam when we got information that Viswa's end had come suddenly. I have nothing more to add. Don't ask questions.'

(My (this writer's) mother, Ammani's second daughter, who was ninety-three at the time of her death, used to maintain that she had a hazy recollection of being carried on the arms of her mother at Kumbakonam and witnessing a lot of hustle and bustle following a funeral, people passing in and out of the house and some boxes being locked and sealed by the police and a motley crowd milling around.)

I asked my grandmother, 'What happened to that woman and your very young step-mother?'

'I don't know, I have no idea.'

'No inquest, no investigation, no questioning of that woman?'

'I don't know. We could not stay away from Nagapat-tinam too long since the collector, an Englishman, was coming for inspection and the magistrate was required to be present. We had to leave. My brother Dr Swaminathan came down from Kolar, and took charge of the situation and father's assets. I can't tell you anything more about it. All I know is what I could gather from my brother later. He spoke to our neighbours who mentioned to him the woman's schemes; the pleader had a lot to say about that woman's ambition and manoeuvres to grab the wealth and property. My brother could not stay on for long either, but before going back to Kolar he made some arrangement for the disposal of that house . . . that's all we know.'

Guru

Guru

All alone in a big house he became a prey to a jumble
of thoughts as he sat at the window overlooking Vinayak
Street. Reclining on his ancient canvas chair, he gazed
ahead at nothing in particular, an old Raintree on which
were assembled crows of the locality, passing clouds,
bullock carts, cyclists, and uninteresting passers-by. His
wife had left him months ago, his two daughters seemed
to have abandoned him too. His first daughter, Raji, the
best of the lot, was in Trichy and his second in Lawley
Extension only a couple of miles away but as far as he was
concerned she might be on Mars or the Moon, displaying
an indifference which was inhuman.

'I am past sixty and am orphaned though I slaved
all my life to bring up the family . . . I have no craving
for their company. Only I want them to realize that I do
not need anyone's help, strong enough still, thank God
to look after myself. That Pankaja Lodge man sends me
food in a brass container for four rupees a meal, enough
quantity for two and I save a portion for the night meal
too . . . if I feel hungry in between, a bun from the shops

across the street costs only ten paise. In all I do not have to spend more than one hundred and fifty rupees a month, whereas my wife used to demand one thousand for house-keeping! I am surviving much to their surprise, a tiny portion of the self-generating interest from my savings is more than enough to keep me alive. And then there is the rent from the shops in Grove Street. Assets built up laboriously, risking my reputation and job.

'My family never cared to understand. How I wish they were appreciative and grateful! God is my only ally. He will never forsake me, I need no one else. I get up at six in the morning, bathe and worship the images in the pooja room, read the *Ramayana* all afternoon. (I am not the sort to sleep in the afternoon.) I feel elated when I hold that ancient volume in my hand, the only treasure that could be named my ancestral property, which my brother claimed and gave up since I firmly told him that I would not tear out its pages in order to provide him a share; and in compensation he grabbed a copper bowl, a deer skin on which my father used to sit and meditate, and also a bamboo staff.

'I tell God, first thing in the day and again at night before sleep overcomes me, "Sir, You have been extremely considerate, whatever others might say, You have been gracious although my colleagues and the public includ-ing my family talk ill of me. You know they speak out of jealousy and malign me, but you are All-Knowing and no thought can be hidden from You. You are my friend in a friendless world."

'I have accepted only gifts and cash given out of good will by those whom I have served. Never demanded them. What one gives out of good will must be accepted with grace, say our Shastras, otherwise one will be hurting a good soul who wants to have the pleasure of giving.

'Apart from the *Ramayana*, I inherited from my father only commonsense and the courage to face life under all circumstances. Through Your divine grace I rose from the smallest job in the revenue department to the present position in the red building occupying the Tahsildar's seat.'

The Tahsildar's office was the focal point where peasants seeking various relief measures offered by the government and the government agencies met. Mr Gurumurthi was the 'agency'. Peasants had to come to him for a variety of favours and present their applications for fertilizers, pesticides, spare parts for tractors, and cash loans. All applications had to be rubber-stamped on his desk and initialled by him, and for each touch of his seal on any paper he had to be paid a certain sum of money, depending on the value of the request, discreetly isolated from the quantum meant for the Treasury.

The isolated amount was propelled into the left-side drawer of his desk, only then did the applicant's paper become animated. When he closed the office for the day, Gurumurthi scooped out the contents of the drawer with loving fingers, and transferred them to a specially tailored inner pocket of his shirt, next to his skin where it gently heaved with his heart-throb. He enjoyed the feel of the wad nestling close to his heart.

He often reflected with satisfaction, 'No pickpocket will have a chance. If everyone follows my method, pick-pocketism will be eliminated, and those rogues will have to turn to honest jobs . . . perhaps to agriculture, and come to me for favours, who knows?'

A questioning mind might ask at this point, 'Who is the real pickpocket?'

He was always the last to leave, after making sure there was no embarrassing presence lurking in any corner of the office except the old attender at the door wearing a red sash around his shoulder, displaying a badge announcing, 'Peon, Tahsildar's Office'. He was a discreet man who had watched a succession of Tahsildars in his career.

Gurumurthi's wife Saroja used to be a quiet-going, peace-loving sort, even-tempered and minding her business. But with years, she began to play the role of a better half, and became questioning, righteous, and argumentative. He noticed her transformation after the birth of their first daughter Raji, who proved to be the best of the lot, the only one in the family who was at peace with herself and with the world.

She married the boy from a family who did not demand a dowry and were satisfied with a simple, inexpensive wedding. His wife Saroja suspected that the boy suffered from some deformity, and that his parents were anxious to marry him off anyhow. It was all an exaggeration, of course (Gurumurthi avoided too close a scrutiny). They turned out to be the happiest couple known, begetting three children in four years – twins at first and a single one later. They kept themselves, which was the best part of it.

Occasionally, Raji came down with her children; somewhat trying times those were, since her children were noisy and restless. Gurumurthi was not fond of grandchildren. Fortunately, the maximum time Raji could spare was one week, her husband needing her constant attention. Gurumurthi always felt relieved when she proposed to leave. Not so his wife, thoughtless woman, who would press her to stay on, until he put his foot down and said, 'Leave her alone; after all Raji knows her responsibilities.' He organized her departure with zest. He engaged a jutka to take her to the railway station, making sure that the girl had sufficient funds to pay the fare. At the ticket counter he held out his hand to her for money. He was in acute suspense till he bundled her and the children into a compartment within the five minutes' halt of the six o'clock Fast Express towards Trichy, and heaved a sigh of relief when the engine whistled and pulled out.

He never permitted his wife to accompany them to the station, explaining, 'I want to walk back, but if you come we may have to hire a jutka.'

'Not at all necessary. I can also walk.'

'Don't be argumentative,' he sternly told her, and left her behind to watch Raji's departure from the doorstep. At the railway platform when the train moved he became emotional, ran along with it, shouting, 'Raji, take good care of yourself and the children, and convey my blessings to your husband.'

His second daughter Kamala was married two years later. The family priest who generally carried a sheaf of horoscopes of eligible brides and grooms in his circuit was a busybody who, when not performing poojas, proposed marriage alliances among his clientele. One afternoon he sat down beside Gurumurthi's easy-chair and asked, 'Have you heard of Dr Cheema of Lawley Extension?'

'Of course, who does not know him?' said Gurumurthi.

'His clinic is crowded all the time like a temple festival.'

'I know, I know,' said Gurumurthi. 'What about him?' It was a Sunday, and he relaxed all day in his easy-chair. The priest sat cross-legged on the floor as became an orthodox brahmin, who would not touch the leather covering on a sofa (though it might be only Rexine, resembling leather, who could be sure? He had two religious functions ahead and would have to take a bath if he touched leather and he avoided risk of pollution by sitting cross-legged on the floor, which also pleased his patrons who were wealthy).

The priest continued, 'His son is twenty-one years old, and is studying for an auditor's job . . . I don't know what degree he will get. Very bright boy, whenever I see him I think of our Kamala, just a perfect match. I always keep in hand our Kamala's horoscope, I compared it with that boy's, just out of curiosity. The horoscopes match perfectly – perfectly means, I do not know how to say it – like – like,' he quoted a sanskrit verse from the *Vedas* which said, 'No power on earth or heaven could keep apart a couple whose stars are destined to merge.' He concluded by asking, 'May I show them our Kamala's horoscope?'

The priest's instinct turned out to be sound, as there never was a happier couple in the world. Only the alliance proved acrimonious, and continued long after Kamala had left her parents' home and was happily settled in Lawley Extension with her husband. The doctor realized when the wedding ceremonies were over that Gurumurthi was unreliable. The doctor had agreed to a simple, unostentatious wedding, as suggested by Guru. 'Let us perform the ceremony at the hill temple and hold a reception in Malgudi. I don't believe in wasting money just for a show and in feeding a crowd. We could save that money and endow it as a fund for the young couple, so that they may have a good start in life.' The doctor appreciated the idea, since his son planned to go to America for higher studies and could utilize the fund thus saved. The priest was a go-between for the negotiations. Gurumurthi kept his wife and daughter out of ear-shot when discussing financial matters with the priest. He told them from time to time, 'Leave it to men to talk about these matters. Women should not interfere but mind their business.'

After the wedding the doctor kept reminding him of his promise to give fifty thousand rupees saved from the wedding expenses. Gurumurthi prided himself secretly on managing to marry off both his daughters, without eroding his bank balance. Gurumurthi had simplified Kamala's marriage to such an extent that even Raji was not invited properly, and he spurned the idea whenever his wife reminded him to send them a formal announcement.

'All right, all right,' he said, brushing her off. 'Leave it to me. I know when to write.' And he reflected, 'Why should Raji be bothered to come with her crippled husband and the restless children, travelling all the way. Our outlook must change – a revolutionary change is needed in our society. Inviting a motley crowd for every wedding is senseless, I wonder whoever started this irrational practice?'

The doctor kept reminding him of the money due to his son, who was preparing to leave for America. Gurumurthi had perfected the art of dodging. He kept explaining that the delay was due to certain government bonds, which would mature soon. Gurumurthi had also promised the bridegroom two suits fit for American wear, for which, he explained, he had ordered imported material from a firm in Madras, and as soon as it was received the young man could go straight to his tailor and get himself measured out. He added, 'I know an excellent tailor who stitched suits for European planters settled in Mempi estates. His father also was a tailor to the British Governors.' The proposal was gradually allowed to fade away.

Next, for the Deepavali festival, Guru had promised a solitaire diamond ring for his son-in-law. After waiting for three months, the doctor himself arrived one afternoon to remind him. Guru received him with a lot of fuss, summoned his wife and daughter to come out and do him obeisance. Kamala was counting the days before she could join her husband. Her father was putting it off on the plea that they were passing through an inauspicious part of the year. But his real motive was to avoid the expenses of an orthodox nuptial ceremony. Guru felt that our whole civilization was rotten and involved wasteful expenditure at every turn. There was no one to whom he could confide his thoughts. His wife was too narrow-minded and conventional and would not understand his philosophy of life. Best thing was to drift along without taking any decision; the inauspicious months giving him a sort of reprieve. The young couple met now and then and went out together; he was not so narrow-minded as to object to it – after all they were husband and wife. Once again it was his wife who displayed narrow prejudices – what would people say if a couple before the consummation ceremony met and roamed about? That was her upbringing, she was free to think as she liked, but he did not mind it, even hoped secretly that they would settle it between themselves and live happily ever after.

When the doctor on his present visit, after accepting all the snacks, broached the subject of the diamond ring, Guru hummed and hawed, 'Eh, ring, ring, of course,' he repeated reflectively. 'That goldsmith is very, very slippery. What shall I do? Impossible man? Every day I go there and shout at him. But what's the use? He promised and swore by all the gods and his ancestors that he would give the ring before Deepavali. But you see . . . '

'Shall we both go and tackle him? He seems to be a crook. Why not tell the police? I know the superintendent,' said the doctor.

'Yes, yes, of course, but only as a last resort. He has been our jeweller for generations . . . '

The doctor got up and left. The lady of the house, who had been watching the scene from a corner came out like a fury. 'You are bringing shame on us. Is there no limit?'

'What limit?' Guru asked aggressively. 'He is avaricious, thinks diamond rings grow on trees . . . '

At this point Kamala came out, her eyes swollen with tears.

'Father, why did you promise it then?' she asked.

'Oh! Oh! You too! You should not be overhearing your elders talk.'

'I am not a baby,' she said. 'You should keep your promise, it is awkward for me. I can't face them if you dodge like this.'

'Oh, you have become their lawyer!' he said, laughing cynically. 'I did not expect you to talk to me like this. You are more interested in those people – your father-in-law earns thousands every day. Why can't he buy a diamond ring for his son, if he cares so much for him?'

'My husband does not care for diamonds or anything.'

'In that case why bother me? You will mind your business. Leave these matters to my judgement. Don't imitate your mother's manner. I'll see that you don't feel any embarrassment later. Be grateful I found you a husband – '

Her mother said, 'It's no use talking to him,' turned round and tried to take her daughter away.

But the girl stood firmly and persisted in saying, 'He doesn't care for diamonds or any ring, it's *you* that offered and promised.'

'Well, that's all an old story, such promises are a formality between in-laws during any Deepavali. One should not take such talk literally.'

Kamala could find no words to express her indignation, but burst into tears, and withdrew. Her mother came out again like a fury and shouted at Guru. He felt enraged and shouted back. 'It's impossible to live in this house! Everyone heckles me.' He briskly got up, put on his sandals, and walked out. He reached the corner of Vinayak Street, where he saw Rao the stamp-vendor standing at his door. 'These are bad days,' said Guru. The other readily agreed with him and added, 'What, with the prices going up, do you notice the price of brinjals? Impossible to buy vegetables, and such extravagant public expenditure by the Government everywhere with no sort of consideration for the public.'

'Even in private life so much extravagance we see, our women are old-fashioned and still continue old practices and ceremonials and presents, with Deepavali growing into a sort of trade – what with crackers, and fireworks, silks, and diamonds! Such a waste! The only solution is education. Our women must be educated,' said Guru.

'When they get educated they become arrogant,' said the other man. 'Do you know how my brother's wife talks to him, because she is a B.A.? We are passing through hopeless days, on the whole. Even without a B.A. my wife insists on this and that and must have her own way in everything.'

'It is bound to get worse if we don't do something about it.'

'True, true,' said the stamp-vendor, feeling satisfied that he had sounded agreeable to a Tahsildar, and did not contradict him in any manner. A Tahsildar exercised his authority in several directions, and it was safer to be on agreeable terms with him. His seal on an application was indispensable especially to a stamp-vendor whose livelihood depended on vending all denominations of special paper for legal documents.

When Guru reached home he found the street door ajar with no one in sight. He stood at the doorway and shouted 'What is the matter? Where is everybody hiding and why?'

His wife screamed back from an unseen corner, 'Why do you get into the habit of shouting? No one is playing hide and seek here.'

'Oh, you aren't? I am glad to hear that. Where is Kamala?'

'She was writing a letter, must have gone out to post it.'

'Letters. Oh, letters! To whom?'

'She doesn't have to declare it to anyone.'

'Oh, is that so? It was a mistake to have sent her to a college. Women become educated and arrogant.'

His wife shouted back from her room, 'What has come over you today?'

'That's what I want to ask you all. I made a mistake in staying away from the office today. You people don't seem to appreciate my company at home ... I will go back to my work.'

'Yes, do so. It's profitless to be away from your office table, I suppose!' she said emerging from her room.

'But for my drudgery, you would not live in a house like this, or have those bangles and necklace . . . '

'Why this kind of talk?'

'Something has gone wrong, you have lost all sense of humour, you take everything literally and seriously like our Kamala's doctor-father-in-law, I only wanted to remind you that you came with a battered tin trunk . . . as a new bride, even the railway porter did not demand more than four annas to carry it on his head.'

'And what did you bargain him down to actually?' she asked.

He laughed and said, 'You have still got your sense of humour – I was wrong in saying that you had lost it. The trunk did not weigh much, I am sure, otherwise the porter would have demanded one rupee.'

'The box had in it forty sovereigns only, which my father gave me, these bangles and a chain also . . . they don't weigh much inside a trunk. After that there was no addition in my box or on my person.'

'What happened to the sovereigns?'

'Don't you remember that the two daughters are married but they could not be presented bare-necked and without bangles on their wrists at their wedding, and had to be provided with a minimum of jewellery.'

'Why didn't you tell me?'

She spurned to answer his question and left his company. He kept looking in her direction and reflected, 'Impossible to carry on any useful talk with women, always ready to squander and argue about it. Forty sovereigns to be squandered on tinsel to impress in-laws! After all, her father chose to give her a mere pittance but did not have the courtesy to tell me! What do I care what that battered tin box contained, so long ago? That box itself, where is it? Lost with all the junk when we moved here.'

It was a provocative subject, revived whenever the lady wanted to score a point. 'You have managed to bring along all your old things, particularly that unsightly, uncomfortable sofa in which no one could sit in peace,' she would say.

'I did not bring it in, knowing what you would say,' Guru replied.

'Not a word could I ever say about your treasures, although I wanted to keep my trunk and repair it – that would have made it new – '

'It was too battered, broken, rusty, discoloured in patches, had only a single handle on the side, the other came off when the porter touched it. No wonder your father chose to put his forty sovereigns in it. He knew no one would be tempted to touch that tin trunk.'

'Not worse than the sofa, your heirloom which you chose to bring all the way though it'd have saved money to break its legs and use them for heating water for a bath.'

Guru explained, 'I brought it along with other goods in that bullock-cart – I didn't have to pay extra money for it. With a little polish and a pat here and there, it will fetch at least two hundred rupees.'

'Then why don't you sell it?'

'Why does it bother you? After all, I have dumped it in the cowshed – '

'Cowshed! When are we buying the cow for the shed? If it comes, the sofa will be in the next lane, I suppose, for any vagrant looking for trash or firewood.'

'Aren't you terrified of the milk price today?' he asked, changing the subject.

'No need to worry about it, as you have successfully abolished coffee at home,' she said.

'The smell of coffee is nauseating,' he said.

'But I love coffee, I find it hard to do without it.'

'No use thinking of it, you must have got used to being without it by now. It is not indispensable. I have brought up our daughters without coffee, they never had a craving for it. Two meals with good rice and vegetables will be sufficient to make one a giant.'

'Our daughters have left this house because they didn't want to grow into giants under your care . . . '

'Why do you say *daughters*? Only Raji is gone, and in Trichy.'

'Have you not noticed that Kamala who went out to

post a letter has not returned, even after three hours? She won't come back. I promise it. She does not want to talk to you again.'

'It's a conspiracy.' He looked angry and upset. 'When will she come back? Where is she?'

'She packed up her clothes and left for Lawley Extension in a jutka.'

'I should not have left you both alone to hatch this plot.'

'Don't call it a plot, she has only joined her husband. Thank God he loves her and could persuade his father not to bother about the gifts you promised.'

'What about the formal nuptial ceremony?'

'They will manage it without public fuss, between themselves.'

Guru let out a hearty laugh. 'Very clever, without a paisa expense – '

'You know my father spent ten thousand rupees for our nuptials at our village, inviting a hundred guests for a three day nuptial celebration. You welcomed it then.'

'I was young and let my elders decide things.'

'Also because the money they squandered was not yours.'

He was in his seat transacting business as usual, with a crowd of villagers waiting for his favours. His badge-wearing door-keeper who usually stood outside came in excitedly and whispered, 'Collector is coming.' Before he could complete his sentence the collector, the chief officer of the district, walked in, and Gurumurthi rose to his feet deferentially.

The peon tried to disperse the crowd of applicants, but the collector said, 'Leave them alone.' He said: 'Sit down' to the Tahsildar, who, however, kept standing since the collector himself did not sit but moved around inspecting the office, its furniture, and the load of files in a shelf at the back of the Tahsildar. He asked, 'Those are applications in front of you?'

'Yes, sir.'

'Give me those papers.'

With trepidation the Tahsildar handed over the papers. The collector flicked through them still standing.

'Please take your seat, sir,' Gurumurthi said offering his seat.

The collector went over and occupied the seat, spread out the papers on the table, and scrutinised them. 'Why have you kept them pending so long?'

'Some details are awaited – some of the applications are incomplete.'

The collector picked up a couple of applications, studied them, and asked, 'Who are these applicants?' Before the Tahsildar could find an answer, two men from the group came forward.

'They are our applications, your honour.'

'When did you present them at this office?'

'Four months ago, sir.'

'Why have you not sanctioned those loans yet?'

'They are not able to produce their birth certificates, sir.'

The collector asked them, 'Why have you failed to produce the certificates?'

'Our village Karnam is dead and the new man . . . '

The collector turned to Gurumurthi and said, 'Very unsatisfactory. You could have taken their sworn statements and attested them.'

'We have been coming here, your honour, every day – walking from our village, leaving our work – '

The collector summoned Gurumurthi to his office next day and said, 'You may go on leave from tomorrow.'

'May I know the reason, sir?'

'Not one reason, but several. I get reports and know what's going on.'

'Oh, sir, there are gossip-mongers and tale-bearers all around.'

'Farmers come all the way to seek help and relief promised to them, and you delay and play with them some game.'

'I am doing my best, sir, but they won't follow the procedure.'

'I know what you are trying to say – excuses you are inventing. I don't want all that – I know what's going on in your office. You are a senior official – I don't want to be too hard on you. I could take disciplinary steps, but

I'm giving you the choice of taking all the leave at your credit and seeking voluntary retirement at the end of it. If you don't want this choice, I'll have to recommend to the government an enquiry and further steps.'

Gurumurthi was shaken at first, but survival seemed more important. He remembered a saying, 'If the head is threatened, let the headgear be blown off.' An enquiry would ruin him; they could withhold his pension and confiscate his property. Gurumurthi acted also as a money-lender on the side, made possible by his delaying tactics when the villagers approached him for interest-free loans offered by the government.

He got over the initial shock in the course of time and adjusted himself to a retired life. He assured his wife, 'We have enough to live on. Our daughters are married, and we have this house, the rents from those shops and my pension. What do I care? That young man, the collector, seems to be an upstart, I don't care. Everyone says he has been doing this sort of mischief in every district. He demanded certain explanations, but I firmly told him that I don't care to explain and am prepared to go. I demanded all the leave at my credit and then retirement. I told him that I have drudged for this ungrateful government long enough.'

'What caste is he?' Saroja asked.

'I don't know. Whatever it may be, he is an upstart

out to eliminate all the seniors in the service. When he found I was tough, he came down a step or two and tried to coax and cajole me to stay, but I was firm, made him understand that they do not deserve a conscientious hard-working man but only a hollow, showy scoundrel who would cringe for their favours.'

'But it was rumoured that you were not helpful to the villagers and so the collector – '

He cut her short. 'Nonsense, don't listen to gossip-mongers. You would not be living in this style if I didn't work hard. After all your father was only a school master!'

'And yet you demanded a dowry from him!'

'Why do you bother about it now, so long ago! If he hadn't found the resources for a modest dowry, he'd have got a bankrupt son-in-law, not one who could support a family.'

He organised his retired life satisfactorily. He left home every morning, went out and spent his time in the free reading room at the corner, a little den with newspapers old and new, piled on a small table at the centre, and a shelf full of odd volumes discarded in the neighbourhood. Some evenings he went and sat on a bench at the Jubilee Park, where pensioners like him were gathered, and Rao the stamp-vendor would of course be there. They discussed the state of the nation and the problems of each other's health. From time to time he visited his banker on Market Road to watch the savings burgeoning with monthly interest. Such moments away from home seemed to him beneficial as he could avoid his argumentative wife. Morning hours were her worst time according to him, as she seemed too tense. After lunch she mellowed, at about seven o'clock in the evening she visited the temple. When she was away he relaxed in his canvas chair and got absorbed in some odd volume picked up at the free reading room. After dinner was a tranquil and peaceful time unless she opened her gambit with, 'I met so and so in the temple, do you know what she remarked?'

'You women seem to have no better business than gossiping.' It would start thus and then go on until both got tired and sleepy.

Time passed. One day Gurumurthi brought out a proposition, which sounded light at first but proved portentous. He had hesitated till he found his wife in a receptive mood, and then brought out the proposition.

'Saroja, we must have a son.'

She was taken aback. 'What! At our age?' she exclaimed, and was amused.

He explained, 'Not that way. We can adopt.' She still treated it as a joke. Sitting on the pyol after dinner and enjoying the night breeze and listening to the rustle of leaves of the rain-tree, they were in a pleasant mood.

She asked, 'Adopt? How? What do you mean?'

He elaborated. 'We are old, our daughters live their own lives away from us – '

'Why not?'

He fumbled on, 'We are aged . . . '

'Nothing surprising. No one grows younger in this world – ' At this point she heard the rattle of vessels in the kitchen and dashed away, muttering, 'It's that cat again . . . '

He reflected, 'I don't know how to talk to her. She either laughs or gets angry and argues.'

Next day he was determined to get it out of his system. He called suddenly, 'Saroja, come here. I am serious about this.' She was cleaning a corner of the hall with a broom and mop. He was sitting, as usual, in his canvas chair beside the window.

'I want to explain something.' She dropped her broom and stood beside him. 'Now listen – as we grow old, we need a son to look after us.'

'Why this sudden decision? Are you serious?'

'I've told you I am serious. I can do many things without waiting for your opinion but now – '

'Yes, that's how I have lived. Even daughters' marriages, you never waited for my opinion, you were the one who made all the decisions. Women must not listen when you talk to the priest about financial matters. You are convinced that I don't know how to count cash over two rupees, I don't even know if you are rich or poor.'

Gurumurthi realized that he had started her off on a different track inadvertently. 'You are the Supreme Lord and I
am only a dependant not worth talking to,' she concluded.

He realized that he had no chance to broach the
subject which was obsessing his mind. Though normally
he was the master of any situation, today he felt somewhat
puzzled, yet decided to bully her to listen to him, the only
way to get along in family affairs as he had known all his
life.

He said firmly, 'I want to adopt a son, and that
is all there is to it.'

She took a little time to understand the implications,
stood silently awhile, and asked, 'What do you expect
me to say?'

'Show some interest, that's all.' She turned round
and went back to her corner. He felt infuriated, got
up, followed her, caught her by the shoulder, turned
her round to face him, looked into her eyes, and repeated
firmly: 'You must hear me fully.'

Tears flowed down her cheeks as she shook herself
free. 'Do what you like, why should you bother me?'

'Adoption means by both parents – you have a part in
the ceremony. Otherwise I do not have to ask you. You
don't even ask who is the son?'

'I have said do what you please.'

'Should you not know who is going to be the son?
I'll tell you though, since it's my duty, even if you are

indifferent. My brother Sambu's third son. He is ready to give him to us.'

She said, 'You mean Ragu! He is a monkey – I won't live in this house, if you bring him here!'

Gurumurthi shouted, 'You are challenging me?' and went back to his chair, fretting. 'She thinks she can order me about because I am gentle and considerate. I won't allow this sort of thing anymore and must put her in her place. I have refrained from mentioning why a son is needed to save her feelings, but I'll tell her even if it upsets her, I don't care.'

He got up resolutely, went up to her and shouted, 'You know why? When I die, I want a son to light the funeral pyre and perform the rites, otherwise . . . '

'Otherwise what?' she asked. He glared at her speechlessly. She continued, 'Life or death is not anyone's choice, we can't know.'

He laughed ironically, 'Oh, you are becoming a philosopher too, hm! You are listening too much to discourses in the evenings. Hereafter you had better stay away from those discourses at the temple . . . '

'You had better stay away from the stamp-vendor at the corner house. Ever since you retired from service you have nothing better to do than listen to his advice and gossip at the reading room.'

'Why do you talk ill of him! Shut up and don't talk of people you do not know!'

Now that she had got over the initial shock, she got into a taunting mood, and added, 'Did that stamp-vendor not mention also that if a son is not available your grandchildren can perform the rites? Anyway, why do you cultivate these unhappy thoughts?'

Gurumurthi pursued his plan methodically. He called his family priest and consulted him in whispers, while his wife ignored them and all their activity and minded her business. He wrote to his brother in Dindigul, a closely-written postcard every day and awaited the arrival of the postman morning and evening, and kept talking about the arrangements as the date approached. What made him uneasy was that he was expected to buy new clothes for his brother and his wife and for himself and his wife too. He felt he could save on this item, as he had preserved the clothes presented to him and Saroja at festivals or other occasions by village applicants seeking his goodwill.

Saroja warned him, 'They have been in storage for years and may have a musty smell.'

He said, 'Don't create problems, please put them out for airing. I'll get some naphthalene balls also . . . I don't mind the expense.'

'You get a dozen for half a rupee,' she said puckishly.

'You seem to know everything,' he remarked.

The priest had explained, 'Adoption is a very sacred

matter, holier than all other activities. You must realize the sanctity of it. All gods and planetary deities must be satisfied with offerings in Homa through Agni the God of Fire. You will be acquiring a new entity, body and soul, and assume the responsibilities for his welfare. Your brother has five sons and it will be no loss to him to give one away; at the same time you will also gain merit by adopting a son. He must solemnly vow before the fire that he will be your dutiful son all his life and perform all the necessary rites when you join your revered ancestors.'

Gurumurthi had also heard on the park bench a general statement from a member, 'When you bring up a minor son in your custody, you can also demand a rebate on your tax.'

With the arrival of Ragu, a lanky youth of twelve, Saroja made her exit, having remained monosyllabic and silent all through. She had performed her duties mechanically, just obeying the directions of the priest who had told her to sit beside her husband and join him in offering oblations in the holy fire. She prostrated at her husband's feet when directed, clasped his hand, received Ragu with open arms formally when told to, seated him on her lap and fed him with a piece of banana, sugar, honey and milk, sniffed his forehead, and touched it with sandal paste.

The smoke from the holy firehouse permeated every corner of the house, the smell of burnt faggots lingered in the air, irritating their eyes long after the ceremony, which ended at midday. The priest and four brahmins departed at three in the afternoon. After they left Gurumurthi rested in his easy-chair and fell asleep. Ragu sat on the pyol and watched the street. He would have loved to go out and wander about but his 'father' had warned him not to go out alone, and so he sat there moping. His own parents had left soon after the ceremony.

When everybody was gone Saroja came out of her room carrying a small jute bag and a roll of bedding. A jutka stood at the door. She stepped out softly, after hesitating for a minute in front of her husband, unable to decide whether to wake him or not. She felt it would be unnecessary to take leave of him. She had already told him she was leaving after the adoption ceremony, explaining that she was going back to her village in Karur in order to take care of her old mother who was lonely and helpless after her husband's death two years before.

Ragu lived as the son of the house for four days, greatly puzzled by his new life. He had never thought he would have to live permanently in the company of his uncle, who insisted upon being addressed as 'father'. The boy felt uneasy in his grim company, and found it difficult to laugh at his jokes, listen to his observations, suggestions, obvious advices and moralizing, and above all his awkward story-telling. Gurumurthi depended on Pankaja Lodge for his sustenance, but the boy did not find that food adequate or acceptable. His 'father' watched him all the time, he was never allowed to go out except in Gurumurthi's company, to sit on the park bench and listen to his cronies. The boy stood it for four days, secretly longing for his companions playing cricket in Dindigul streets, and one afternoon slipped away while his 'father' was asleep.

Gurumurthi searched for the boy here and there and spent sleepless nights until a postcard arrived from Dindigul to say that the boy was back there and would soon join him after obtaining his school leaving certificate. Obviously it was never obtained. The boy kept away, and his father did not write to Gurumurthi again. Gurumurthi wrote once or twice, never got a reply, and decided not to waste money on postage anymore.

He reflected, 'After all, it is all for the best, why should I keep that boy here? What for? Difficult to understand him. It has cost me less than seven hundred rupees and a hundred and fifty in rail fare for the parents to come for the ceremony and fifty rupees for feeding the priests; after all it made only a slight dent in my bank balance, that's all. And my brother's demand for a "loan" of five thousand rupees, which I promised to consider though fully aware that it was a veiled price tag on the boy, need not be given now, that would have been another extravagance if that boy had stayed on. Also, the boy was too demanding, always wanting something to eat, frowning at Pankaja Lodge food. He was a glutton who could not be satisfied with a simple nutritious meal.' It was also a strain to keep him amused or entertained, the fellow sticking to him all the time. Raji and Kamala as children were never like this fellow, they left him alone unless called to his side. Good riddance on the whole. He felt complacent, except when he was told by the stamp-vendor, 'The boy is only twelve, but when he attains majority he may legally demand a partition and a share of your property, especially if he should come over and perform the funeral rites when you die.'

Gurumurthi felt uneasy at this prospect but comforted his mind with the proviso, '*Only if* he performs my funeral ceremony, but why should I tell him or anyone of my death?'

Salt and
Sawdust

Salt and
Sawdust

Being a childless couple Veena and Swami found their one-and-a-half-room tenement adequate. A small window opened on to Grove Street, a pyol beside the street door served for a sit-out, there was a kitchen to match and a backyard with access to a common well. The genius who designed this type of dwelling was Coomar of Boeing Silk Centre, who had bought up an entire row of old houses adjoining his Silk Centre, demolished them, and rebuilt them to house his staff working in the weaving factory beyond the river. It proved a sound investment and also enabled Coomar to keep his men under his thumb.

Swami left (on his bicycle) for his factory at seven-thirty a.m., but got up at five, while his wife was still asleep. He drew water from the common well, lit the stove and prepared coffee and lunch for two, packing up a portion to carry. Veena got up late, gulped down the coffee kept on the stove, swept the floor and cleaned the vessels. After her bath she lit an oil lamp before the image of a god in a niche.

After lunch, she sat on the pyol, watched the street

with a magazine in hand, and brooded over a novel she was planning to write, still nebulous. She felt she could start writing only when she got a proper notebook, which Swami had promised to bring this evening.

While returning home Swami stopped by Bari's Stationery Mart on Market Road, and announced, 'My wife is going to write a novel. Can you give me a good notebook?'

'How many pages?' Bari asked mechanically.

Swami had no idea. He did not want to risk a conjecture. 'Please wait. I'll find out and come back,' he said and tried to leave.

Bari held him back. 'I know what you want. We are supplying notebooks to novelists all the time. Take this home.' He pressed into his hand a brown packet. 'Two hundred pages Hamilton Bond, five rupees. Come back for more – our notebooks are lucky. Many writers have become famous after buying from us.'

Veena was thrilled. She gazed on the green calico binding, flicked the pages, and ran her finger tenderly over the paper.

'Now I can really start writing. I have been scribbling on slips of paper – old calendar sheets and such things.' She flicked the pages again, and cried, 'Lined too!'

'Lined sheets are a great help. When you want another one, tell me, and I'll get it,' he said.

'I want four hundred pages, but this will do for the present.' She was so pleased that she felt she should do him a good turn, she hugged him and asked, 'Shall I cook our dinner tonight?'

'No, no!' he cried desperately.

On earlier occasions when Veena cooked he had to swallow each morsel with difficulty, suppressing comment and silently suffering. He felt that they might have to starve unless he took over the kitchen duties. He realized that she was not made for it. Boiling, baking, spicing, salting, blending, were beyond her understanding or conception. He was a good eater with taste and appetite. 'A novelist probably cannot be a good cook,' he concluded, 'just as I cannot write a novel. She has not been taught to distinguish salt from sawdust.' He quietly took over the kitchen leaving her free to write whatever she fancied.

However, he would enquire from time to time, 'What progress?'

She answered, 'Can't say anything now, we have to wait.'

Several days later, when he asked for progress, she said, 'The heroine is just emerging.'

'What do you call her?'

'Oh, names come very last in a novel.'

'In that case how can a reader know who is who?'

'Just wait and see, it is my responsibility.'

'I could write only two pages today,' she said another day.

'Keep it up. Very soon you will fill four, eight, sixteen

pages a day.' His vision soared on multiples of four for some obscure reason. 'I think I had better buy another two-hundred-page notebook before Bari's stock is exhausted. He said that the demand from novelists is rather heavy this season.'

'Did he mention any novelist's name?'

'I will ask, next time I will find out.'

Swami went to his room to change into a garb to suit his kitchen work. When he came out, changed to a knee-length dhoti and a towel over his shoulder, Veena said, 'I was asking if he had met any novelist.'

'Bari has met any number. I know only one novelist and she stands before me now.' He then asked, 'What kind of man is your hero?'

She replied, 'What do you imagine him to be?'

'Tall, and powerful, not a fellow to be trifled with.'

'So be it,' she said, and asked, 'is he a fighting sort?'

'Maybe, if he is drawn to it.'

She completed his sentence, 'He won't hesitate to knock out the front teeth of anyone – '

Swami found the image of an adversary minus his teeth amusing, and asked 'What about the rest of his teeth?'

'He will deal with them when he is challenged next.'

'You almost make him a dentist,' he said.

'A Chinese dentist has opened a clinic at New Extension, and a lot of people sit before him open-mouthed.'

'How have you come to know it?'

'Sometimes I lock the door and wander about till it is time to return home. Otherwise I cannot get ideas.'

'When will you find time to write if you are wandering about?'

'Wandering about is a part of a writer's day. I also carry a small book and jot down things that interest me.'

'Excellent plan,' Swami said, and disappeared into the kitchen as he smelt burning oil from the frying pan.

Veena developed the idea further, and said when they settled down on the hall bench after supper, 'I think a Chinese dentist is the hero, it is something original, no one has thought of him before. Chinese dentists are famous.'

'But how can a girl of our part of the world marry a Chinese?'

'Why not?' she said and thought it over and said, 'Actually, in the novel, he is not a Chinese. He only had his training in China.'

'Why did he go to China?' asked Swami.

'When he was a boy he ran away from home.'

'Why?'

'His schoolmaster caned him one day, and in sheer disgust he went and slept on a bench at the railway platform for two days and nights. When a train passed at midnight, he slipped into a carriage and finally joined some monks and sailed for Peking in a boat.'

'Very interesting, very interesting,' Swami cried. 'How do you get these ideas?'

'When one writes, one gets ideas,' Veena explained, and continued, 'the monks left him at the port and vanished . . . '

'Were they supernatural beings? Could you explain their presence and help?'

'God must have sent them down to help the boy . . . '

'Why should God be interested?' Swami asked.

'God's ways are mysterious.'

'True, God's ways are certainly mysterious,' he endorsed her philosophy.

She continued, 'And the young fellow wandered here and there in the streets of Peking, without food or shelter for a couple of days, and fainted in front of a dentist's clinic. In the morning when the dentist came to open the door, he saw the boy, and thought he was dead.'

'What do they do in China with the dead?' he asked in genuine concern and added, 'they probably bury.'

'No, no, if he was buried that would end my story.' She added, 'Chinese are probably careful and cautious, unlike in our country, where they immediately carry away a body and dispose of it.'

'Not always,' Swami said, showing off his better knowledge of the situation, 'once, when I was working in a cloth shop, a body was found in the veranda and they immediately sent for a doctor.'

'Why a doctor when he or she is already dead?'

'That's a routine in such circumstances,' he generalized.

'I want you to find out from someone what the Chinese do when a body is found at the door. I must know before I proceed with the story.'

'Since he becomes the Chinese dentist of your story later, he was not really dead – so why bother about it?' asked Swami.

'Of course,' she agreed, 'when he came back home, he knew how to work as a dentist, and became prosperous and famous.'

'Readers will question you . . . '

'Oh, leave that to me, it is my business,' Veena replied.

The story was taken one step further at the next conference. They had both got into the habit of talking about it every evening after dinner, and were becoming, unconsciously, collaborators.

'He fell in love with a girl, who had somehow lost all her teeth and come to have new ones fitted . . . Day by day as he saw her with her jaws open to be fitted up, he began to love her, being physically so close to each other.' Veena gloated over the vision of love blossoming in a dentist's chair.

Swami became critical. 'With her jaws open and toothless gums, do you think it is possible for a man to be attracted? Is any romance possible in that state?'

'Don't you know that love is blind?'

Not wanting to appear to cross-examine or discourage her, he said, 'Ah, now I understand, it is natural that a man who bends so close to a woman's face cannot help it, and it's his chance to whisper in her ears his passion, though if a toothless person came before me, I would not care for her.'

Veena took offence at this point. 'So that means if I lose my teeth, you will desert me?'

'No, no, you will always be my darling wife. But all that I am trying to say is, when the teeth are lost both the cheeks get sucked in and the mouth becomes pouchy, and the whole face loses shape.'

Veena was upset at this remark, got up and went away to the corner where her books were kept and started reading, ignoring him. By the time they sat down again the next night after dinner, she relented enough to say, 'He need not be a dentist, I agree it's a difficult situation for lovers. Shall I say that he is something in a less awkward profession, a silk merchant or veterinary doctor?'

Swami was pleased that she had conceded his point, and felt that it was now his turn to concede a point and said, 'No, no, let him be what he is, it's very original, don't change it – this is probably the first time a dentist comes into a story . . . ' And on that agreeable note, peace was established once again. The dentist had to work on the heroine's gums for a long time, taking moulds and preparing her denture, trying them out, filing, fitting and bridging, all the time Cupid was at work. It took the dentist several weeks to complete his task and beautify her face. When it was accomplished he proposed and they married, overcoming all obstacles.

As the notebook was getting filled, Veena took an afternoon off to spend time at the Town Hall library to browse through popular magazines on the hall table and romances on the shelves, desperately seeking ideas. Not a single book in the whole library on the theme of a dentist and a bare-gummed heroine. She returned home and remained silent all through the evening, leaving Swami to concentrate on his duties in the kitchen. She sat in her corner trying to go on with the story until Swami called from the kitchen, 'Dinner ready.'

One evening she confessed: 'I have not been able to write even two lines today. I don't know in which language I should continue.' She was suddenly facing a problem. She was good in English and always remembered her sixty per cent in English literature in her B.A. At the same time she felt she should write in Tamil, that it was her duty to enrich her mother tongue so that all classes of people could benefit from her writing. It was an inner struggle, which she did not reveal even to her husband, but he sensed something was wrong and enquired tactfully, 'Want anything?'

'What is our language?' she asked.

'Tamil, of course.'

'What was the language of my studies at Albert Mission?'

'English.'

'How did I fare in it?'

'You always got sixty per cent.'

'Why should I not write in English?'

'Nobody said you should not.'

'But my conscience dictates I should write only in my mother tongue.'

'Yes, of course,' he agreed.

'You go on saying "Yes" to everything. You are not helping me.' Swami uttered some vague mumbling sounds. 'What are you trying to say?' she asked angrily. He remained silent like a schoolboy before an aggressive pedagogue.

'Don't you realize that English will make my novel known all over India if not the whole world?'

'Very true,' he said with a forced smile. 'Why is she grilling me?' he reflected. 'After all I know nothing about writing novels. I am only a weaving supervisor at Coomar's factory.' He said to himself further, 'Anyway, it's her business. No one compels her to write a novel. Let her throw it away. If she finds time hanging heavily, let her spin yarn on a Charka.'

He suddenly asked, 'Shall I get you a Charka?'

'Why?' she asked, rather alarmed at his irrelevancy.

'Mahatma Gandhi has advised every citizen of India

to spin as a patriotic duty. They are distributing Charkas almost free at Gandhi Centre . . .'

By this time Veena felt that something was amiss, she abruptly got up and went over to her canvas chair in the corner, picking up a book from her cupboard. Swami sat in his wooden chair without moving or speaking. He began to feel that silence would be the safest course, fearing, as in a law court, any word he uttered might be used against him. He sat looking out of the window though nothing was happening there, except a donkey swishing its tail under the street lamp. 'Flies are bothering it,' he observed to himself, 'otherwise it could be the happiest donkey.' His neighbour was returning home with a green plastic bag filled with vegetables and passed him with a nod. Swami found the silence oppressive and tried to break it. 'Mahatma Gandhi has advised that every individual should spin morning and evening and that'd solve a lot of problems.'

'What sort of problems?' she asked gruffly, looking up from her book.

He answered, 'Well, all sorts of problems people face.'

'What makes you talk of that subject now?'

She was too logical and serious, he commented to himself. Has to be. Novelists are probably like that everywhere. He remained silent, not knowing how to proceed or in which direction. She sued for peace two days later by an abrupt announcement.

'I have decided to write both in Tamil and English, without bothering about the language, just as it comes. Sometimes I think in English, sometimes in Tamil. Ideas are more important than language. I'll put down the ideas as they occur to me, if in English, it'll be English, if the next paragraph comes in Tamil I'll not hesitate to continue in Tamil, no hard and fast rule.'

'Of course there should be no hard and fast rule in such matters. To be reduced to a single language in the final stage, I suppose?'

'Why should I?' she said, slightly irritated. 'Don't we mix English and Tamil in conversation?'

He wanted to say, 'If you knew Hindi, you could continue a few paragraphs in Hindi too, it being our national language as desired by Mahatma Gandhi,' but he had the wisdom to suppress it. Another mention of Gandhi might destroy the slender fabric of peace, but he asked solicitously, 'Will you need another book for writing?'

'Yes,' she said, 'I'm abandoning this notebook and will make a fresh start on a new notebook . . . ' His mind got busy planning what to do with the blank pages of the present notebook. 'I don't want to look at those pages again. I'll start afresh. You may do what you please with the notebook. Get me another one without fail tomorrow.'

'Perhaps you may require two books, if you are writing two languages it may prove longer.'

'Difficult to say anything about it now, but bring me one book – that will do for the present.'

'I will tell Bari to keep one in reserve in any case,' he said.

It went on like that. It became a routine for her to fill her notebook, adding to the story each day. They used to talk about it, until one day she announced, 'They are married. It is a grand wedding since he was a popular dentist, and a lot of people in the town owed their good looks to him. His clinic was expanded and he engaged several assistants, and he was able to give his wife a car and a big house, and he had a farm outside, and they often spent their weekend at the farm.'

'Any children?'

'By and by, inevitably.'

'How many are you going to give them?'

'We will see,' she said, and added, 'at some point I must decide whether to limit their offspring to one or several.'

'But China has the highest population,' he said.

'True, but he is not a real Chinese, only trained there,' she said, correcting him.

'Then he must have at least four children. Two sons and two daughter, the first and the third must be daughters,' he said, and noticed that she looked annoyed, too much interference she suddenly felt, and lapsed into silence.

'Suppose they also have twins?' he dared.

'We can't burden them that way having no knowledge of bringing up a child ourselves.'

'God will give us children at the appointed time.'

'But you assume that we could recklessly burden a couple in the story!' she said.

She wrote steadily, filling up page after page of a fresh notebook ... and with a look of triumph told Swami, 'I won't need another notebook!' She held it up proudly. He looked through the pages, shaking his head in appreciation of her feat in completing the work; not entirely her work, he had a slight share in her accomplishment, of the two hundred pages in the book he had contributed ten pages, and was proud of it. In the story, at the dentist's wedding an elaborate feeding programme was described for a thousand guests. The feast was very well-planned – two days running they served breakfast, coffee and Idli and Dosai and Uppumav and two sweets and fruit preparations, a heavy lunch with six vegetables and rice preparations, concluding with a light, elegant supper. Fried almonds and nuts were available in bowls all over the place, all through the day. The bridegroom, the dentist, had expressed a wish that a variety of eatables must be available for those with weak teeth or even no teeth, he had all kinds of patients capable of different degrees of chewing and mastication.

Food had to be provided for them in different densities and calibre. Arrangements were made not only to provide for those who could chew hard food, masticate a stone with confidence, but also for those who could only swallow mashed, over-ripe banana. The doctor was saying again and again, 'It is my principle that a marriage feast must be remembered – not only by those endowed with thirty-two teeth, but also by the unfortunate ones who have less or none.'

At this stage Swami and Veena lost sight of the fact that it was a piece of fiction that they were engaged in but went on to chart every meal with tremendous zest. Swami would brook no compromise. It had to be the finest cuisine in every aspect.

'Why should you make it so elaborate and gluttonous?' Veena asked.

He answered, 'The guests may have a wide choice, let them take it or leave it. Why should we bother? Anyway it is to cost us nothing. Why not make it memorable?' So he let himself go.

He explained what basic ingredients were required for the special items in the menu, the right stores which supplied only clean grains and pulses imported from Tanjore, and Sholapur, honey and saffron from Kashmir, apples from Kulu valley, and rose-water from Hyderabad to flavour sherbets to quench the afternoon thirst of guests, spices, cardamom, cinnamon and cloves from Kerala, and chillies and tamarind from Guntur. Swami not only knew where to get the best, but also how to process, dry, grind, and pulverize them before cooking. He also knew how to make a variety of sun-dried fritters, wafers and chips. He arranged for sesamum from somewhere to extract the best frying oil and butter from somewhere else to melt and obtain fragrant ghee.

Swami wrote down everything, including detailed recipes on the blank pages of the notebook that Veena had abandoned. When he presented his composition to Veena, she said, 'Too long. I'll take only what is relevant to my story.' She accepted only ten pages of his writing, rewrote it, and blended it into her narrative. Even with that Swami felt proud of his participation in a literary work.

Swami took the completed novel to Bari, who looked through the pages and said, 'The lady, your missus, must be very clever.'

'Yes, she is,' said Swami, 'otherwise how could one write so much? I could only help her with ideas now and then, but I am no writer.'

Bari said, 'I can't read your language or English very much, but I'll show it to a scholar I know, who buys paper and stationery from me. He is a professor in our college, a master of eighteen languages.'

It took ten days to get an opinion. Ten days of suspense for Veena, who constantly questioned Swami at their night sessions after dinner, 'Suppose the professor says it is no good?'

Swami had to reassure again and again, 'Don't worry.

He'll like it. If he doesn't, we will show it to another scholar.' Every evening he stopped by at Bari's to ask for the verdict, while Veena waited anxiously for Swami's return.

'Wait, wait, don't be nervous. Scholars will take their own time to study any piece of work. We can't rush them.'

One evening he brought her the good news. The scholar's verdict was favourable. He approved especially the double language experiment which showed originality. Veena could not sleep peacefully that night, nor let her husband at her side sleep, agitated by dreams of success and fame as a novelist.

She disturbed him throughout the night in order to discuss the next step. 'Should we not find a publisher in Madras? They know how to reach the readers.'

'Yes, yes,' he muttered sleepily.

'We may have to travel to Madras . . . can you take leave? If Coomar refuses to let you go, you must resign. If the novel is taken, we may not have to depend upon Coomar. If it becomes a hit, film-makers will come after us, that'll mean . . . ' Her dreams soared higher and higher. Swami was so frequently shaken out of sleep that he wondered why he should not take a pillow and move to the pyol outside.

Bari stopped their plan to visit Madras. 'Why should you go so far for this purpose? I have paper and a friend has the best press . . . '

'Where?' asked Swami.

'You know Mango Lane just at the start of Mempi Hill Road?'

'No, never been there . . . '

'Once it was an orchard, where mangoes were culti- vated and exported to Europe and America, till my friend bought the place, cleared the grove, and installed a press there, he prints and publishes many books, and also gov- ernment reports and railway timetables. I supply all the paper he needs, he's a good customer – not always for our Hamilton Brand but he buys all sorts of other kinds. His name is Natesh, a good friend, he will print anything I want. Why should you wait upon publishers in Madras – they may not accept the novel, having their own notions, or if they take it they may delay for years. I know novelists who have aged while waiting and waiting.'

'Impossible to wait,' said Swami, recollecting his wife's anxiety and impatience to see herself in print.

Next day Bari had the printer waiting at his shop. He told Swami 'My friend came to order some thin paper for handbills, and I have held him back.'

Natesh was a tall, lean, bearded person who wore a khadi kurta and dhoti, his forehead smeared with vermil- ion and holy ash. Natesh wished to see the manuscript. Swami produced the notebook for the printer's inspection next day. But when he suggested he'd take it with him to Mango Lane for estimating the printing charges, Swami felt embarrassed, not being sure if Veena would like to let it out of sight.

He said, 'I'll bring it back later, the author is still revising.'

Natesh went through the pages, counting the lines for about fifteen minutes, noting down the number of lines and pages, and declared, 'I'll give an estimate for printing and binding in two days.'

'I'll give an estimate for the papers required – that's my business,' added Bari.

On this hopeful note they parted for the evening. Coming to brass tacks a couple of days later, Bari made a proposal. 'I'll supply the paper definitely as a friend. Natesh has calculated that you will need twenty reams of white printing for the text, extra for covers. We will print five hundred copies at first. It would have cost less if the text had been in a single language but now the labour charges are more for two languages, and Natesh wants to print Tamil in black ink and English in red ink on a page, and that'll cost more. I can supply printing ink also. It would have been cheaper if your missus had written fewer pages and in her mother tongue only.'

Swami said, being ignorant of the creative process, 'I will tell her so –'

'No, no,' cried Bari in alarm. 'I'd not like to offend her, sir. Novelists must be respected and must be left to write in as many languages as they choose. Who are we to question?'

The printer at their next meeting said, 'I can give a rough estimate, not the final one unless I go through the text for two days, and I won't undertake printing without going through the text to assure myself that it contains no blasphemy, treason, obscenity or plagiarism. It's a legal requirement, if there is any of the above I'll be hauled up before a magistrate.'

Swami became panicky, he had not read the manuscript, even if he had he could not say what offence Veena might have committed, but protested aloud, 'Oh, no! Bari knows me and my family, and our reputation . . . '

Bari endorsed this sentiment. 'Such offences are unthinkable in their family, they are very well-known, of high class, otherwise they can't be my customers. I would not sell Hamilton Bond paper to anyone and everyone unless I am convinced that they are lawful persons belonging to good families. If I gave my best paper to all and sundry, where would I be?'

Swami had no answer to this question as he could not follow the logic of Bari's train of thought. They were sitting around on low aluminium stools and Swami's back ached, sitting erect and stiff on a circular seat which had neither armrest nor a back. He stood up.

Bari cried, 'Sit, down, sit down. You must have tea.' He

beckoned his servant, an urchin he had brought with him from Aligarh, whom he never let out of sight. 'Jiddu, three cups of tea. Tell that man to give the best tea, otherwise I'll not pay.'

While the boy dashed out for tea, Natesh said, 'Apart from other things I must guard against plagiarism.'

Swami had heard of plague, but not plagiarism. 'Please explain,' he said.

When Natesh explained, he grew panicky. He wondered if his wife visited the Town Hall library to lift passages from other books. As soon as he went home, he asked his wife, 'Did you go to the Town Hall library?'

'Not today.'

'But when you go there what do you generally do?'

'Why this sudden interest?' she asked.

He retreated into his shell again. 'Just wanted to know if you found any story as good as yours in the library . . . ' She brushed off his enquiry with a gesture.

He coaxed and persuaded her to give the novel for the printer's inspection the next day. With many warnings she let him take the notebook away with him, expressing her own doubt, 'What if he copies it and sells it?'

'Oh, no, he can't do that. We will hand him over to the police, if he does. Bari will be our witness. We'll take a receipt.'

Next day at Bari's Swami met Natesh and handed him the notebook. Natesh took three days to complete

his scrutiny of the novel and brought back the manuscript, safely wrapped in brown paper, along with the
estimate. They conferred once again behind a stack of
paper. They were silent while Jiddu went to fetch three
cups of tea. After drinking tea Bari said, 'Let us not waste
time. Natesh, have you the estimate ready?'

'Here it is,' said Natesh, holding out a long envelope.

Bari received it and passed it on to Swami with a
flourish. Then he asked the printer 'How do you find
the novel?'

'We will talk about it later . . . '

Bari said, 'If you are not interested, Swami's missus
will take it to the Madras printers.'

'Why should she?' asked Natesh. 'While we are here?'

'If so, come to the point. I'll supply the paper at
less than cost price, when the book is sold you may
pay . . . '

Swami felt rather disturbed. 'But you said the other
day, you would supply it . . . '

Bari said, 'I am a businessman, sir, I said I'd supply
the best paper at only cost price, and three months sight.'

'What is "sight"?' asked Swami, now completely bewildered.

'Let us not waste time on technical matters,' said Bari
briefly. 'When I said I'd supply, I meant I would supply,
nothing more and nothing less.'

At this point Natesh said, 'You have not seen my

estimate yet. Why don't you look through it first?'

Swami felt he was being crushed between heavy-weights. He opened the estimate, took a brief look at the bewildering items, and then at the bottom line giving the total charges, felt dizzy, abruptly got up and rushed out into the street without a word, leaving the two agape.

Veena was standing at the door as usual. Even at a distance she could sense that something had gone wrong, judging from Swami's gait and down-cast eyes. When he arrived and passed in without a word, she felt a lump in her throat. Why was he uncommunicative today? Normally he would greet her while coming up the steps. Today he was silent, could it be that the printer had detected some serious lapse, moral or legal, in her novel and threatened him with action? They ate in silence. When they settled down in their seats in the front room, she ventured to ask, 'What happened?'

'Nothing,' he said, 'I have brought back the book.'

'I see it. Are they not going to print it?'

'No, unless we sell ourselves and all that we have, to pay their bill. Even Bari has proved tricky and backed out though he had almost promised to supply the paper.'

He went over to his cupboard and brought out the estimate. Veena studied it with minute attention, tried to understand the items in the bill, then let out a deep sigh, and showed symptoms of breaking down. Immediately Swami shed his gloom, assumed a tone of reckless cheer and said, 'You should not mind these setbacks, they are incidental in the career of any writer. I do not know very much about these things, but I have heard of authors facing disappointments all through life until a sudden break of good fortune occurred. Even Shakespeare. You are a first class literary student, you must have read how downhearted he was till his plays were recognized.'

'Who told you? I have never seen you read Shakespeare!'

Swami felt cornered and changed the subject. She did not press him further to explain his acquaintance with Shakespeare. This piece of conversation, however, diverted her attention, and she said, overcoming her grief, 'Let us go away to Madras, where we will find the right persons to appreciate the novel. This is a wretched town. We should leave it.'

Swami felt happy to see her spirit revive, but secretly wondered if she was going to force him to lose his job. Without contradicting her, he just murmured, 'Perhaps we should write to the publishers and ask them first.'

'No,' she said. 'It will be no use. Nothing can be done through letters. It will be a waste of time and money.'

He felt an impulse to ask, 'On reaching Madras are you going to stand outside the railway station and cry out, "I have arrived with my novel, who is buying it?" Will publishers come tumbling over each other to snatch up your notebook?' He suppressed his thoughts as usual. She watched him for a while and asked, 'What do you think?'

'I'll see Coomar and ask him for a week off.'

'If he refuses, you must resign and come out.'

This was the second time she had toyed with the idea of making him jobless, little realizing how they were dependent on Coomar for shelter and food. Somehow she had constituted herself Coomar's foe. This was not the time to argue with her. He merely said, 'Coomar will understand, but this is a busy production season, lot of pressure at the moment.'

She grumbled, 'He wants to make more money, that is all, he is not concerned with other people's interests.' Swami felt distressed at her notion of his boss, whom he respected, but he swallowed his words and remained silent.

Four days later, in the afternoon they had a visit from Bari and Natesh. It was a holiday and Swami was at home. He became fussy and drew the available furniture here and there, dashed next door and borrowed a folding chair, and managed seats for everybody. Veena threw a brief glance at the visitors, and walked past them unceremoniously and was off, while Swami fell into a state of confusion, torn between surprise at the arrival of visitors and an impulse to go after Veena. His eyes constantly wandered to the corner of the street while greeting and welcoming his visitors.

'Your missus going out in a hurry?' asked Bari.

'Yes, yes, she has an engagement in the Fourth Lane, busy all day . . . '

'Writing all the time?' asked the bearded man, whose bulging eyes and forehead splashed with holy ash and vermilion gave him a forbidding look.

'Yes, yes, she has to answer so many letters every day from publishers in Madras . . . before we go there . . . '

The two looked at each other in consternation. 'No need, no need,' they cried in unison, 'while we are here.'

'But she has definite plans to take her novel to Madras . . . '

When they said, 'No sir, please, she will bring fame to Malgudi.' Swami felt emboldened by their importunity, and said in a firm tone. 'Your charges for printing will make me a bankrupt and a beggar.' He looked righteous.

'But sir, it was only a formality, estimates are only a business formality. You must not take it to heart, estimates are provisional and negotiable.'

'Why did you not say so?' asked Swami authoritatively. He felt free to be rude.

'But you went away before we could say anything.'

Swami gave a fitting reply as he imagined. Veena's absence gave him freedom. She would have controlled him with a look, or by a thought wave as he sometimes suspected, whenever a third person was present. He realized suddenly his social obligations. 'May I offer you tea or coffee?'

After coffee and the courtesies, they came down to business. Natesh suddenly said. 'I was in prison during the political struggle for Independence, and being a political sufferer our government gave me a pension, and all help to start my printing press – I always remind myself of Mahatmaji's words and conduct myself in all matters according to his commands.' He doubtless looked like one in constant traffic with the other world to maintain contact with his Master. 'Why am I saying this to you now?' he suddenly asked.

Bari had the answer for it, 'To prove that you will always do your best and that you are a man of truth and non-violence.'

The other smiled in satisfaction, and then remarked to Swami, 'Your wife has gone out, and yet you have managed to give us coffee, such good coffee!'

'Oh, that's no trouble. She keeps things ready at all times. I leave her as much time as possible for her writing too.'

They complimented him on his attitude and domestic philosophy. Bari said, 'We will not allow the novel to go out, we will do it here.'

Natesh said, 'I am no scholar or professor, but I read the story and found it interesting, and in some places I was in tears when the young couple faced obstacles. I rejoiced when they married. Don't you agree?' he asked, turning to Bari.

'Alas, I am ignorant of the language. If it had been in our language I'd have brought it out famously, but you have told me everything, and so I feel I have read it. Yes, it is a very moving story, I'll supply the paper and Natesh will print it.'

'Where?' asked Swami.

'In my press of course,' replied Natesh. 'At Madras I learnt the ins and outs of the publishing business. Under the British, publishers were persecuted, especially when we brought out patriotic literature, and then I had to give up my job when Mahatmaji ordered individual *Satyagraha*. I was arrested for burning the Union Jack, and went to prison. After I was released, the Nehru Government helped us to start life again. Now I am concentrating on printing . . . but if I find a good author, I am prepared to publish his work. I know how to market any book which seems good.'

'So you think this novel will sell?' asked Swami, buoyed up.

'Yes, by and by, I know when it should be brought out. In this case the novel should be published later as a second book, we will keep it by. Your story portion stands by itself, but without spoiling it we can extract the other portion describing the marriage feast as a separate part, and publish it as the first book, with a little elaboration – perhaps adding more recipes of the items served in the feast – it can then become a best-seller. While reading it, my mouth watered and I felt hungry. It's so successfully presented. With a little elaboration it can be produced as a separate book and will definitely appeal to the reader, sort of an appetizer for the book to follow, that's the novel, readers will race for it when they know that the feast will again be found in the novel. If you accept the idea we may immediately proceed. I know how to sell it all over the country. The author is at her best in describing food and feast. If you can give me a full book on food and feast, I can give you an agreement now, immediately. On signing it I'll give you one thousand and one thousand on publication. We will bring it out at our own cost. When it sells, we will give you a royalty of ten per cent, less the advance.'

Later Swami explained to Veena the offer. Veena immediately said dolefully, 'They want a cookery book, not a novel.'

'I think so,' Swami said, 'but he will give a thousand rupees if you agree. Imagine one thousand, you may do many things.'

'But the novel?'

'He will publish it as a second book, after your name becomes known widely with the first book.'

'But I don't know any cookery . . . '

'It doesn't matter, I will help you.'

'You have never allowed me in the kitchen.'

'That should make no difference. You will learn about

it in no time and become an authority on the subject . . . '

'Are you making fun of me?'

'Oh, no. You are a writer. You can write on any subject under the sun. Wait a minute.' He went up to a little trunk in which he kept his papers, brought out the first green-bound notebook in which he had scribbled notes for the dentist's marriage feast. Veena went through it now carefully, and asked, 'What do you want me to do?'

'You must rewrite each page of my notes in your own words – treat it as a basis for a book on the subject.'

'What about the novel?'

'That will follow when you have a ready-made public.' Veena sat silently poring over the pages which she had earlier rejected, now finding the contents absorbing. She thought it over and shook him again that night while he was sound asleep, and said 'Get me a new notebook tomorrow. I'll try.'

Next evening on his way home, Swami picked up a Hamilton notebook. Veena received it quietly. Swami left it at that till she herself said after three days, 'I'll give it a trial first . . . '

That afternoon, after lunch Veena sat in her easy chair and wrote a few lines, the opening lines being: 'After air and water, man survives by eating, all of us know how to eat, but not how to make what one eats.' She wrote in the same tone for a few pages and explained that the pages following were planned to make even the dull-witted man or woman an expert cook . . .

She read it out to Swami that evening. He cried 'Wonderful, all along I knew you could do it, all that you have to do now is to elaborate the points from my notes in your own style, and that'll make a full book easily.'

Swami signed a contract on behalf of Veena and received one thousand rupees advance in cash. Veena completed her task in three months and received one thousand rupees due on delivery of the manuscript. Natesh was as good as his word and Bari supplied the best white printing paper at concessionary rates. They called the book *Appetizer – a guide to good eating*. Natesh through his contacts with book-sellers sold out the first edition of two thousand copies within six months. It went through several editions and then was translated into English and several Indian languages, and Veena became famous. She received invitations from various organizations to lecture and demonstrate. Swami drafted her speeches on food subjects, travelled with her, and answered questions at meetings. They were able to move out of Grove Street to a bungalow in New Extension, and Veena realised her long-standing desire to see her husband out of Coomar's service. All his time was needed to look after Veena's business interests and the swelling correspondence, mostly requests for further recipes, and advice on minor problems in the kitchen.

Though Swami offered to continue to cook their meals, Veena prohibited him from stepping into the kitchen and engaged a master cook. In all this activity the novel was not exactly forgotten, but awaited publication. Natesh always promised to take it up next, as soon as the press was free, but *Appetizer* reprints kept the machines overworked, and there was no sign of the demand slackening. Veena, however, never lost hope of seeing her novel in print and Swami never lost hope that some day he would be allowed to cook, and the master cook could be secretly persuaded or bribed to leave.

THE PRINTER OF MALGUDI

Fresh from the presses of the Truth Printing Works, the weekly edition of The Banner enjoys a certain distinction. Srinivas, its editor and sole contributor, concerns himself with artistic and intellectual problems: Mr Sampath, its printer, amicably shoulders the financial burdens. When the paper folds – a surprise to them both – Mr Sampath sees a way to save an equable partnership. With splendid magnanimity he arranges for Srinivas to write the filmscripts for Sunrise Productions. Unfortunately, the glamour of it all goes quite to Mr Sampath's head, and his sudden change of fortune leads to sublime, unmitigated chaos . . .

'A charming examination of the chaos of Indian film-making . . . Recommended to anyone who wishes to embark on Narayan's oeuvre.'
IRISH TIMES

'Narayan is a grave and lovely writer.'
HOWARD SPRING

THE ENGLISH TEACHER

At the Albert Mission College, Malgudi, the Lecturer of English was himself once one of the two hundred-odd pupils having Shakespeare and Milton drummed into their heads. But if Krishna sometimes despairs of a certain futility in the routine of his vocation, nothing can equal his delight when his young wife is at last able to join him in the small rented house which permits the couple to enjoy a life of undiluted bliss. Then tragedy strikes, and life in Malgudi can never quite be the same . . .

'An exquisite experience'
COMPTON MACKENZIE

'An idyll as delicious as anything I have met in modern literature for a long time. The atmosphere and texture of happiness, and, above all, its elusiveness, have seldom been so perfectly transcribed'
ELIZABETH BOWEN

'The hardest of all things for a novelist to communicate is the extraordinary ordinariness of human happiness. Jane Austen, Soseki, Chekhov: a few bring it off. Narayan is one of them'
SPECTATOR